WYRMEWEALD
RETURNER'S WEALTH

Paul Stewart and Chris Riddell

GALAXY

PLUS

First published 2010 by
Doubleday, an imprint of
Random House Children's Books
This Large Print edition published 2011 by
AudioGO Ltd
by arrangement with
the Random House Group Ltd

ISBN: 978 1405 664851

British Library Cataloguing in Publication Data available

Printed and bound in Great Britain by
CPI Antony Rowe, Chippenham and Eastbourne

P.S.—For Julie
C.R.—For Katy

WHITEWYRME

The most ancient of the great whitewyrmes turned his mighty head towards the horizon. His nostrils flared.

It was there again. The odour on the wind; rank and fetid, and threatening to taint everything it touched. The great whitewyrme's barbels trembled at the sides of his mouth.

It was the stench of the two-hides. And it was closer than ever.

On the highstacks and festercrags around him, the whitewyrmes turned enquiring eyes towards him, awaiting the signal to depart. All but one, a female.

She was perched alone on the speckled stack, cramped up and writhing, her jaws contorted with pain, her scales flushed. The fire from deep within the chimney-like stack fluttered on her spread wings, and on her swollen belly, made large by the egg that had grown inside her.

She let out a keening cry, and her whole body quaked. She squatted down, her wings raised and tail arched. Her haunches cramped. She craned her neck back and opened her jaws, and her cry grew louder and more desperate.

It was happening. The wyve was coming.

The fading rays of golden sunlight caught the gleaming shell as it protruded from the opening in her front. Slowly it grew. With each contraction, more and more of the mottled white egg appeared until, with a gentle thud and a puff of dust, the huge boulder-like wyve dropped into the cushioned nest of hot ashes the female had prepared for it.

Still shaking, she turned and inspected the wyve closely, prodding it with her horny snout, dragging ash around it with delicate claws. Her body stilled and the vibrant purple sheen of her scales faded back to white. She turned and saw the great whitewyrme perched at the top of the adjacent highstack, staring back at her, and inclined her head.

The whitewyrme raised his wings in response, and flapped them vigorously back and forwards. All round, the whitewyrmes heeded the signal and launched themselves into the air. From the black needle, the broken back and white pillar stacks, they rose in waves, until the sky was thick with the giant creatures and the rockscape below fell dark with their shadows as they blotted out the sun.

And then, as one, the great wyrmehost wheeled round, and flew off. Thousands of them, large and small, old and young. The female stole one last lingering look at the wyve, then launched herself off from the edge of the speckled stack. The ancient whitewyrme joined her. Together, flying side by side, the pair of them followed the departing host, soaring towards the red ball of the setting sun.

Soon the wyrmehost was gone and the land and the towering highstacks were empty. Almost. For a few wyrmes had remained.

They were sleek and strong, and reluctant to follow the rest. Now, more than ever, the wyve would need protecting—as would the others that nestled at the tops of other crags. They would not abandon them. They could not.

ONE

The eyes would be the first to go once the
scavengers landed. Already, sharp-
eyed, keen-nosed carrionwyrmes with
cropscythe claws and teeth like
hackdaggers were circling overhead.

Micah stared down at the corpse. It was
lying on its front, face down on the
blistered rock. One hand was reaching out,
its grasping fingers dustblown and stiff.

The youth prodded the body tentatively
with the tip of his boot. His toes, poking
up through split bootleather, grazed the
hard nubbed ribs of the dead man's side.
He shoved a boot-toe into the shadowed
hollow of the stomach, braced his legs and
rolled the body over. A cluster of broken
teeth remained on the rock where the
face had lain. They were pitted and
smokeweed-yellow, their roots set now in a
small patch of red stained sand. The head
whiplashed back then forward again, and
the body came to rest on its back with a
soft thump and a puff of dust.

Micah crouched down beside the body,
his hands on his hips. There was congealed
blood around the crushed nose and at the
corners of the dust-encrusted mouth. The
face was hollow, puckered with lack of
water, and dark desperate eyes stared
blindly up at him.

The dead man wore the clothes of a

3

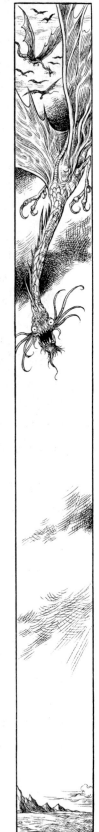

seasoned traveller. Birdhooks and arrowheads were carefully tucked into the band of a leather hat which was creased and worn and sweatstained at the brim. His jacket, a sturdy hacketon of buckhide, was worn thin at the elbows and frayed at the cuffs, while his breeches bore the evidence of years of patching and mending. His backpack lay beside him, turned half inside out and empty of supplies, while the watergourd next to it was unstoppered and bone-dry. But the boots—they were mighty fine. Tooled leather, soft and well-oiled, with sturdy hobnailed soles and iron-tipped toes. But fine as the dead traveller's boots were, they hadn't helped him when his water ran out.

Micah reached out and pulled off the right boot. The foot appeared from inside, blue-grey like moulded metal, puffy round the toes, as though it had been wading through water, and the skin as smooth and blister-free as Micah had known it would be. The smell, though, sour and acrid like rancid curds, he had not foreseen.

Suddenly, from far above his head, he heard keening cries, and he squinted up to see the black shapes against the high sun, wheeling round in the sky. He turned his attention to the second boot, awkward fingers fumbling with the lace, and tugging hard. Glancing up as it came free, he could make out the jagged wings of the carrionwyrmes now as they wheeled round lower, their rapier claws and hackdagger teeth glinting. Kicking his own boots hurriedly aside, he pulled the new ones onto his feet, first one, then the other, and knotted them tightly, then jumped to his feet—just as the first of the carrionwyrmes landed, head cocked and screeching with indignation.

4

Micah backed away. He reached down for his heavy walking stick. Two more of the creatures landed, blood-red eyes and ridged skulls gleaming. They shrieked discordantly as they hopped towards him. Screaming back at them furiously, Micah swung the heavy wood at them, driving them back—then abruptly turned and ran.

Behind him, the creatures squealed and jabbered in a frenzy of vicious squabbling. He glanced back. None were giving chase. Instead, they were clustered round the dead body, which had disappeared in the midst of the writhing mass of flapping wings, scratching claws and snapping teeth . . .

The next moment, the air filled with a gutwrenching stench as the carrionwyrmes slashed the stomach open. Micah retched and stumbled on.

Only when the raucous frenzy of the feeding creatures had faded away completely did he look round a second time. The bloody scene had disappeared behind a low ridge, though far in the distance, he thought he could make out the shape of the jagged wings flapping back into the sky. He came to a halt and bent double, panting hard as he stared at his fine new boots.

His own watergourd, he knew, was almost empty.

TWO

'Concentrate on your work, Micah,' Caleb bellowed, 'or you'll feel my whip on your back!'

It was three months earlier. Micah lowered his head and gripped the parallel staves as tight as his blistered fingers would allow, and as the ox plodded forward, he endeavoured to keep the heavy plough moving as even as he could. He watched the blade bite into the hard ground, and the black earth fold over onto itself as he continued the line.

He looked up and stared into the hazy distance once more; over the fields, through the shimmering heat of the dusty plains, and away towards the far-off horizon.

Somewhere beyond the flat featureless plains lay the mountains of the high country—a land of impossibly high crags and deep verdant valleys, of thundering waterfalls and crystal-clear lakes; a land of bitter cold winters and furnace-hot summers, of driving rain and great swirling duststorms; of precious metals and priceless gemstones. And of wyrmes.

Micah's eyes lit up. Wyrmes!

He had never seen one, not down here on the plains, though he'd heard stories enough. Many left for the high country, and though few ever returned, those who did brought riches back with them—returner's wealth—and the stories of the strange and terrifying creatures they'd encountered there . . .

'Micah!'

Micah flinched as the voice bellowed in his ear, and the heavy open hand that followed struck him so hard on the side of his head that he was knocked away from the plough and ended up sprawling over the fresh-turned mud. He looked up.

'Didn't I warn you?' his brother Caleb demanded. His face was flushed red; his neck, cabled. 'Didn't I tell you to drive a straight line?'

Micah swallowed, and nodded. 'You did,' he said meekly.

'And this is what you give me,' Caleb roared, his hand wiggling like a swimming fish as he indicated the furrow Micah had ploughed. 'I ain't going to have you holding me back, boy. Y'understand me. The master has charged me with getting the fields ploughed good.' He nodded ahead. 'And this is *not* good.' He aimed a muddy boot at Micah's chest. 'Too busy daydreaming 'bout the master's daughter, I'll wager,' he said, and sneered. 'I swear, one smile from her and you're as lovesick as a stable donkey, and about as useless!'

Caleb grabbed Micah by the hair and hauled him roughly to his feet.

'Now get on with your work!'

Micah stepped between the curved staves of the plough once more and gripped them with renewed

7

determination. The ox turned and surveyed him with doleful brown eyes. Micah twitched the reins and the ox turned away and trudged on.

This time he was careful to keep his gaze on the line between the creature's swaying rump and stout horns, and to ensure that the furrow he cut maintained the same line. He tried to empty his mind—to concentrate on his ploughing.

But it was no good. Thanks to Caleb, Micah's thoughts were now full of the master's daughter, Seraphita.

THREE

'No way back,' Micah breathed.

He clung to the rockface with bandaged hands, and gulped at the scorched air. Sweat ran down his cheeks and plashed onto the rock, dark grey circles that shrank and disappeared in moments. Below him, the clatter and grind of the rockfall he'd triggered petered out.

Don't even consider looking down, he told himself, then did just that. He groaned, feeling sick and vertiginous.

One slip would send him plunging to certain death on the jagged boulders far below. A rock, tardier than the rest, gathered speed then dropped, and Micah counted fully to ten before the sharp crack signifying its landing echoed back to him.

He craned his neck. Some way above, the grey rock gave way to brown rock. He had a notion it would be more dependable than the stratified shatterrock he was clinging to, which frost and sun had crazed and loosened. Even from this distance, the brown rock looked hard, and there seemed to be hollows where he might pause to allow his body the rest it craved.

One step at a time, he counselled. One goddamn step at a time . . .

He inched upward and prised his fingertips into a narrow fissure; then, taking good care not to kick off with excess

9

vigour, brought first one leg higher, then the other. His breathing came in short gasps. His pale eyes scrunched up. It was like climbing the shattered tiles of a lofty pitched roof.

He paused, reached up and grasped the brim of his hat, and tugged it forward. A slice of welcome shade slipped down over his face.

Hunched over, he reached for a likely handhold—then cried out with shock and fearfulness as the snarling head of a bearded rockwyrme sprang up from the very same crevice. He started back, his arm flailing. His boots slipped. The rockwyrme, no bigger than a jackrabbit, scrabbled out of the rock with a screech and skittered away on its back legs, tail raised and scaly wings erect.

Suddenly, everything else was in hectic motion too. The grey rock was shifting; slabs, large and small, slid and fell away all around him. Micah scrabbled desperately with his hands and his feet, seeking out purchase on the shifting rockface. His fingertips were grazed raw; his chin got cut. The thud and grind of the tumbling rocks echoed around the high mountain crags.

At that very moment, the toe of his boot found a crack, where it lodged, jarring his leg painfully at the hip but holding firm. He closed his eyes, pressed a cheek to the hot rock and raised a shaking arm above his head in the hope it might protect him from the rocks that were slipping and slewing by him in such a rush, and waited for the rockfall to cease.

When it did, he opened his eyes once more.

He arched his back and raised his head. The crazed and cracked grey rock had fallen away to

10

reveal a layer beneath, as yet untouched by the elements, that gleamed like the skin of a fresh-sloughed wyrme. It was rougher to the touch and, when Micah finally summoned the courage to proceed, proved somewhat easier to climb than the weathered rock it had replaced. Yet the ascent was still hard going, what with the ache in his leg and his throbbing fingers that left blood marks where they touched, and he grunted with relief when he climbed the last stretch of shatterrock.

Now that he could see it close up, the brown rock was a disappointment. It wasn't hard at all, but pitted and crumbly, though the veins of white granite that ran through it offered a more reliable, if slippery, hold for his boots. Red dust rose as he clambered over its surface. He came to the first of the hollows he'd seen and slipped into the shallow indentation, twisting round and setting himself down, back to the cliff-face, his legs stuck out over the edge.

He fumbled for the calfskin gourd that hung at his side, tooth-tugged the stopper, tipped back his head and hurried the open top to his flaking lips. Water that was warm and tasted of stewed meat dribbled into his mouth, and then it was gone, every last drop. He let his arm fall into his lap, and a look of resignation settled upon his features.

He needed to find water. If he didn't, he would die. That was the plain fact of the matter.

He started to climb, his cloak crowtattered and his sweatlick feet hot and sore inside his simmering boots. He grunted and groaned up a narrow chimney in the brown rock, taking care to trust his weight only to the granite striations. Pausing for a moment, he wiped the back of his bandaged hand

11

across his cracked lips and was fascinated by the saltiness that found its way to his tongue. He breathed in the searing air.

Water. He needed water.

At the top of the chimney at last, he came to a sheer rockface. Beneath their bindings, his blistered fingers throbbed. He had to go on. He blew on his fingers tenderly, easing the pain before wedging them into a narrow crevice. He found a foothold at knee height, kicked up and reached higher. Sweat gathered in his frownlines and overflowed. A single drop ran down the bridge of his nose, hesitated, then fell from the tip. He caught it on the end of his tongue. It was as salty as the sweat-drenched bandages.

What wouldn't he give for a sip of cool clear deepdrawn wellwater . . .

With a grunt, Micah heaved himself up over a jutting crag and onto a narrow ledge, and froze. Close by, faint but unmistakeable, was the soft, bell-like sound of water trickling into a pool. He cocked his head and listened, his thirst more acute than ever now there was a chance it might at last be slaked.

The sound was coming from the far end of the ledge, where the rockface was undulated like a drawn curtain. Micah inched towards it, face turned to one side and arms spreadeagled against the burning rock. His boots scraped along the ledge, dislodging shards that clicked and clattered as they tumbled down the cliff-face below. He came to a crack in the folds of rock. It was narrow and dark and chill, and echoed with the tantalizing sound of running water.

Micah hesitated, his eyes blanched with anxiety

12

as he peered into the crevice. Red dust, wet with sweat, emphasized the lines that scored his brow. The muscles in his jaw and temples twitched with indecision. Ahead of him, the water trickled and plashed with thirst-quenching promise, yet the unknown blackness filled him with dread.

But he could not turn back. No, not having come so far.

Unable to stop himself, Micah eased his body through the narrow fissure, into the darkness, and towards the sound of water.

FOUR

'Hold still, Micah, and put those hands of yours to your sides where I can see them.'

Micah chuckled. As he'd stepped inside the threshing barn, two arms had enfolded him from behind and a blindfold had covered his eyes. 'Seraphita?' he said. 'I might have guessed! What fool notion is this?'

'I told you to drop those hands, farmboy!' she said sharply.

Micah obeyed.

'That's better,' she said, her tone more amenable. 'Now, don't you move.'

He heard her strain softly as she reached up, and felt her elbows lightly graze his shoulder blades, a sensation that sent a shiver of anticipation through his body. She tugged hard at the blindfold, jerking his head back, then pressed her thumb firmly against the silk and knotted the two ends securely.

'How's that feel?' she asked, taking a step back.

'Tight,' he said. 'So tight I can't even open my eyes.'

'You're not supposed to open your eyes,' she said, and his head turned, following the sound of her voice as she moved round him. 'You're not meant to see a thing, Micah. I want you as blind as old Jeptha for what's about to follow.'

Micah swallowed. 'What *is* about to follow, Seraphita?'

'Wait and see,' she said, laughter concealed just behind her words.

He felt her hands reach for his own. They were cool and soft where his were hot, calloused and clammy, and her manicured nails dug softly into his rough palms. He let himself be guided by her, stumbling slightly as she pulled him towards her.

'At least tell me where you're taking me,' he said.

'And spoil the surprise?'

Taking small cautious steps, he allowed her to lead him outside, noting how the straw underfoot gave way to irregular cobblestones, and that the dust-filled air of the threshing barn had been replaced by the sharp tang of the ox-yard.

A while later she spoke again. 'Nearly there.'

He pictured her heart-shaped face, her full lips, her delicate upturned nose. And those eyes, so dark in candlelight that the pupil and iris seemed to fuse together to form two bottomless wells of blackness. When amused, she would toss her long hair, so black it looked blue, back behind her head and laugh like a stipplejay. When angered, she'd sweep it forward like a glossy curtain, through which she'd stare with a smouldering intensity; one hand gathering her bright red cloak at her neck, the other balled in a fist . . .

'What are you wearing?' he asked, surprised to

15

hear his thoughts finding voice.

Seraphita giggled. She pushed her face into his, and he felt his cheeks redden under her hot spicy breath. 'What would you like me to be wearing, Micah?' she breathed.

Micah swallowed, flustered. 'I . . . N . . . nothing, I wasn't . . .'

'*Nothing*, Micah?' she broke in. 'That's very forward of you . . .'

'No, I didn't mean that,' he protested, his scalp prickling. 'I just wondered . . .'

'Whether I might be standing before you, naked?'

When he protested a second time, she hushed him softly and squeezed his hands in hers, a motion that made Micah feel as weak-kneed as a new-born foal. They came to a place he did not recognize. It was cool and fresh, and he noted how their footsteps echoed softly from all sides as though they were in a walled courtyard.

Seraphita let go of one of his hands and took him by the arm.

'Take a step backwards and set yourself down,' she said, steering him as she spoke.

The backs of his knees came into contact with something firm, and he eased himself down onto a hard seat. It had a high back and straight arms, and he rested his own arms upon them and gripped the smooth carved bearpaws at the ends. Seraphita took a hold of both of his forearms with a firm grip, skin on skin, and Micah trembled as she leaned forward and he felt the warmth of her body so close to his.

'The trial is about to begin,' she announced. Her breath was sweet and moist.

16

'Trial?' he said. 'What trial?'

'You'll see,' she said. 'Or rather, you won't,' she added, and laughed. 'Just mind you don't touch that blindfold, Micah. I don't want any peeking.'

He nodded. She pulled away. The residue of her touch lingered on his arms like fingerprints on a windowpane.

'Don't move,' she told him. 'I shall be ready for you directly.'

Micah remained where he was, sitting bolt upright in the highback chair, his own arms as rigid as the wooden arms he gripped. He could hear faint birdsong, and the distant creak and grind of the ploughs working the fields; there was water splashing into a pool somewhere behind him. And when he breathed in, he detected the fragrance of rose blossoms on the air.

'Open wide.'

'No,' he muttered through clenched teeth. 'Why?'

'Just open your mouth,' she replied, a wheedling element creeping into her voice. 'Trust me.' She paused. 'You do trust me, don't you, Micah? Just open that mouth of yours.'

He sensed something hovering close by his lips.

'What is it?' he said. 'Is it something nice, Seraphita? Will I like it?'

'Why, Micah,' she cried out, the time for wheedling abruptly over, 'I swear you are acting as hickety as a pack-mule in a paddy-saddle. Now, I do not want to have to tell you again, open your mouth, and hold your tongue—and I don't mean that literal. For the duration of the trial, Micah, your tongue belongs to me.'

He parted his lips a little, and smooth metal

clinked against his bottom teeth. It was just a spoon, though there was something upon it, and his face screwed up in mistrustful anticipation.

'Well?' she said gleefully. She pulled the spoon slowly from his mouth.

He frowned. 'It's sweet,' he said.

'Sweet,' she repeated. 'Is that all?'

The liquid coated his tongue. 'It's thick and sticky . . . is it maltsyrup?'

'Maltsyrup?' She laughed. 'It's a might better than maltsyrup, Micah.'

'It's good,' said Micah, and nodded earnestly, his nose crinkling with pleasure as the sweet viscous liquid slipped down his throat. 'Could it be honey?'

'It could be and it is!' she exclaimed. 'The finest honey from my father's hives, served only at the top table—and then only on feast days!'

Micah nodded. 'I don't believe I have ever tasted anything so good.'

He felt a soft finger remove an errant drip of honey from below his chin and pop it into his mouth. He sucked the finger clean.

'Did you like that, Micah?'

'I did,' he replied. 'I liked it a lot.'

'I told you to trust me.'

'I know it,' said Micah, 'and it is to my shame that I did not.'

He reached up for the blindfold, only for Seraphita to grasp him by the wrist.

'The trial's not over yet,' she laughed, and Micah felt the ends of her hair sweep across his arm. 'Did you think I would set everything up so orderly for a single spoonful of honey, however fine it might be?'

This time Micah heard the chinking of glass on glass. He opened his mouth unbidden, and waited.

'You'll end up swallowing flies if you're not careful,' she laughed. 'Now hold still.'

He felt a glass press against his lower lip and his mouth filled with a cold liquid. Micah swallowed.

'Aaah!' he breathed. 'Seraphita, this trial just gets better and better.'

'What was it?'

'Liquor, of course,' he said.

But not just any old liquor. The only liquor Micah had ever tasted came from the clay jars at the back of the oxsheds, rough and home-distilled. It burned like the devil and tore at the back of the throat like a cornered wildcat. The liquor Seraphita had given him was smooth and warm and aromatic; it set his mouth to tingle and chest to glow.

'From my father's cellar,' Seraphita laughed, and Micah caught the smell of the liquor on her own breath. 'Older than both of us, and kept in a vessel of green glass with a waxen seal . . .'

'You stole it?'

'What my father doesn't know can't vex him,' she told him. 'It's time for your next challenge. Open wide.'

Micah obliged, and was rewarded by the touch of Seraphita's finger and thumb resting lightly on his lips. They probed his mouth and deposited something upon his tongue, then withdrew. Micah closed his mouth.

What new and exciting luxury might this be? he wondered.

'Well?' she said, excitement in her voice.

'Well,' said Micah, rolling it slowly around his

19

mouth with his tongue. 'Is it some kind of fruit?'

It was the size of a grape, cold and waxen smooth. And when he breathed in, he got the faintest hint of mown grass.

'Chew it,' said Seraphita. 'There's no use on earth you trying to suck the taste out of it, Micah. You gotta crunch down with your teeth.'

He did so, and a sour liquid squirted from the ruptured skin. He chewed some more. Leathery seeds got between his teeth and under his tongue. It was a vegetable . . .

A moment later, he felt an explosion of burning pain. With a cry of distress he bent double and spat the mushy, half-chewed boll from his mouth and tore the blindfold from his eyes.

'Chilli . . .' he gasped.

That was what it was. A cheap old black chilli pepper, fiery hot and fit only to spice half-rotten meat.

Seraphita's peals of laughter echoed around the courtyard. Micah's eyes watered, and he spat and spat, but not sufficient to spit away the burning sensation. Worse, it was on his lips now, making them feel like they had been freshly branded. He climbed to his feet, sucking in the cool air, trying to douse the fire in his mouth.

He wiped his streaming eyes and looked round. Seraphita had stopped laughing and was now staring at him.

'Why did you *do* that, Seraphita?' he asked her, his voice wounded and cracked.

'I . . .' Seraphita fell still and lowered her head. Her dark eyes glittered from behind a veil of black hair.

Then, suddenly, she was upon him, burying her

hands in his matted hair and pulling his face to hers. He felt her lips pressing against his lips, sharing his fiery pain, her tongue grazing his lower lip and probing his mouth, soothing the chilli pepper's fire. He closed his eyes, and as their tongues touched, he was pitched into a seething confusion as another fire raged through his body. It was excruciating and unendurable, intoxicating and bewildering, painful and delicious, and he never wanted it to end.

It was Micah's first kiss.

Five

From up ahead, the water sang out, siren-like seductive.

Micah twisted round and continued sideways on, but like a tightening vice, the walls of the crevice pressed in against his back and his chest until he could barely fill his constricted lungs. With a sickening lurch of panic, Micah realized that if he continued, he might end up wedged stoppertight and unable to wriggle free.

Go back, his fear advised him. Go on, his thirst beseeched.

Gasping for breath, Micah skitched his way forward until, with a dry gritscratched heave, he wriggled free of the tunnel and found himself in a vast cavern. He paused to catch his breath, his heart beating against his ribs like a caged crow.

The cavern was illuminated by a faint chink of light that penetrated from somewhere in the vaulted roof high above his head. For countless millennia, water must have seeped through the rock above, depositing particles of limestone that had built up to form a forest of bleached rock extrusions; fluted trunks, latticed branches and stippled roots . . .

And there, spiralling down a glistening white stalactite at the centre of the cavern and trickling into a vast ink-black pool below, was the water Micah craved. At last.

His parched tongue scraped across his flaking lips. He fumbled for the gourd at his side and was about to rush forward when a scratching, scuffling sound, like a rat in a corn barrel, and just as unwelcome, stopped him in his tracks.

Something was there.

Cussing his poor fortune to hell and back, Micah retreated into the shadows, pressed his back hard against the roughness of the cold rock and drew his hackdagger. He kept rigid still, scarcely daring to breathe as chilled sweat trickled down the back of his neck. Eyes slit narrow, he scoured the dimly lit cavern before him.

It was an angular snout he saw first, followed by a paw, tipped with curved talons that glinted as they reached round from behind a low limestone-glazed mound on the far side of the dark pool. The snout jerked upwards and a long tongue, black and forked, flicked out and lapped at the air. The next moment, with a thin wheezing cough, a pale runty-looking wyrme, knee-high and pot-bellied, scuttled out into plain view.

Micah held his breath.

Tarnished scales, cracked and misshapen, gilded the wyrme's skin, which hung in folds on its bony frame like an outsized oilskin. It was limbwithered and shrivelwinged. Thin twists of pus-coloured smoke dribbled from the scabbed nostrils of its bony carapaced skull. On the end of its thin twisted forepaws and spindly hindlegs, vicious curved talons gleamed like rapiers, and looked as though they came from a creature ten times its size.

But more than anything else, it was the creature's eyes that filled Micah with horror. They were huge and cataract-white, swivelling independent of each other in their scab-pocked sockets.

Bile rose in Micah's throat. He tried in vain to press back further into the rock, as though he hoped the shadows might swallow him up and make him disappear completely. But he could still hear his heart thumping; still smell his own fear.

And, as its tongue flicked in and out with a horrible probing delicacy, so too, it seemed, could the wyrme.

Tentatively it started forward, clattering on those tottery dagger claws. Glistening strands of drool spilled from the corners of its mouth and hung trembling from its chin. It wheezed and coughed, its scrawny neck extending and contracting with each lurching step as it skirted the rim of the ink-black pool and headed slowly but remorselessly towards the spot where Micah stood, wrapped in shadow.

He wanted to turn and run, but knew he had already left it too late. The wyrme would give chase and Micah had no desire to get caught in the narrow confines of the black tunnel with a rapier-taloned wyrme slashing at his heels. He would have to stand and fight.

On the nearside of the lake now, the white-eyed wyrme, guided by its flickering tongue, came inexorably closer. Crossing the cavern floor in short skittering steps, the wyrme gulped at the air, and Micah caught the sour whiff of dead meat. It paused, its bony skull tilted to one side as if listening.

Micah gripped the shaft of his hackdagger. Suddenly, the wyrme reared up on its bony hindlegs, the keening whine coming from its gaping jaws rising to a high-pitched screech as it sprinted towards Micah and lunged . . .

SIX

The kingirl leaned easily to one side of the whitewyrme and looked down, the long lance she held trembling in her grasp as the wind seized a hold of it. Far below, their single elongated shadow swept smoothly over grey slabs and black fissures, and the glistening waters of a broad turquoise lake, fringed with sparkling crystals of salt.

The wyrme peered back at her through dark questioning eyes. The jagged scar on his sinuous neck was black against the white scales. The girl returned his gaze, and nodded.

The great white creature tipped his wings, folded them close to his body and dived. The girl straightened up, raised her lance in both hands and braced it at her shoulder. As the clear water came closer, the wyrme unfolded his wings and glided over the lake at a shallow angle, just above the surface.

'Steady, Aseel. I see them!' said the girl.

Her voice was low and even, though creaked slightly through lack of use. The wyrme and the girl were kinclose and had no need for words. She had spoken not for the wyrme, but so that she might hear the sound of her own voice and remind herself that she still could speak.

The girl braced herself against the

creature's clavicle and vertebral spur. A ripple of acknowledgment passed along the creature's neck as they plunged into a swarm of giant damsel flies hovering low over the surface of the water. The insects had bright jewel-like bodies, long tails of iridescent blue and four gossamer wings that buzzed in a whirr of motion as they hovered above the water.

The girl gripped with her thighs, her muscles tensing beneath the tight silken soulskin that encased her body. She leaned forward and aimed the slender lance with both hands. With the brittle sound of cracking carapaces, the girl neatly skewered three of the damsel flies on the end of her lance before the whitewyrme pulled out of the dive and soared back into the sky.

The girl held the lance out to the whitewyrme and, arching his neck, the creature nibbled delicately at the tender morsels until the shaft was clean. Then, listing to one side and angling his wings, he wheeled round in the sky and flew back down.

Again the whitewyrme skimmed the lake while the girl expertly speared the damsel flies hovering above its surface. The girl proffered the skewered insects to the whitewyrme once more, but this time the creature did not eat. Instead, with a guttural roar, a jet of white flame emerged from his parted lips and enfolded the laden lance-tip. The wings, carapaces and legs were incinerated in an instant, and the girl judged the toasting of the damsel flies by the charred fragrance that wafted back.

When they were done to her liking, she pulled the lance away and wedged the shaft back under her arm. She pulled off the pieces of charred meat with her fingers and ate hungrily. Sated, the girl licked the grease from her fingertips and pressed back with her heels.

The creature beat his vast leathery wings in response and soared higher still, veering eastwards in the sky towards a thin ravine that sliced through the heart of the imposing wall of mountains ahead. The girl noted the clusters of stunted trees far below, their gnarled roots clinging to the bare rock; the blind gulleys, overhanging bluffs, rockfalls and shattered buttes. The next moment, as the wyrme listed to one side, his left wing dipping and right wing raised, she pressed in hard with her legs and braced her body, and the pair of them whistled into the narrow ravine.

The vertical rockface smudged past them, slate-brown and sparkling, as the wyrme's wingtips grazed the sheer sides of the crevasse. Moments later, they emerged into sunlight on the other side of the sheer wall of rock and continued to soar high above the mountains beyond, now spread out beneath them in a jagged chaos of skyscratch summits and shadow-dark gullies.

With a hand against the whitewyrme's neck, she surveyed the land below with a practised eye, noting the long chains of ragged ridges, together with the solitary peaks. Black needle, broken back, white pillar and speckled stack . . .

There, high up on the black speckled rockstack, just below its jagged pinnacle and wreathed in swirling smoke, was a point of red light, like a jewel glinting from a bed of velvet. They swooped down in a low looping curve, circling the pinnacle. Embedded in a nest of warm ash at the top of the speckled stack was the whitewyrme wyve they'd been watching over. Glowing intensely, the egg was close to hatching, the wyrmeling within already testing out its festerbreath on the inside of the shell.

Whitewyrmes had laid their wyves in the high stacks for untold centuries, safe in the knowledge that they would remain there undisturbed until the time of their hatching. But that had changed with the coming of the two-hides.

A charge, like a stray tendril of lightning, seemed to pass through them both. The whitewyrme switched his tail in agitation. The girl's face clouded over.

Far down in the dark shadows at the bottom of the peak, were two men, their heads down and shoulders sloped. They were making their way up the speckled stack with steady determination, slowly approaching the pinnacle. Each was dressed in a hood, heavy wyrmehide boots and leggings, and capacious jackets, every pocket bulging with the various tools of their trade.

The whitewyrme let out a long low groan. The kingirl gripped her lance fiercely and raised the soulskin hood that mantled her shoulders, cowling her face in impenetrable blackness.

'Wyrmekith,' she breathed.

SEVEN

With a howl of terror, Micah jerked back
as the wyrme lunged, striking his head
hard on the rock wall behind him. A
shower of stars filled his vision. Saliva
spattered his face, and the stench of dead
meat filled his nostrils, warm and vile and
churning his stomach . . .

He raised his arms, hackdagger in one
hand, the other balled into a fist. Before
him the creature seemed frozen in mid air
in defiance of all natural laws. The scales
at its neck constricted and buckled, and
it let out a high strangulated cry. Its
outstretched tongue flexed as its hideous
chalk-white eyes bulged. The next moment
it came crashing to the ground.

As the wyrme jerked backwards, Micah
noticed the thin metal choke-collar that
encircled its neck, biting into the tarnished
scales. And the slender, thread-like golden
chain that stretched out taut behind it.

Wild with rage and frustration, the
creature thrashed violently at his feet.
Micah lashed out with his boot, kicking the
creature hard in its snarling, slavering
mouth. The wyrme yowled and scuttled
backwards out of harm's way. The chain
slackened, then went taut again and tugged
hard.

With a choked shriek, the stunted
wyrme scrabbled to its feet and shook its

head from side to side to loosen the constricting fetter at its neck. Smoke dribbled from its nostrils as it teetered backwards. Again the chain tugged, and as the creature was dragged backwards, legs braced and claws scoring the soft rock, its fight seemed to ebb away.

Turning its back on Micah, it retreated, meek now, head down and stuntwings drooping. It headed for a black tunnel opening on the far side of the lake into which the thin thread of chain, barely discernible in the dim cavern light, seemed to disappear. Micah caught sight of something white and gleaming lying before him on the ground. He stooped down and picked it up.

It was one of the creature's fangs, smooth and pitted. He traced the needle point across his forearm, and winced. It was deadly sharp. There was dark blood and tags of tissue around the root.

He swallowed, but there was no moisture to lubricate his throat. He sheathed his hackdagger and reached for the leather gourd. On the other side of the lake, the wyrme melted into the darkness of the tunnel.

The cavern fell still. Only the sound of the water trickling down into the ink-black pool broke the silence.

Micah scurried forwards, all haste and urgency. He glanced round the dim-lit cavern twitchily as his boots crunched over the whitesplash gravel. At the water's edge, he hunkered down and cupped his hands. He plunged them into the cool clear water, then raised them trembling to his parched lips. He sipped—then spat it out and retched emptily.

The water tasted bad. Real bad. Stale, stagnant,

31

rotten; as though dead decaying things had been steeped in it.

Micah straightened up and stared about him, miserable and bewildered. He had to get some water inside him—but not this water; this water that had lain motionless for who knew how long, turning brackish and undrinkable.

His gaze fell upon the huge stalactite, and the thread of water coiling down its length and trickling into the fetid lake below. He waded in, trying hard not to gag. Water gushed over the top of his boots till his feet were sloshing. The lake bed was slimy and, by the time he hit knee deep, Micah was bracing his legs for balance with every step as the soles of his boots squelched and skidded through the sludge. The water was up to his thighs by the time he reached the stalactite.

He looked up. The point of the rock stopped six feet or so above the surface of the lake. The water glinted as it twisted down through the air. He reached out, his bony fingers crushed together so hard the skin went waxen white. He collected up the water as best he could, then raised it tentatively to his face and sniffed.

The water was slipping through his fingers. He pushed his lips into his bandaged palms and sipped at what remained before it all drained away.

It tasted good.

He raised his hands a second time, and watched impatiently as the water collected slowly in his cupped palms. The fact was, more seemed to be trickling through his fingers than ever was collecting. Dropping his arms to his side, he tilted his head backwards and shuffled forward till the thin line of water was pouring directly into his open mouth. He swallowed, then he swallowed again. The water sluiced down his throat, cooling his burning insides. He swallowed some more, and kept on swallowing, only stopping when fear began to replace his quenching thirst.

He hesitated, his ears pricked and eyes peering into the shadows.

The water trickled down into the pool before him. Ripples fanned out and away. He couldn't leave; leastways, not yet. He eased himself back a tad, taking care not to slip. Then he shifted the leather gourd round, pulled the stopper and held the neck out. He braced his arms. The water began trickling inside.

Come on, Micah urged, and glanced nervously over his shoulders.

He felt the water splash onto his wrists and returned his attention to the gourd, realigning it beneath the dribble of water. He tilted it from side to side, and was disappointed to note how modest was the amount of water that sloshed about inside.

Come on, come on . . .

The water was mule stubborn. It would not be hurried. Eyes darting this way, that way, Micah held rigid. The air was brittle. The darkness heaved. Shadows seemed to swell and contract, and as he stared into them, he was unable to persuade himself that the glittering shards of schist and mica were not the eyes of bloodcrazed predators sizing him up.

Come *on* . . .

He shifted the swelling gourd around, supporting its weight in the crook of his arm, and cradled it like a babe in arms. He was hot and cold. His body was trembling; his legs were numb.

It seemed like an eternity and a day had passed before the gourd was full. Micah rammed the stopper back into place, splashed to the shoreline and, draining the stinking water from his boots, made a dash for the tunnel. The gourd was heavy and the leather strap dug sharply into his shoulder. Not that he was complaining, for Micah now had the water he'd sought, and was grateful for it.

He entered the tunnel and the light was abruptly extinguished. He smelled the fetid odour rising from his boots and breeches. Soon the rock started pressing in on both sides once again, and Micah turned sideways, taking care to protect the precious bulging gourd.

The water would last several days if he was careful. Special careful. He'd taken a terrible risk venturing inside the rock, and he had struck lucky. But the next time his gourd was empty, he would take no chances. He would seek out a waterfall or a tarn, even a fly-flecked rainpuddle—anything rather than enter the darkness again.

As he scrambled out of the fissure, the sky crackled and flashed with tendrils of white lightning. He resumed his climb. The image of the hideous runty wyrme filled his head; its swivelling white eyes, its outsized claws, its drooldrip fangs, and the chain . . .

Micah swallowed as the thought struck him. If there was a chain, then who or what was at the other end?

34

EIGHT

Let one of the others be taken, Heppy prayed. Any of the others. Just not me . . .

She could not rightly remember how many there were just now. So many had come and gone. Why, she hadn't even learned their names.

She peered round anxiously, trying to put faces to the soft moans and muted whimpers that sounded in the shadows. But it was too dark to see clearly. Three, she reckoned there were. Maybe four.

All at once, there came the scratching of claws and click-click of metal on stone.

She raised her legs and lowered her head, closed her eyes and clamped her arms about her ears. She didn't want to see anything. She didn't want to hear anything neither.

She kept her head bowed as the sound of curdled snarling and shrill yelps mixed with muffled screams and whimpers. And, as she felt the hot stinking breath on her face, she flinched and clamped her arms even tighter round her head. The next moment, she cried out as the top of her arm was pinched with plier force.

'Skin and bone . . .'

She shuddered. Not me. Someone else, just not me.

35

NINE

Micah picked his way along the sharp ridge
of naked rock, the mountain falling away
as steep shattered cliffs on both sides. He
was stooped forward, hat tipped and
crowtattered cloak flapping. His empty
leather gourd hung limp at his side. The
cave water had lasted him for three days,
but he'd had the last gulp of it that
morning and in this arid dustblown
landscape, Micah couldn't see where he
might come by more.

He thrust his arms out shakily at his side
and flailed for balance as, the higher he
climbed, the more unsteady he became.
His boots skeetered on the slippery
windbuffed rock.

'Godammit to hell!' he cussed as he
missed his footing and lurched perilous
close to the edge.

The words echoed in the air. Feeling
like a fool for exclaiming out loud, he
scrambled back to the apex of the ridge on
hands and feet.

He pulled himself up to a cautious
stoop, then continued, the cloak tatters
fluttering as his arms dipped and swayed.
The sun rose above a distant line of
mountains. Two raggedy winged creatures
tumbled across the sky, one after the
other, rawking loudly. He noticed neither,
his gaze fixed instead on the perching rock

up ahead. It marked the end of the ridge and the beginning of a plateau.

His face looked old, the grime ingrained in the wince and grimace lines like scars. His hair was spiked rigid with grey-white mud and his clothes were mired with the evidence of hard climbing and dry grit-laden winds.

Since he'd fled the cavern, Micah had spent one night curled up in a rock hollow while the sky had raged and splintered with tumultuous thunder and blinding forks of lightning. He'd remained there the whole of the following day, holed up until the storm had passed, and then walked through the next night by the silver light of a full moon. On the afternoon of the third day, with his food and water running low, the distant sky had turned chestnut red, and he'd watched it billow closer, intrigued by the accompanying roar, which sounded like a stampede. Then the duststorm had struck, thick and impenetrable, and caused him to hole up again till it had blown over. Then he'd found the ridge and followed it up to the plateau in the distance.

Micah stumbled over the high flat ground, the rock beneath his feet as hot as forge coals, until he came to a gulch in the flat landscape, a deep fissure, invisible at a distance. He lurched to a standstill and peered over the side.

Some way off, a slender yet vigorous torrent of water erupted from a chasm in the cliff wall and cascaded into a pale-green lake that nestled in the vastness of the rock basin below. He slipped and slithered his way down the steep sides of the gulch to the water's edge.

Close to, the mountain-clasped lake was enormous, with the waterfall so far away at its

37

distant end that Micah could barely hear its rushing sigh. There were angular trees dotted around among the toppled boulders, and grass and weeds fringed the lakeshore. A flat apron of white rock jutted into the lake before him.

Micah stumbled to its end, dropped to his knees and cupped water gratefully to his mouth till his thirst was satisfied. Then, dropping his backpack, he pulled off his hat, cloak, jacket and boots and stepped down into the lake. The gravel jabbed the soles of his feet as he waded deeper.

He crouched down and his gaze fell upon his hands, smooth and sallow-white where the water had washed away the disintegrating dust-caked bandages. He thrust his arms down into the lake and wiped the skin clean. Fine golden hairs glistened on his forearms. He removed his calico shirt and undersmock, rolled them into a ball and tossed them onto the rock. Then, releasing his braces and standing first on one leg, then the other, he pulled off his fieldpants, and they joined the rest.

He knelt down slowly. The water rose up his body, cool and delicious. It came up to his neck. Dipping forward, he splashed it over his head. Grime dissolved. He ducked his head completely, and a milky-white cloud haloed his hair as he massaged his scalp with his fingertips and rubbed the back of his neck. He resurfaced, probed his earholes and wiped away the dust that had gathered in the corners of his eyes, then dunked his head a second time.

Little by little, like sloughed skin, the layer of filth and grime washed away. The dust melted and his hair turned from grey to dark blond.

Micah climbed to his feet and splashed across to the rock. His clothes buzzed with flies, and his nose crinkled up at their sour odour. He couldn't bring himself to put them back on, not now his body was clean, so he washed them as best he could; cloak, shirt, vest, breeches and all, and laid them out to dry. Then he crouched down and, reaching into his pack, took out the last of his supplies.

It wasn't much—some precious chunks of dry fungus, and a handful of black salsify roots.

He placed them on the flat rock. He fetched fallen branches from the stunted lakeside trees, then made a circle of small rocks and constructed a nest of the twigs. He pulled a wad of bollcotton from a side pocket of his jacket and teased away a small twist, which he settled down among the kindling. Then, taking two flintstones from another pocket, he struck them together to create sparks that showered down on the dry fibres.

Pink and yellow flames lapped across the crackling twigs as he blew, head down and hands cupped. He broke a bleached branch across his knee and placed it over the fire. It caught with welcome spits and sputters. He added more wood, and satisfied that the fire was not about to die on him, he returned to the pack for the copper pot that he kept stowed at the very bottom. He filled it with water and set it over the flames. Then, having cleaned the fungus and sliced up the black salsify, he dropped the meagre handful into the water.

Sharp pangs of hunger writhed in the pit of his stomach, but the dish could not be hurried. The roots had to be boiled to rid them of their harsh bitterness and render the thin gruel that resulted at least half edible. It wasn't enough, but it was all he had. As Micah caught his reflection in the still lakewater, gaunt and stick-thin, ribs painfully visible beneath stretched skin, he realized he was beginning to starve.

A chill breath of air fluttered across the lake. The sun was losing its heat. Below, in the green depths, shadows glinted like old gold as large fat lakefish darted to and fro. Micah's stomach constricted painfully, and he cursed aloud his lack of a fishing net or spear. Here he was, weak with hunger, standing beside a lake full of abundant food just beyond his grasp.

Behind him, he could hear the water coming to the boil and caught the first whiff of the softening salsify roots as their fragrance was slowly released. He would have to nourish himself with this thin soup, and hope that he'd have the strength to forage round the lakeshore the next day.

Micah picked up a small stone and tossed it bitterly into the lake. He was watching the ripples spread out across the still water when the lake changed. It swirled and heaved, and a great dome-like bulge rose up at its centre, then burst into a cascade of crashing white water as a monstrous head broke the surface.

Micah stumbled backwards.

The great head was broad and low-browed, with skin like rough bark and two ridges of jagged bone edging its skull like turret castellations. A long thin snout descended from two enormous heavy-lidded eyes before spreading out into a vast flat plate, like the bill of a monstrous duck.

As the lakewyrme rose higher out of the water, its scaly neck came into view, thick as the trunk of an ancient pinetree yet as sinuous as buckreeds. Its

40

back broke the surface, snail encrusted and wide as a barn, and upon its flexing shoulders were affixed the stubby vestiges of wings. The water waked and welled as the creature swayed to and fro.

A deep mournful roar churned the brittle air and echoed around the lake. The monumental lakewyrme was staring directly at Micah. Barbels that dangled from the corners of its mouth trembled and dripped. Its huge flat beak quivered. Its lidded eyes narrowed to dark slits.

Naked and defenceless, Micah stared back at it, open-mouthed.

The creature slowly raised and lowered its head. Then, with a deep sigh, it slipped beneath the water, like a blade cutting through silk. Chevron ripples lined the surface for a moment, then they too were gone.

Scrambling over the rock, Micah was about to gather up his things when there was a colossal explosion of movement beneath the water, and a torrent of bubbles rose to the surface. With a roaring rushing sound, the lakewyrme broke through the water and launched itself high into the air, its back arched and twisting.

The sunlight gleamed on its burnished scales as it reached the top of its prodigious leap and came down again. Its head dipped and its body hit the water with an almighty crash, its broad tail thrashing down after it. And as the creature dived, it seemed as if half the lake was displaced. A gushing geyser of water exploded back into the air and showered down onto the lakeshore.

Micah was doused.

When the downpour subsided, he pushed his wet hair back and surveyed the water. As suddenly

41

LAKEWYRME

as it had appeared, so the great lakewyrme had disappeared again. The turbulence receded and the water grew calm. Then a flip-flop agitation caught his eye, and Micah looked down to see a fat lakefish thrashing about on the rock at his feet.

Another lay some way off, with a third flopping about beside it. And, as Micah looked round, he saw that the shore was littered with dozens of others, writhing and squirming on the silt. A broad grin spread across his face, creasing the corners of his blue-grey eyes.

The fire fizzed and spluttered beneath the upturned pot, damp and half-quenched and smoking badly. But Micah didn't mind. The great lakewyrme had bestowed upon him a special favour. He bent down, picked up a lakefish.

Tonight, he thought, turning the plump succulent fish over in his hands, he was going to dine like a lord.

He didn't notice the shadow flickering across the lake, a shadow cast by a great whitewyrme, high in the early evening sky. A great whitewyrme and its rider.

TEN

Eli Halfwinter looked up, his eyes narrowed behind heavy lids, his stubbled jaw silver in the flickering light. Shifting the heavy pack on his shoulders, he surveyed the rockstrewn slope before him, and the line of the horizon, slate-grey on polished black, beyond.

Nightfall had eased the suffocating heat. The shrubpocked rocks and scree slopes had cooled, while overhead, the black sky fizzed and crackled with tendrilled sprays of lightning.

The cragclimber withdrew the knot of gulchroot he was chewing and surveyed the pulped end, his brow furrowed, before clamping his teeth back down on it.

Just then, the darting filaments of lightning overhead coalesced into a sheet of brilliance that lit up the sky and illuminated the barren rockscape around him. And there, black against the white sky, was the drystone roundel of a craghut.

Spitting out the pungent gulchroot, the crag- climber gave a throaty chuckle as he straightened up and strode towards the stone shelter. He would sleep well that night.

He approached the craghut, noting with satisfaction that there was no smoke coming from the hearth-hole at the centre of the stone roof, nor light seeping through the cracks in the walls. He had no desire for company.

Stooping down, he stepped through the doorway and inside. The air smelled hot and smoked, like charred parchment, and, he fancied, was laced with the faint tang of liquor. There were the remains of an old fire in the hearth, crumbs on the stoneslab table and several filthy-looking blankets in a heap by the far wall. He swung the pack from his shoulders and set it down before him, then unstrapped his bedroll and laid it out in one of the sleeping-hollows. He unhooked his lamp and, lifting the mantle and striking a match in one fluid motion, put the flame to the wick.

The craghut was transformed into a brooding upturned pot of grey shadows and yellow glow. Sootblackened rocks encircled the hearth-hole in the roof, through which lightning could still be seen, shattering the black sky at irregular intervals.

He sat himself down on the edge of his bedroll, dragged his pack towards him and wrapped his legs about it. Then he unbuckled the straps, loosened the ties and pulled it open.

He removed a folded wyrmepelt and laid it across his knees. His face creased into a satisfied smile as he held up the pelt. The smooth metallic patina glowed like quicksilver.

Laying it to one side, Eli Halfwinter rummaged in his backpack. He pulled an earthenware pot from the pack, removed the cork stopper and peered inside.

The scentsac of a mistwyrme, smooth and round, its membrane intact, floated in thick yellow oil. A heady fragrance, musk-dark and spicerich, filled the air. The cragclimber breathed deep and

45

smiled again.

All at once, a straining groan and exaggerated yawns erupted from the far side of the craghut. The man looked up, surprise turning to anger. He'd been careless. He stoppered the jar grimly and wrapped it in the wyrmepelt. Opposite him, the heap of blankets shifted. He stowed the pelt inside his pack and closed it.

'Is it company I have on this dark stormcrossed night?' a croaky voice enquired.

The cragclimber climbed to his feet, raised his lamp and strode across the hut, the yellow light swaying to and fro over the trampled earth. From the depths of the blankets he'd overlooked, a figure sat bolt upright and squinted into the light.

He was bone-thin and unshaven. His shaggy beard and tangled hair formed a matted clump, like a giant seedhead. His eyes were round and dark and open so wide that a circle of eyewhite surrounded each iris. All at once, a broad smile split his face.

'So,' he cried, 'a fellow traveller!'

His voice was harsh with brightness. He scrambled to his feet, letting the blankets drop to reveal a frayed shirt and tattered wyrmeskin breeks, covered in scrawled signs and symbols. At his neck were several strings of tiny wyrmeteeth threaded on leather thongs. He thrust out a grimy hand.

'Ichabod, the truth-seeker,' he said. 'Stone prophet and visionary.'

The cragclimber winced, both at the piercing nature of the man's voice and the tenor of his words. He had no truck with fanatics. He lowered the lamp, but kept his guard up. He seized the man's thin hand and squeezed it for an instant, then let it go, surprised by how hot it felt.

'Eli Halfwinter,' he said. A gruffness had crept into his more familiar drawl. He cleared his throat. 'Pleased to make your acquaintance . . . stone prophet.'

The two men fell silent. The dry lightning storm was all but above them now. A ferocious wind had got up and was whipping round the craghut while the thunderclaps rattled the stones. Crackling across the sky like burning tinder, the flashes of sheet lightning filled the drystone hut below with a spectral silver blue.

Eli shuddered.

Ichabod laughed, his eyes wild. 'The voices of the ancestors, friend Eli,' he proclaimed. 'I hear them calling down to me.' He threw back his head, his arms wide apart and jerking at his side as he gazed up through the hearth-hole above. 'We are all lost children in this unforgiving land . . . There is no hope unless we see the light!'

He looked round, and Eli found his gaze being held by Ichabod's intense stare. The stone prophet jittered forward and grinned. Every movement he made was twitchy and fitful, like some strange, jerky dance, and Eli found himself exaggerating his own naturally measured pace in response.

'But I am forgetting my manners, friend Eli,' Ichabod announced. 'A wild night such as this requires a remedy, does it not?'

Eli watched the ragged creature skip round on his leathery heels and scamper back to the heap of blankets, where he untangled a shabby wyrmeskin longjacket from their folds. He thrust his hands into the sleeves, then again into the pockets. His

47

brittle grin flexed broader than ever when he turned back, a leather flask twirling in his fingers.

'Green spirit, finest in all the wyrmeweald,' he proclaimed.

Eli placed his hands on his hips and shook his head, a lopsided grin stretching his tanned skin. It explained the odour his nose had first detected on entering the craghut. 'Forgive me, Ichabod, but I was unaware that preachermen drank intoxicating liquors.'

Ichabod cocked his head to one side and stared at the flask, intense concentration furrowing his brow. He ran a bony finger over its pitted surface, then looked up at Eli, smiling as he pulled the cork.

'It soothes my nerves,' he said. 'And quietens the voices on nights such as this!'

He took a long hard swig. As the liquor hit the back of his throat, his face screwed up and his feet performed a brief jig. Then, in a flap and flurry of movement, he spun round in a full circle and handed the flask to Eli with a flourish.

'Join me, friend Eli.'

A smile passed slowly over Eli Halfwinter's face as he took the flask and sniffed at the open top.

'Smells smooth,' he said.

'Smooth as soulskin,' Ichabod confirmed, nodding encouragingly.

'Course, I'm not that used to strong liquor,' said Eli. 'Not no more. Tends to go straight to my head.' He smiled that lopsided smile again. 'But it smells *good*.'

Raising the flask high, he took a long draught. He breathed in and smacked his lips. He took a second slug, and a third, then staggered backwards, liquor sloshing from the neck of the flask as he did so.

'Steady there, friend Eli,' said Ichabod, his face pinched with exaggerated concern.

Eli smiled, and sat down heavily on his bedroll. More of the pungent liquid splashed down his front. Mumbling something indistinct, his eyes closed and his head slumped forward on his breastbone.

Ichabod knelt down in front of the old crag-climber and watched him closely for a few moments. Then he took the flask gently from his grasp and restoppered it.

'Told you it was good stuff,' said Ichabod. He pushed the flask into his pocket. 'Now let us see what manner of merchandise you've been trading in . . .'

He swivelled round on his knees and began tugging at the leather buckles on the sleeping man's pack with filthy cracked fingernails. Eli Halfwinter opened his eyes and spat out the unswallowed liquor he'd been holding in his mouth. He reached out.

'That's enough, preacherman.'

His voice was soft and purring, yet the grip he had on the stone prophet's wrist made Ichabod squeak with pain. The stone prophet turned his head away, only to feel the tip of a sharp blade press against the side of his neck.

'Don't, don't, *don't*,' he screeched, straining to pull back.

'You move, and I'll slit your throat,' said Eli calmly.

'I didn't mean no harm, friend Eli,' Ichabod protested, his voice shrill and indignant. 'I . . . I was just looking, is all. Just wondered what a fellow traveller might be carrying with him . . . Perhaps we could barter. Trade.' He wriggled and squirmed. 'You know. Share what we both have . . .'

'Share,' Eli repeated, and snorted. 'What do you take me for? Some greenhorn plainsman new to the crags and wet behind the ears? You'll have to do better than a liquor-cosh to take me down, preacherman!'

'Please!' squealed the stone prophet. 'Have mercy!'

Eli clamped a hand round Ichabod's jaw and pressed the blade more firmly against the straining, sinew-taut neck. He could smell the fear oozing from the stone prophet's pores.

All at once, the craghut was shaken by a tumultuous thunderclap, so loud and violent that Eli twitched involuntarily. Ichabod let out a small cry. High up above the hearth-hole, the blood-red sky turned white and shattered into a thousand jagged pieces.

A single lightning bolt crackled and hissed as it doglegged out of the sky. It blistered the air and scorched the wind as it zigzagged down the craghut chimney like a bony finger. It touched the upturned face of the stone prophet at the very centre of his forehead.

Eli Halfwinter was thrown aside.

For an instant, the lightning bolt dangled down the chimney like a sparkling fishline. Hooked at its end, fringed with light from the tips of his bare toes to the seedhead splendour of his wild hair, was the preacherman. His eyes were wild and staring, his taut mouth drooled, while his bony body performed a tortured jerking dance.

50

Then the lightning bolt snapped. Eli waited for Ichabod to fall.

But he didn't. He remained standing. Then, as Eli Halfwinter watched, the stone prophet turned and hurtled out into the raging storm, stumbling and smoking and shrieking at the skies.

ELEVEN

Micah's boots slammed into something hard. He fell heavily to the ground, ending up winded and wrist-jarred. He glanced back to see what had tripped him, and a small cry escaped from his lips.

'Sacred Maker,' he breathed.

It was a dead body, lying supine in the shadows of one of the highstacks. The carrionwyrmes hadn't got to it yet. The corpse still had its eyes.

Micah crouched down, reached forward with cramped fingers and eased the eyelids shut. The touch of the moist skin made him shudder, and as he sat back on his haunches, he brushed his hands together as if to wipe away the unpleasant feeling.

Micah craned his neck backwards and squinted up. He was at the base of a speckled stack of dark rock, hard and crystalline, pockmarked with lumps of gypsum, each one the size of his fist.

The body was dressed in heavy clothes. A wide neckback hood, grey skin boots, padded leggings and a capacious jacket, its pockets bulging with snares and wires, and a skinning knife with a carved handle and serrated blade.

He noticed a faint dark stain down the front of the dead man's jacket. He reached forward with trembling fingers, unbuttoned the bone toggles and pulled it open.

His breath caught in his throat.

A huge patch of blood was spread out over the shirt beneath; dry and brown at the edges, but still bright red and glistening at the centre. It emanated from a dark wound in the middle of the chest, inflicted by something thin and hard, like a lance or a pike.

Micah glanced up. There was a second corpse.

It was above him, draped backwards over a jutting spur of rock. One arm was reaching out, its hand extended in a mockery of supplication, while its head lolled upside down, staring blindly down at him. The thin-lipped mouth was fixed in a silent scream.

Like the body on the ground, there was a deep wound in the chest, but it was the ornate spyglass, banded with copper and brass, dangling from a chain around the man's neck, that caught Micah's attention.

He climbed to his feet and reached up. His hand closed round the spyglass. He flicked the chain free. The body jerked and the dead man's sightless eyes seemed to bore into his. He was slipping the chain of the spyglass over his head when the blow struck . . .

It hit him colossal hard in the chest, sending him toppling backwards. He came down heavily and lay there winded for a moment. Then, despite the bewildering pain that racked his body, he rolled himself over and scanned the gathering darkness, his eyes wide with panic.

He drew his hackdagger.

Dusk had fallen, and a mist had descended, clammy and brimstone sour. With a grunt of pain, he climbed awkwardly to his feet, his chest throbbing like the devil. He reached up and touched a hand gingerly to the source of the pain. His fingertips discovered a hole in his leather jacket, and something viscous and sticky.

It was blood; his blood.

Just then, a wild jarring screech echoed round the rock stacks. In a flurry of movement and a rush of stale air, a giant angular shape appeared before him out of the mist. There was a blur of slashing talons, and blazing eyes bored into his for an instant as flames scorched his skin and singed his hair.

With the flat of his hand pressed hard against the wound, he ran. The air was still, and he could hear nothing but the sound of his own footfalls.

Then it was back, whatever it was. The air swept past him in a swirling rush, tugging his cloak and plucking at his hat, and he felt something slash at the pack on his back.

He glanced behind him. A vicious-looking lance jabbed at his head. He ducked, and felt it glance off the side of his shoulder.

He stumbled through the labyrinthine chasms of rock, stooped and cowering. His hand was sticky with blood that oozed through his fingers. He dodged tumblerocks and boulders, and stumbled through sanddrifts, his head swimming and his legs weak.

Drops of blood splashed onto the rock. His breathing faltered and lurched.

He kept running. He kept running until the towering peaks were far behind him. He kept running until he was sure that whatever it was pursuing him had given up the chase; until the

54

clammy night mist had swallowed him up. Then he kept running some more.

But he was tiring, his legs heavy and threatening to buckle with every step he took. He swallowed, then gasped for air, and the pain in his chest intensified like a blade twisting in his flesh. He collapsed, then pulled himself to his feet once more. He stumbled on.

And then he saw it, just up ahead, a yellow light in the thick air, as though the rocks themselves were ablaze. He hesitated, then staggered towards it.

A thin trickle of blood spattered the rocks as he passed. It gathered in small puddles every time he paused, and marked a line across the threshold of the doorway as he tumbled inside.

He fell to his knees, and clasped both hands to the copiously bleeding wound, battling to catch his breath as great waves of pain and nausea broke over him. His head spun in a blur of flickering light and shadow as, with a soft and empty whimper, Micah fell forwards into nothingness.

TWELVE

The clamour of liquor-touched voices roused Micah in his hiding place behind the rainwater butts in the far corner of the courtyard. Night had fallen. Guests were departing and Seraphita's balcony windows were bathed in golden lampglow.

He climbed stiffly to his feet and waited for the voices to subside, then crept across the courtyard till he was standing beneath her balcony. He looked up, raised his hands to his mouth and hooted like an owl. The windows stayed shut. He hooted again, and his heart quickened as the windows opened and Seraphita appeared.

'Micah,' she whispered. 'Is that you?' She gripped the balustrade and looked down. Their eyes met. She frowned. 'I didn't think you were coming.'

'I'm truly sorry, Seraphita.' He shuffled with embarrassment. 'But I was waiting for the guests to leave. I have something for you—for your maidenfeast . . .'

'Well?' she said. 'You gonna stay down there all night, scratching about like a lone rooster, or are

56

you coming up to greet me proper?'

Micah climbed the trellis that lined the walls and clambered over the balustrade. Seraphita took his hands in hers and pulled him across the balcony, through the open doors and inside her bedchamber. A smile spread across Micah's face.

'You sure look pretty tonight,' he said.

Seraphita released his hands and stepped back. She reached up, undid the silver clasp, and shook her hair down loose. She winked at him, then twirled around. The finely embroidered dress she was wearing sparkled as it billowed, and Micah longed to wrap his arms around her slender waist.

'My father had it made special,' she explained, 'for my maidenfeast . . .'

Micah undid his jacket and took out the bundle cradled to his chest. He carefully unwrapped the cloth to reveal a beechwood carving of a horse in mid gallop, its mane flowing and nostrils flared.

It was Seraphita's stallion, Peshneg.

'It . . . it's for your maidenfeast,' he stammered.

Seraphita took it and gave it a cursory glance. 'Oh, Micah,' she said, setting it down carelessly on the dressing table, 'how sweet of you.'

Micah looked at the carving—the carving he'd spent long nights toiling over, his fingers blistered and blue with cold; the carving that Caleb had beaten him over, for wasting good flax oil; the carving that he hoped would show her how much he loved her, cared for her . . .

He stared at it miserably. It was useless. Crude and lifeless.

A brooch lay beside it. It was made of filigree gold, its circumference studded with jewels, while at its centre, picked out in a black precious stone, was the silhouette of a rearing horse. It was delicate and finely wrought . . .

'You gonna stand there all day gawping, ploughboy?' said Seraphita.

She pulled him towards her warm body, and dragged him to her bed . . .

THIRTEEN

'You care for some more?'

Micah looked up wearily. He saw the leather flask being proffered and licked his lips. The liquor had tasted good. He glanced at the man proffering it. His pale-blue eyes were surveying him coolly. The man shifted a piece of chewed root from one side of his mouth to the other with his tongue.

'Well?'

'You sure?'

'Wouldn't have offered it if I wasn't willing to part with some,' he drawled. He jiggled the flask. 'Take it or no. 'S all the same to me.'

They were seated at the end of a long stone table. Micah reached for the flask, wiped the top with the palm of his hand and took a deep swig. He exhaled noisily, expressing his approval.

The quality of the liquor lay somewhere between the rough hooch from a farm still and the smooth aromatic liquor he had once tasted, taken from a vessel of green glass, its waxen seal broken. It burned his tongue some, but did not make his eyes water, and he took pleasure from the way it kept on burning as it slid down. He wiped the back of his hand across his lips.

'Like it?'

'I like it a lot,' said Micah. He handed

the flask back to the man, who put it to his lips and took a sip.

The man frowned, his eyes creasing up at the corners, then leaned forward. 'See, the thing is,' he said slowly, 'you didn't want to be doing that.'

Micah was puzzled. 'Doing what?'

The man rubbed the palm of his hand over the top of the open flask. 'That,' he said. 'Some folks might take it as a sign of disrespect.'

'Disrespect?' Micah's scalp began to tingle. His mouth dried up.

'Disrespect in the sense that, before drinking from it, you should choose to wipe the flask clean.' His unblinking gaze hardened. '*Clean*, you understand me? With the implication that it was dirty before. That I am dirty.'

Micah took a sharp intake of breath. 'I . . . I didn't mean . . .' He swallowed. 'I had no mind to offend or to disrespect you, sir.'

The man's face relaxed, and the twinkle returned to his pale eyes. 'I guess you didn't, son, but it's as well to be aware. It's easy to make enemies in the wyrmeweald, and though I'm not generally one for company, I've got to concede that there have been times when I've needed all the goodwill I could muster.'

Micah nodded. And when the man held the flask out a third time, he took it and put it straight to his mouth. He swallowed quickly and returned it. The man stood the flask on the table and reached out his hand.

'Name's Eli Halfwinter,' he said.

Micah shook it firmly. 'I'm Micah,' he said eagerly. He smiled, his face suffused with a mixture of gratitude and relief. 'And I am pleased to make your acquaintance, Eli,' he said. 'If I may call you Eli, sir?'

'You may, son, since that is my name,' he said. 'And since we have shared a flask of green spirit liquor together.' He frowned. 'How's that wound of yours?'

Micah looked down and put his fingers gingerly to his chest. 'Feels a little better,' he said.

'Possibly on account of the liquor,' said Eli drily.

'It's on account of all the help you have provided me with,' said Micah. 'I am truly thankful for everything you've done.'

' 'S all right,' Eli told him, climbing to his feet. 'Don't you fret none.'

Micah watched as Eli crossed to the centre of the craghut, fed the fire, stirred a pot and flipped over the sizzling contents of a pan. He returned with a battered metal plate of smoked lakefish and greens, which he set down on the table before him. The food tasted good, but Micah had little appetite.

'You're the first person I've met in weeks,' he told Eli. 'First *live* person leastways,' he added.

Eli nodded thoughtfully. 'The wyrmeweald's a harsh place, ain't no doubt about it.'

Micah took a mouthful of smoked fish and swallowed. 'First one died of thirst,' he said. 'And the other two . . . Can't rightly say what happened to them, but they didn't die a natural death judging by their wounds . . .'

He cleared his throat, stifling a rising cough, and pushed the plate away. Eli frowned and looked at Micah closely, his eyes crinkling up.

'Deep wounds?' he said quietly. 'Likely caused by a pike or a lance?'

Micah nodded. 'How did you know?'

'Your wounds were the same.'

The cough rose again and this time wouldn't be stifled, and with it came a sharp stabbing pain. Micah groaned and pressed a hand to the bindings at his chest. His eyes watered and his face reddened, and he grimaced as the hacking cough seemed to turn a blade in the wound. Eli passed him the flask of liquor, which Micah swilled round his mouth and gratefully swallowed.

'Troubling you, ain't it?' said Eli, nodding towards Micah's chest.

'It . . . it's all right,' said Micah, short of breath, but when he pulled his hand away, he found his fingers sticky with blood. A patch of dark red was spreading out across the bandages. He coughed again, and there were blood flecks in the saliva.

Eli shook his head. 'I'd hope to have stopped the bleeding, but the healing of a wound such as yours requires more skill than I possess. I'm wyrmekith. I make my living trading in wyrmepelts and scrimshaw. I ain't no healer.'

He noticed the panic in Micah's face.

'But don't vex yourself, lad. I know someone who might help.'

Micah clamped his lips together, struggling not to cough.

'Though you'll need all your courage to submit to her savage healing.' Eli's eyes widened. 'There's only one kind who can treat the wound that afflicts you—the same kind that caused it.'

Micah swallowed. 'Who . . . who's that?'

Eli took back the unwiped flask. 'Wyrmekin,' he replied.

FOURTEEN

'I am wyrmekin,' the woman proclaimed.

She lowered her hood to reveal a face caked in heavy make-up and framed by bleached white hair. Beneath black painted eyebrows, her deepset eyes, too close together, glinted with ferret-like cunning.

'And I have travelled far, from the distant high country . . .'

The crowd oohed.

'A harsh and desolate rocky wilderness known as the wyrmeweald . . .'

The crowd aahed.

'And I bring with me a living breathing creature, for your delight and delectation, the like of which has seldom ever been seen here in the beautiful cultivated lands of the plains.'

The crowd exploded in whoops and gasps, happenstance neighbours muttering excitedly and nudging one another in the ribs. Everyone jostled for a better view.

'Show us!' someone shouted out.

'Yeah, let's see it!'

A drunken farmhand darted boldly forward, his

eyes glittering. He ducked down by the side of the patchwork covering and reached for one of the ties that secured it. He turned and winked at the crowd, who egged him on with approving cries. The next moment, there was sharp movement from beneath the blanket, a choked roar, and the man was hurled roughly aside.

The woman smiled slyly. 'The beast is mighty proud and quick of temper,' she confided. 'But as wyrmekin, I have the skill to control this extraordinary creature.'

A hush of anticipation fell over the crowd. The woman raised the tether high above her head and gestured towards the concealed beast.

'For the right price, I shall exercise this skill and display the creature to you.'

There was a clinking of coins in pockets, and someone tossed a handful of coppers. The woman stared down at them disdainfully.

'Seems I was woefully misinformed about you folks,' she said. 'Seems I must be on my way . . .'

'Twenty-five ducats!' a voice called out from the balcony of the tithe-house. 'That is what I am prepared to offer you to show us the wyrme.'

The woman smirked. 'You're indeed in luck, sir,' she said, as all eyes turned to the balcony, then back at her. 'For twenty-five ducats is precisely what I am prepared to accept.'

The crowd erupted with a roar of gratitude for the generosity of the handsome young man on the balcony, who threw a purse down to the woman. She pocketed the money, then crouched down at the creature's front. She unbuckled the ties that fixed the covering to the forepaws, then moved round to the back and did the same. The tension in the crowd grew as she stepped forward and seized a wad of blanket in her hand.

'Behold!' she cried out. She tugged hard, and the covering fell away.

For a split instant, there was absolute silence. The next, the square was filled with hollering and screaming, shrieks of amazement and yowls of fear.

Micah gasped. He had never seen such a creature before.

It had broad wings that, freed from the covering, now rose up and flapped, the mottled skin glinting in the lantern glow. Its claws appeared razor sharp and, when it opened its blistered mouth, rows of yellowing teeth were revealed that looked like they could tear apart a team of oxen in seconds flat. Around its neck, digging into the skin, was a vicious choke-collar, to which the tether was attached. Raising her hood, the woman made great show of jerking the tether hard, and bringing the wyrme coughing and choking to its knees.

Delighted by her mastery over the wyrme, the crowd yelled out for more. In answer, the woman shifted the lance in her grasp, stepped forward and jabbed it into the creature's flank. The wyrme's pus-crusted eyes rolled. It reared up on its hindlegs, supported by its tail. It craned its neck, opened its jaws and a plume of fire roared from the depths of its throat and shone bright against the darkening sky.

The crowd screeched with appalled delight. The woman jerked hard on the chain, and the wyrme fell back with a wheezing gurgle.

'Do it again!' someone cried out, and a chucked rock struck the side of the wyrme.

It swung its head round and roared a second time. The flame was less impressive, and soon petered out. The wyrme wheezed and coughed, and a forked tongue flickered limply out from between its jaws.

'Again! Again!'

More rocks, along with sticks and the occasional drinking mug slammed against the side of the wyrme. It roared, but feebly, then dropped back down onto all fours and lowered its wings. Micah watched closely as it raised a back leg and scratched listlessly at a red-raw sore on its flank, dislodging a couple of cracked scales, which fell to the ground.

A disappointed murmuring began to ripple through the crowd.

The woman strode forward and jabbed the point of the lance sharply into one of its smoking nostrils, and the wyrme reared up once more, furious, roaring and flapping, and the crowd bellowed louder than ever. Once more, she brought the enraged creature under control with the vicious collar and chain. It cowered miserably, its fight spent. It looked sick and half-starved, its ribs pressed against sagging hide.

Micah's elation at the sight of the creature had turned to horror. The great wyrme from the vast freedom of the high country had been reduced to a servile tortured beast here on the hot dusty plains. As he gazed into the wyrme's bloodshot eyes, he was overwhelmed by a deep sense of pity.

Looking away, Micah scanned the cluster of rapt faces on the tithe-house balcony, and his gaze fell on one that was familiar to him. He tensed.

It was Seraphita.

Her hair was up, and her eyes were bright with excitement. She was wearing a white dress, low-cut and sparkling, with a white fur stole wrapped around her slender neck. Micah didn't think he'd ever seen her looking so beautiful. Then he noticed the brooch with the circle of gems and rearing black horse pinned to the front of her dress.

As he watched, Seraphita's full lips parted and her white teeth gleamed as she cheered and shouted, and she tossed her head and broke into peals of stipplejay laughter. Like everyone else, she was enchanted by the captivating antics of the tormented wyrme.

A hand alighted on her shoulder, and she turned. Micah's stomach cramped up as he realized that she had a companion. He swallowed hard. It was the handsome young man who had paid for the sordid spectacle down in the square.

Seraphita reached up and pulled him towards her. Then, as Micah watched helplessly from the jostling crowd below, up on the tithe-house balcony the two of them melted into a passionate kiss.

Fifteen

'Wyrmekin,' the woman whispered. 'Wyrmekin did this.'

Her voice was soft and fragile, but her hook-nailed fingers caused Micah to flinch as they probed the inflamed wound in his chest. She pulled away, the nails gleaming like talons as she held her hands out before her, fingers spread wide as if calming a nervous colt. Her eyes narrowed as they scrutinized his face.

She was beautiful, her pale skin translucent and seeming to glow from within. Despite the frown lines that scored her brow and creased the corners of her mouth, there was something youthful and intense about her large dark-green eyes. She flicked back her long straight silver hair and pressed her face close to his. Her breath smelled of wet mud.

'You are a wyve collector?' she rasped accusingly.

*   *   *

Micah and Eli had set off from the craghut shortly after daybreak . . .

Micah was weary and in constant pain. He stumbled across the rising rocky terrain, a crown of jagged mountain peaks glowering at him from all sides. The sun slammed down out of a sullen sky;

rockscree slipped beneath his boots, and more than once, as he leaned on Eli's shoulder, the cragclimber had to catch him and pull him back upright.

'How much farther?' he asked, his hand pressed to the throbbing wound.

'Less far than before.'

Eli's response was always the same, but Micah's need to enquire persisted.

The sun had travelled halfway across the sky when Micah saw the dark line across the windswept plateau. As they drew closer, the line widened, revealing itself as a crack in the flat rock that seemed to grow broader and deeper the closer they came, until Micah found himself standing at the very edge of a chasm.

Ferns and grasses, shrubs and trees clung to the near-vertical rockface all the way down to the mistswirl in its shadowy depths. Towards the narrowing end of the chasm, a waterfall emerged from a subterranean spring and tumbled down in a glistening cascade. Fisherwyrmes, pitchwyrmes, screechwyrmes and snatterjabs wheeled in the air above it, diving for prey, and sometimes at each other . . .

'Green havens, some call places such as these,' Eli told him.

They skirted the ravine edge until they came to a narrow track that took them down into the vast chasm. Giant trees, moss-encrusted and strung with vines, competed with waxen-leafed ferns and towering conifers, all anchored in shadowed cracks and crevices and growing up towards the brightness of the sky.

Micah stumbled and tripped continuously as Eli

helped him down the steepening track through the ravine forest. Sweat beaded his forehead. His bandages were soaked through with blood.

Just as Micah felt he could go no further, they came to a vast overhanging spur, the windcarved rock smooth and handhold-free. The track narrowed to little more than a ledge, and they were forced to continue sideways on, Eli in front and Micah close behind, clinging to Eli's arm. The air roared with the sound of falling water, and Micah looked up to see the waterfall directly in front of them.

Eli inched himself along the ledge, wet and slippery from the swirling spray. He abruptly disappeared behind the curtain of falling water and pulled Micah in after him.

Micah looked around blearily. He was standing at one end of a vast cavern concealed behind the waterfall—a cavern that was alive and shrieking with wyrmes of all kinds, the atmosphere ripe with their scaletang and scorched breath.

There were tiny, translucent wyrmes with long tails and jagged ruffs at their necks prowling the walls and ceiling. Larger wyrmes—some white and tatterwinged, some dark and gnarled, and some with scales of red and green and mustard gold—stalked the stone floor or scuttled in and out of crevices, their talons tapping and scratching on the rock. Others, their wings folded, perched on every available surface, from the moss-covered rockledges to the rough troughs and earthenware pots clustered in the cavern's dark recesses.

Their rawking and screeching bounced off the walls as territory was breached and squabbles broke out. Underlying it all, Micah noticed another noise besides—a wheezing panting sound, rumbledeep and snuffle-filled, as though the chamber itself was alive and breathing. He fancied it was coming from the shadows at the back of the cavern.

A slim silver-grey-clad woman stepped silently out of the shadows, her hands raised in a solemn greeting. She walked towards them, her hollow-cheeked face and bone-thin body gathering years with each step she took. Her age did nothing to diminish her beauty. Her eyes looked feral fierce, and there was something almost predatory about her stabbing gait. Yet when her gaze focused on the cragclimber, her face softened.

'It is a long time since the last time, Eli Halfwinter,' she said in a soft voice, cracked and quaver-flecked from underuse.

She turned her unblinking gaze from Eli to Micah, and he felt a frostlicked shudder run down his spine . . .

*   *   *

'You are a wyve collector,' the woman said again, a harsh edge to her fragile voice.

Micah shrank back as the talon-nails pressed into his cheeks.

'He ain't no wyve collector,' came Eli's voice.

The woman nodded in terse acknowledgement of the words, though Micah was unable to determine whether she believed him or not.

'He's just a greenhorn departer, happened upon the wrong place at the wrong time, I reckon,' Eli was saying as he crossed the cavern floor, indignant wyrmes scattering before him in a scritching of

71

talons and a skirring of wings.

He stood beside her, crossed his arms, and the pair of them looked down at Micah, who was seated on a rock.

'He stumbled into a craghut I was sheltering in, over in the highstacks country . . . He needs help, Jura.'

The woman breathed in sharply, the air hissing over pointed teeth.

'You are a wyve collector?' she repeated for a second time.

Micah's head buzzed. 'Wyve?' he said, and turned to Eli questioningly.

'I done told you, Jura,' the cragclimber told her gently. 'He's a departer from the plains, don't know squat about life here in the wyrmeweald.'

'Hold still,' she hissed.

She clamped her bony fingers to the sides of Micah's head, the nails grazing his scalp. Micah froze, his heart thudding like hail on a flat roof. He felt her thumbs reach round, tracing his burning cheeks. They sought out his eyes, closing the lids and pressing the eyeballs hard into their sockets.

Her skin was oily smooth. Her hair brushed against his exposed chest, soft and pungent with the tang of sulphur.

She pressed harder with her thumbs, and Micah began to see flashing lights and pools of red behind his eyelids. From the far end of the cavern he heard a soft wheezing groan. The pressure on his eyes increased and he feared she was about to put them out completely. Then, abruptly, she released her grip.

'I shall help,' she announced. She pulled away.

Micah blinked. He could still feel where the

probing hands had held him tight. 'Thank you,' he said simply.

Jura snorted. 'Soon, you may not thank me.'

She turned away, and Micah watched her heading towards the shadows at the back of the cavern. Several wyrmes rubbed at her legs as she went, affectionate and proprietorial. She disappeared into the shadows and Micah heard the grinding sound of something being sharpened on a whetstone.

When she emerged a moment later, his horrified gaze fell on the gleaming spike she held in her hand. One end was splintered, and it looked as though it might once have been the sharp end of a much longer lance or spear, though it looked no less lethal for that.

Jura crossed the floor towards the far corner of the cavern and was lost from sight once more. Micah glanced round at Eli.

'What's she doing?'

Eli shrugged and shoved his hands deep into his pockets. Micah, though, had noticed a slight twitch in the man's usually impassive face.

He heard soft whispering coming from somewhere deep in the shadows. It was answered by the deep rumbling groan he'd heard before. He glanced at Eli again, but the man's expression was fixed once more, stoneset grim.

All at once, there was a roar from the far end of the cavern, and Micah looked back to see a patch of deep red glowing in the darkness. It bathed the surrounding rock, it cast the woman in a crimson halo, and it fell upon something of great size but indeterminate shape.

The red light intensified.

It was a stream of fire. Silhouetted against it were the woman's hands, outstretched as she held the spike in the flame.

Micah swallowed.

The roar dwindled to a wheezing gasp, and the red firelight abruptly went out. Jura emerged from the shadows and strode back quickly across the cavern, the spike—now glowing a blinding yellow white—held out before her.

As she approached, Micah could smell the acrid heat. He turned to Eli, to find that he was no longer standing by his side.

He looked back at Jura, who nodded, and Micah realized that Eli had moved round to his back. Before he could move, his arms were grasped and pulled behind him, and he felt both wrists being crushed together and gripped tightly by one of the man's powerful hands. At the same time, an arm was wrapped around his neck, and Micah felt the cables of hard muscle flex at his jaws.

Jura came closer, her deep green eyes avoiding Micah's imploring gaze. She had a stick in one hand; the glowing spike was in the other.

'Bite on this,' she said, thrusting the stick into his mouth.

Micah did as he was told, too frightened not to. He bit down on the wood. The spike hovered in the air as Jura loosened the bandages and tugged them away until the wounds were exposed. The heat warmed his face—then his chest.

He struggled, his eyes rolling in his head like a panicked horse. Eli held him all the tighter.

He felt her hooked nails pluck at the skin around the wound. He felt the heat of the spike get closer . . .

74

'What was done must be undone,' she said softly, in that cracked quaver-flecked voice of hers, her eyes gleaming with a fierce determination.

She pressed the glowing spiketip to the ragged opening of the wound in his chest.

There was a hiss of blood, and the whiff of burned flesh, as the spike plunged deep into Micah's body. He bit down into the piece of wood so hard it felt like his jaw would crack, yet nothing could ease the pain. Pain that seared deep into his very core; scalding, blistering, burning. Pain that could not be endured.

The stick fell from his slack jaw and landed on the floor with a clatter. Micah didn't hear it drop.

SIXTEEN

Seraphita. Seraphita. Seraphita . . .

Her dark eyes were wide with astonishment, unfathomable pools of blackness, as she stared back at him. She had come running into the stables to visit her beloved Peshneg, just as Micah had hoped she would. It was the first time he'd had the chance to talk to her since he'd seen her kissing on the tithe-house balcony.

He'd sneaked out to the stables after work, and had been lying in the hayloft for more than three hours, waiting for this moment to catch her alone. And when he'd heard those tell-tale footsteps in the courtyard, he'd leaped to his feet and climbed down the ladder to confront her outside Peshneg's stall.

But the sight of Seraphita's beauty had snatched his breath away. Now, it threatened to rob him of speech and turn him into a stuttering tongue-tied fool in front of her.

Seraphita's face flushed, a delicate shade of crimson that blossomed in her cheeks and spread down her slender neck. Her glistening black hair

76

was loose and tumbled down over her shoulders, which were bare, for instead of her riding clothes, Seraphita was wearing a tight-bodiced gown, sprinkled with gleaming pearls. At her breast was pinned the jewelled brooch with the rearing stallion motif.

'Seraphita!' Micah said, aware that he should try to keep his voice to a whisper, but failing. 'I had to see you. It's as if, ever since your maidenfeast, you've been avoiding me. Didn't you hear me hooting beneath your window like a moontouched owl? Each morning and evening I've hidden in the hayloft, but you sent grooms to look after Peshneg. That's not like you, Seraphita . . .'

Seraphita seemed rooted to the spot, her eyes wide, her mouth open and a look almost of panic plucking at her beautiful face.

'Seraphita,' Micah continued, and the words he'd wanted to speak to her for four long days now, came tumbling out like apples down a cider chute. 'Who *was* that I saw you with on the tithe-house balcony, and why were you kissing him? . . . Seraphita?'

Micah was painfully aware of the choking catch in his voice; the lump in his throat.

'Seraphita, please . . . say something . . .'

He took a step towards her, and was shocked to see her flinch. It was only then that he tore his eyes away from her face and looked past her shoulder to the doorway of the stables.

There, silhouetted against the evening light, were two figures. As they stepped into the stables and approached Seraphita, Micah recognized them with a sickening jolt.

The shorter of the two, dressed in a rich velvet

cloak with a heavy fur collar, and a large soft daycap of braided silk, was Seraphita's father. His small stoat-like eyes glittered and the nostrils of his sharp nose flared with distaste as he looked at Micah. On the other side of Seraphita, taking her arm and stroking it reassuringly, was the handsome young man she had kissed. He wore an expensive-looking black jacket, fine-tooled silver-tipped boots and a sneering grimace, as though he had caught a whiff of something foul.

'Seraphita, my love,' he said, his voice a soft and silky drawl. 'Do you permit all your grooms to address you in this manner?'

Seraphita glanced at him, then back at Micah, and he saw her face harden, her eyes narrow beneath arched eyebrows and her nostrils flare, until she resembled the two figures on either side of her.

'Oh, this is Micah,' she said, with a light and easy giggle, her black eyes boring into Micah's, intense and wintercold. 'He's not a groom, he's just a silly little ploughboy . . .'

This time it was Micah's turn to flinch.

'Last summer, he got it into his poor tousle-haired head that he was in love with me. Followed me round like a millstone donkey. I thought it was funny at the time, but now it has become rather a nuisance. I should have put a stop to his nonsense, but he seemed so pathetic, Caspar.'

'You're just too sweet and kind for your own good, my love,' smiled the young man, guiding Seraphita gently by the arm towards the stable door. 'Come, you can show me that fine horse of yours another time.'

Seraphita nodded. Caspar wrapped an arm

78

around her and steered her through the door. As she stepped out of the stables, she stole a backwards glance over her shoulder, and for the briefest moment Micah saw a stricken look in her eyes, of tenderness, of regret and heartache. Then she turned back to Caspar and disappeared from view, a brittle bell-like laugh ringing out.

Seraphita's father watched them go, his small eyes twinkling in the middle of a face gone flabby with affection, before turning back to Micah. His face was stoneset once more.

'My Seraphita is indeed a tender-hearted child,' he said in a quiet musing voice, almost as though he was talking to himself. 'And just like with Peshneg over there, she neglects the whip out of kindness . . .'

He raised a hand and clicked his fingers.

'Such sentimentality is not one of my failings. Overseer!' he barked. 'See to it that this ploughboy is soundly thrashed at the whipping-post. I shall not have my daughter's honour sullied!'

A figure loomed at the door, a heavy hide whip in his fist.

'I'll see to it, my lord, don't you worry about that,' came a horribly familiar voice, and Micah's brother Caleb stepped into the stables.

'Make sure you do,' Seraphita's father rasped, turning away and strutting out of the stable.

'Well, little brother,' said Caleb gruffly, seizing Micah by the collar and dragging him out into the courtyard. 'Can't say I haven't warned you. Brother or no, you'll not stand in my way . . .'

He pushed Micah over to the whipping-post and tied his arms to the crossbeam.

'Time has come to prove what a fine overseer

your brother can be . . .'

But Micah was no longer listening. Instead he was gazing ahead, his stare fixed on the far corner of the courtyard, where a little girl sat playing. She was six years old or so, with matted strawcolour hair and a faded dress of blue cotton. She was playing with the beautifully carved wooden horse she'd discovered a couple of weeks earlier, one front leg snapped off from when it had been carelessly tossed from a balcony window.

Before the first blow fell, Micah's eyes had filled with tears.

*   *   *

Micah winced as he bent down. The fiery red weals that crisscrossed his back had cooled some. Now they were tight across his shoulders like an undershirt he couldn't take off, and only really pained him if he moved suddenly. Like now.

He shoved the watergourd down into the stream, listening to the bubbles, watching them wink at the surface as the gourd filled.

Three weeks he'd travelled, three weeks of dusty roads, muddy paths and rocky tracks, the country slowly changing, the air becoming thinner and the going tougher as he left the plains behind and ascended towards the high country. Ahead of him, on the other side of the gently trickling stream, a vast desert of bleached scree and low bluffs stretched out as far as he could see.

This was the barrier. The badlands. The region he would have to cross to reach the high country:

The wyrmeweald . . .

There was wealth to be had there. Returner's

wealth. He would get it, or die in the attempt. And he would fill his pockets and return to the plains and claim his Seraphita with that returner's wealth. He climbed to his feet and swung the swollen watergourd over his shoulder.

But first he'd have to pray that his water held out.

SEVENTEEN

The air smelled of something intoxicating sweet. Light was coming in from somewhere, shining red through his eyelids. There were low voices.

Micah opened his eyes. He was lying on his back on a mattress of aromatic moss. In a cavern. He stared up at the ceiling.

High above his head, a tiny wyrme was stalking a green-carapaced bug, its body rigid as its angular legs picked stealthily over the pitted rock. It hesitated for a moment, then struck with a darting forward motion, seized the insect in its mouth and crunched into the shell with needleteeth. Before it could swallow, a second wyrme, larger and with a purple crest, shot forward, huge jaws agape. It snatched the bug, the wyrme and all, and scurried away across the ceiling.

Two drops of blood splashed onto Micah's chest. He grimaced, and turned his head to the side.

Eli and Jura were seated next to one another on the rockfloor some way off, their backs towards him, silhouetted against the shimmering curtain of water. Eli's half-emptied backpack was resting against one crooked leg, the top open, and as Micah watched, Eli leaned forward and plunged a hand inside.

Micah closed his eyes again.

82

'I travel alone, Jura. You know that.'

'That is true, Eli. You always have . . .' Her fragile voice trailed away.

Micah breathed in and felt the bandages tighten at his chest. He remembered the sight of the glowing spike in the wyrmekin's braced fingers; the heat, the pain, the smell of his own flesh burning. The throbbing had gone now, and the wound was beginning to itch. He didn't move to scratch it, content just to lie there and listen.

'This, this I can use,' Jura was saying, and Micah heard something like the crumpling of waxed paper.

'Take it,' said Eli. 'You've surely earned it.'

There was a small indignant gasp. 'I sought no payment.'

'Take it all the same,' Eli told her calmly.

They fell silent, and Micah listened to the sound of rustling and clinking as more objects were removed from the rucksack and laid out on the stone floor. He heard the other sound too, the one he'd heard earlier, coming from somewhere in the shadows at the back of the cavern; a low wheezing sound that got louder and higher, before collapsing back on itself into a low rumbling groan. Jura sighed.

'I take some of this too,' she said, and Micah heard a clacking sound, like bits of wood being collected together.

'You can use those?' said Eli. He sounded surprised. 'I only keep them on account of their smell. That sack of mine can conjure up a stench that would scare the dead, and them pine nubs do sweeten things.'

'Ground up and boiled, they make a paste that

83

soothes the canker.'

Eli paused. 'The canker?' There was concern in his voice.

'Asra is growing old,' she said quietly. 'We both are . . .'

'We none of us are what we once were, Jura,' Eli observed gruffly.

'But it is not only the canker it soothes,' Jura was saying. 'Boils also, ulcers and such.'

'Here, take as many as you like,' said Eli. 'And I don't know for sure what this stuff might be, but if you've a use for it, Jura, then take it.'

Micah heard her breath hissing through those pointy teeth of hers. 'Wyrmebane,' she whispered. 'Rare white wyrmebane—a powerful weed.'

'Good or bad?'

'It can start a heart that has stopped—from terror, exhaustion, cold,' she said. 'It can stop a healthy heart . . .' Her hand slapped down on the rock. 'Like that! You tell me if that is good or bad?'

'I'd have to think on that,' said Eli as he shifted round, his leather coat creaking, and dragged the backpack across the floor. 'Except for that wyrmepelt and scentsac, Jura, you are most welcome to anything that I have collected which you can favourably employ.'

'But this, it is not right,' Jura objected. 'We should exchange, Eli. You give. I give—'

'It's not necessary. I—'

'Wait.' There was more rustling. 'The rains are coming, Eli. Take this. Rub it into your feet. It will help protect them from whiterot when your boots are wet through. And this . . .'

There was the sound of a stopper being popped.

'Hellfire, Jura,' Eli gasped. 'What is *that*?'

84

'For leeches. One dab, they curl up and drop.'

'Not surprised,' he said, and grunted. 'Whiterot balm. Leech ointment.' He chuckled. 'I swear, Jura, is there nothing in the high country you ain't learned how to cure?'

'Wyrmekin teach wyrmekin.' She paused. 'As wyrmekith teach wyrmekith, no?'

Eli snorted. 'More like every man for hisself, from my experience.'

'But *you* learned.'

'Learned more from you than any kith, truth told.'

'But also others.'

Eli sighed. 'I'll allow I gleaned a few helpful tips along the way,' he said. 'Some of them from kith . . .'

'So,' Jura said, and there was a certain triumph in her voice. 'Which is why you should teach the boy, Eli Halfwinter. If you do not, then someone else will, only they will not teach him what he should know. Only bad things. How to steal and plunder, how to kill . . .'

'Oh, I see,' Eli drawled. 'Back to that, are we? Like I said, Jura, I travel alone.'

They fell silent once more. Micah opened his eyes again and looked across the cavern. Eli and Jura were still side by side in dappled light, each of them staring down at the rockfloor before them, and the small heaps of bartered items between.

'Yet you brought him here to me,' Jura persisted.

'I've brought cracked wyves and injured wyrmes to you in the past, Jura. It ain't no different.'

Micah cleared his throat and sat up on one elbow. Eli and Jura looked round.

85

'So you're awake at last,' Eli said gruffly. 'Soon as I conclude my business here, I'm hitting the trail. I suggest you gather your stuff, Micah, and do the same.'

Jura stood up and crossed the cavern floor to Micah. She crouched stiffly beside him, her beautiful face lined with concern as she lifted his shirt, plucked at the bandage and examined the wound. It was raised and puckered, the black stitches looking like a row of flies. She placed the backs of her taloned fingers against his red skin.

'You are well enough to travel?' she enquired. 'Your pain is less than before?' Her dark-green eyes peered deeply into his own, her gaze as disconcerting as ever.

Micah nodded on both counts. He scrambled to his feet.

'The boy's strong,' said Eli. He fastened his backpack and heaved it up onto his shoulders. 'I'll bid you farewell. May there be less time until the next time.'

He turned brusquely away. Micah grabbed his belongings and hurried after him.

'Wait,' Jura told him. She crossed to one of the earthenware urns that stood in the shadowy alcoves, reached down inside it, and returned with a handful of small, dark-green, waxy-looking leaves. 'Chew on these to keep the pain at bay,' she told him, piling the leaves in his outstretched hands. 'One at a time.'

She pushed a leaf into his mouth when he opened it to thank her, and Micah bit down. The leaf tasted acrid sour and his tongue went numb. And when he swallowed the juices that welled up in his mouth, his body tingled with warmth.

86

Micah glanced up.

The cragclimber was already over by the waterfall at the far end of the cavern, backpack on his shoulders and hat brim down, about to disappear. Micah stuffed the rest of the leaves in a jacket pocket and struggled to catch him up, his own rucksack bouncing awkwardly as he loped over the rockfloor. He paused at the ledge, turned and looked back, intending to wave, or say goodbye, or thank you—something at least to mark his departure.

But the wyrmekin was nowhere to be seen. From the dark shadows at the back of the cave, he heard the sound again—that wheezing panting sound, deep and rumbling, as though the chamber itself was alive and breathing.

EIGHTEEN

Micah emerged from behind the waterfall into bright daylight. He squinted and pulled the brim of his hat low down over his eyes; he tried to blink away the dazzle. Eli was up ahead, making his way determinedly along the narrow path without a backward glance.

Micah hurried along in his footsteps, until the track widened sufficiently for him to walk by the cragclimber's side. Eli showed no sign of acknowledgement, and Micah struggled to think of something to say. Eli travelled alone. He'd told Jura as much when he thought Micah wasn't listening, but, Micah realized with a growing sense of unease, he didn't want to be left behind.

The sun was high and strong, and the air was suffused with the heady scent of the broad pale leaves and heavy blossoms that stewed in its fiery heat.

'I must have slept through the night,' Micah began, as casually as he could.

Eli glanced round at him. 'You slept through *three* nights in all, Micah, boy,' he said.

'Three nights!'

'Thrashing about like a rockwyrme in a snare.'

He fell silent. Micah dropped back a pace. He watched Eli's broad shoulders

88

sway from side to side.

'You waited for me, all that time?' he ventured.

'Only to see if you'd recover,' Eli said, and snorted. 'I agreed to stay as an undertaker,' he told him. 'As it turned out, my gravedigging skills were not required.'

Micah looked down at his boots as he continued through the lush forest that clung to the steep cliffsides of the ravine. It was far harder to climb than it had been to descend, and when his wound started to complain, he chewed on another of the dark waxen leaves. Then another.

Mistwyrmes and fisherwyrmes shrieked overhead. A snatterjab folded its wings back and dived like a falling arrow.

Micah took another leaf, and trudged on. Five minutes passed as the two of them made their way up the track through the steaming ravine forest, to the accompaniment of a skeeling chorus of fisherwyrmes overhead, working the waterfall. Save for the regular *clack clack* of his walking staff as it struck the hard track, Eli was silent.

'Jura said I was attacked by wyrmekin,' Micah said, determined to show Eli that he could keep pace with him *and* keep up a passable conversation at the same time. 'What I don't understand is why,' said Micah. 'I mean, I wasn't doing nothing . . .'

'Nothing you were aware of, maybe,' Eli told him. 'Could have been stomping right past a nest of wyves for all I know.'

'Wyves?' said Micah, wiping the sweat from his face. He remembered Jura's question. *You are a wyve collector?*

'Eggs. Wyrme eggs.' Eli shook his head. 'Kin take it bad when kith stumble across wyves, and they do everything in their power to protect them.'

He kept on striding ahead. Silence closed in around them once again, loud and oppressive to Micah's mind.

'I met a wyrmekin once before,' Micah said. 'Back on the plains.'

'I very much doubt it.'

'I swear, Eli. She had on a suit of oxhide, with a hood that covered her face, and she had this lance which she used to control the wyrme she had— that, and this vicious choke chain . . .'

'That weren't no wyrmekin you saw, Micah,' said Eli disdainfully. 'Just a plainswoman playing the role of such for gain . . .'

'Her wyrme was real enough,' Micah protested, keeping the conversation going despite the negative turn it was taking. 'It was huge. More than twice the size of a fully grown ploughox. It had scaly wings and fiery breath . . .'

'And was more than half dead, I'd wager.'

Micah fell silent as he remembered the wheezing beast's raw sores and pus-crusted eyes. And the way those eyes had rolled in its head when its front legs had collapsed.

Eli grunted. 'Wyrmes are high country creatures. They sicken and die back there on the plains, just like horses and packmules perish up here in the thin air. Mind you, that doesn't stop kith trying in their search for riches. Either way round, the poor creatures don't last more than a season or two.'

They walked on for a while in silence. The forest was beginning to thin out, and the head of the ravine was coming into view. When they reached the top, Micah realized, they would go their

90

separate ways.

I travel alone. Eli's words sounded in Micah's head.

'Eli,' he said, 'how did you and Jura first meet?'

Eli stopped in his tracks, and stood rigid still, staring ahead of him. Micah swallowed. Perhaps he'd gone too far? Eli spoke.

'Boy, I want to assure you that you should not feel obliged to remunerate me for my company in the form of conversation. Y'understand?'

'I . . . I think so, sir.'

'Call me Eli.'

'Eli.' Micah swallowed again, the acrid leaf-juice sluicing down his throat.

The cragclimber lurched back into motion, his head still held high and gaze fixed on some distant point. Micah followed, keeping half a step behind.

It looked like a storm was on its way. Black billowing clouds, fringed with dazzling silver, were poking up over the far side of the ravine and roiling in. A chill wind set the leaves quivering and raised dust on the track.

'Jura and I go back a long way,' Eli said, without looking at Micah. 'And our story is not one I find it easy to tell, especially on so short an acquaintance.'

He peered up at the cliff-face thoughtfully, then turned to Micah. 'But she taught me to respect wyrmes of every shape and description, to use to the full what they offer, but never to take it by force. It is a lesson I have learned well.'

'Will you teach me?' Micah asked, his head swimming and his mouth full of chewed leaves.

Eli marched on up the last stretch of track without looking back, his boots kicking up dust. He reached the top of the ravine and paused, placed his hands on his hips and surveyed the view. Micah stumbled to a halt behind him. He felt giddy. A bit sick. He tottered forward and fell to his knees, then looked up to see Eli staring at him severely.

'One leaf at a time, Jura told you.'

Micah breathed in sharply. Of course she had— and he'd gone and pushed a dozen or more into his mouth at one time. He spat out the fibrous boll of chewed leaves.

'Am I going to be all right?' he said.

Eli shrugged. 'You'll live,' he said, 'though I daresay you'll sleep well tonight.' His tanned features creased up questioningly. 'Which way were you thinking of heading anyhow, boy?'

Micah swallowed. This was it, then. The cragclimber who liked to travel alone was about to do just that. He scanned the distant horizon, then swept an arm vaguely before him, his outstretched hand lingering on a jagged line of far-off crags.

'That direction, I thought,' Micah told him, his voice as confident as he could muster.

Eli had been good to him. He'd saved his life. Micah would not presume further on his kindness.

'North-west, eh?' said Eli, removing his hat and scratching his head thoughtfully. 'Well, that is indeed a coincidence, Micah, for it is the way that I myself am heading.'

'You are?'

'The other side of that pass there,' he said, pointing towards the crag with his staff. 'There's a scrimshaw den down in the foothills I've a mind to visit. Mind you, I'll have to watch myself. You need two pairs of eyes in a scrimshaw den, I swear, one at the front and one at the back.'

Micah swallowed, then took a breath. He wished

the giddiness would subside.

'Maybe *I* could be that second pair of eyes,' he said quietly.

Eli turned to him, a thoughtful look on his face. 'Maybe you could,' he said.

He turned and walked on. Micah watched him stride away. It wasn't an invitation exactly, but it would do, he decided.

Hitching his rucksack high up onto his shoulder as he staggered to his feet, Micah ran to catch up with the cragclimber, and fell into step beside him. Eli turned to him gravely. Micah held his breath.

'We can travel alone, together,' he said with the faintest trace of a smile.

NINETEEN

'The rain season,' Eli Halfwinter observed. 'Makes for hard travelling.'

As if in answer to his words, the wind swirled and the sheets of rain rippled, darkening the air and fuzzing out the distant mountains. Visibility was down to the distance of an outstretched hand.

'That way,' Eli said.

The wind keeled round, and the rain cascading over the brim of Micah's hat blew back into his face. He wiped it away on the back of his hand, the saturated cuff of his jacket cold against his cheek. He looked down at his feet, and noted how the sheet of water that rippled across the rock splashed over the toes of his boots each time he placed a foot down.

A skein of tatterwyrmes passed over their heads, screeching loudly as they glided jerkily on squalled air. Micah wrapped his raggedy cloak tight round his shivering body and tramped after the cragclimber. They made their way through the watery landscape, fording flooded gulleys and bloated streams until, at about midday, they came to a rain-swelled river.

'We cross here,' Eli pronounced, after surveying the torrential waters for a moment.

Micah nodded back, though why the cragclimber had favoured this particular spot to wade across, he could not tell.

'Roll up your cloak and stash it away,' said Eli. 'Then follow in my footsteps.'

He waited till Micah's rucksack was buckled and back on his shoulders, then stepped forward, raising his arms for balance as first one boot, then the other, sank down into the torrent of water. Eli was knee deep. He ploughed forward, dragging one leg after the other, grunting with effort as he did so.

'Come on,' he shouted back.

Micah grimaced, and followed. As he plunged into the water, it gripped him, threatening to spin him round, and he raised his arms—like Eli had done—to steady himself. He held still for a moment, trying to accustom himself to the powerful currents that tugged at his legs. The rain continued to fall, beating down upon his hat and shoulders, and stippling the river's surface.

Micah heaved himself forward, forcing one leg, then the other, through the flooded gulley as he took care to trace Eli's footsteps. The water grew deeper, then deeper still, till it was up to his waist. Ahead of him, Eli continued crossing at an angle, his back turned towards the oncoming stream, and Micah did the same.

As the water reached his belly, something slammed hard into his back, and reaching behind him, Micah grasped a rough and scaly object and found he was clutching a drowned wyrme by the tail. It was the size of a gamebird, but grey-scaled and bedraggled. Its skin was torn and the scales battered, and its sightless eyes stared into mid air.

He pressed on. The currents were vicious and determined. Beneath him, gravel shifted and rocks

95

slammed against his boots. But soon, as Micah approached the far side, the bed of the gulley began to rise. He heaved himself out of the water and collapsed in a heap on the bank, panting with exertion.

The cragclimber looked round, his pale-blue eyes narrowed and unreadable.

'Must have lost its footing,' he observed, nodding at the dead wyrme in Micah's hand.

He took it and examined it quickly, before looping its tail round his belt and knotting it.

'What are you going to do with it?' asked Micah.

'I shall honour it by using to the full what it has to offer,' Eli said.

They rested for a while, then set off again, tramping through the grey rain-filled afternoon.

'A little bit further,' Eli said at last, as the light began to fade, 'and then we'll rest up for the night.'

Their journey had brought them to the foothills of the mountain crags they'd been heading towards all day. They started to climb. The smudge of cragtops was far above their heads, obscured by dark cloud and the approaching night. The higher they went, the more uneven the ground became. Tumps and hummocks dotted the rock, with freshsprung creeks weaving their way between them. They kept on. The darkness grew and, as it did so, the drumming of the rain on Micah's hat and shoulders seemed more insistent than ever.

Eli turned. 'Over there,' he said.

They approached a wedged slab of rock jutting out from the side of the mountain. It offered shelter.

'This should do us,' said Eli. He looked round, his eyes coming to rest on a stunted thornbush that clung to a crack in the rock. 'This should do us just fine.'

Without being told, Micah set rocks for a fire, cut down the thornbush with his hackdagger and turned it to a heap of kindling; then, using his bollcotton and flintstones, soon had a fire lit. Next, he took his gourd and waterflask, together with Eli's canteen, to the edge of the overhanging rock, where thin strings of water were falling. He held out the containers, one at a time, and waited for them to fill with rainwater.

He returned to find Eli knelt down on the ground before the fire. The dead wyrme lay before him on the flat rock. Steam was rising up off the cragclimber's wet clothes and the flames glinted on the blade of his skinning knife. As he approached, Eli looked up. He held up the wyrme.

'Take it,' he said.

Micah hesitated.

'Go on,' said Eli. 'I'll tell you what to do.'

Micah seized the wyrme by the neck and squatted down beside the cragclimber. Eli handed him the knife.

'Use this,' he said. 'It's a mite sharper than that hackdagger of yours.'

Micah did as he was told. He gripped the handle as tightly as his shaking fingers would allow.

'Pierce the skin, just beneath its chin,' Eli told him. 'That's it. Now draw the blade carefully down the creature's underbelly . . .'

As Micah cut through the skin, the wyrme's stomach opened up like a sloppy grin.

'That's the way, lad,' said Eli. He reached forward, pushed his hand inside the wyrme and tugged at its inner organs. 'Intestines,' he said, and slung them into the fire. 'Liver.' It followed the intestines into the flames, where they hissed and spat and gave off odours, both sweet and foul. 'Wyrme liver's poisonous,' he remarked as he thrust his hand back inside the dark cavity, 'whereas the kidneys make fine eating . . .' He laid the two glistening brown organs down on the rock. 'As does the heart. Ain't nothing quite like the heart of a wyrme.' He looked up again, and caught Micah's wide-eyed stare. 'Pass me my canteen.'

Micah set it before him and hunkered down to observe how Eli sluiced out the inside of the wyrme. Then he took back his knife and, with Micah gripping the creature's hindlegs firmly, he set to work slicing off the tattered skin.

'Pelt's useless in this condition,' he was saying. 'Otherwise I'd have strung it up and skinned it proper. Besides,' he added, 'greywyrmepelts are not highly prized—though we might be able to get something for the wingbones.'

Micah nodded, his brow furrowed.

Bit by bit, the scraps of scaled skin fed the fire. When it was all removed, Eli set to work on the body, cutting and slashing with swift dextrous flicks of the blade. He sliced off the legs at the joints, divided the back and quartered the breast, till there were ten pieces of meat lying before him, each of a similar size. Carefully, Eli laid out the meat, together with the two kidneys, and finally the heart, upon the rocks that encircled the fire, so that the flames lapped at them.

Micah leaned back, his hands flat on the rock behind him, the heat of the fire slowly drying out his clothes. Beyond the warm dry shelter of the overhead rock, the downpour continued, and the flickering flames, which flashed and flared as the fat dripped, made the raindrops look like taut wires. As Eli turned the pieces of meat, the air became mouthwatering. He skewered one with his knife.

'Looks about done to me,' he ventured.

Micah drew his hackdagger and did the same, then pulled off a strip of the slightly charred meat with his teeth. His face broke into a smile. It was sweet and succulent. He had a second piece, then a third. Beside him, Eli did the same, wiping the grease from his mouth on his sleeve, and belching when he was done.

At last, Micah looked up to see that only one piece remained. Eli handed it to him.

'The heart,' he said. 'The best part. I saved it for you.'

Micah took it, trying to look pleased. The cooked organ was pale grey and crumbly. He broke off a morsel and pushed into his mouth. The texture was dense and claggy, and it had a strong rusty flavour. He swallowed it, helped by a mouthful of water.

'The heart of the wyrme,' Eli said. 'The taste takes some getting used to, but it is a powerful thing—full of nourishment. It'll ease the aches and pains of today's journey and tomorrow you'll wake up refreshed.'

Eli looked at Micah and smiled, then pulled a stubby length of gulchroot from his top pocket and began chewing.

'You done good today, lad. Real good. It was a hard tramp. Them rainflood gulches are sore perilous to man and beast alike. As our supper bore witness,' he added, his eyes twinkling. He pulled the root from his mouth. 'You made us a good fire, you fetched water unbidden, and I appreciate that thoughtfulness, Micah.'

Micah's cheeks reddened. He picked up a couple of stray twigs lying beside his feet and tossed them into the flames.

'And you picked up the rudiments of wyrme gutting with neither squeam nor relish, which is as it should be. I should have listened to Jura. She charged me with your learning, and she was right to.'

'She was?' Micah said.

Eli nodded. He returned the plug of gulchroot to his mouth, then frowned thoughtfully. When he spoke again, his voice was hushed. 'You asked me a while back how Jura and I first met . . .'

'I know . . . I'm sorry, I didn't mean to pry—' Micah began, but Eli raised a hand to still him.

'Happen the two of us are acquainted well enough for you to hear the tale after all.'

TWENTY

'Jura was a piteous sight when I first clapped eyes upon her, Micah,' Eli told him.

'It was in a scrimshaw den to the west of here, beyond the grey peaks, where the valley country starts—and, at that time, the very farthest we kith had ventured into the weald . . .

'She was hogtied hand and foot, and beat up so bad it'd make you weep. Yet even through all the blood and the bruises, her startling beauty was plain for all to see.

'I was a young trapper back then, new to the high country and trying my luck fishing the falls for eelwyrme and blackwing. I relished the challenge of it, pitting myself against nature in such fashion, though I'd be a liar if I told you I had much success. Which is why I had a notion to hook up with a gang and go after larger quarry. That's why I'd ventured into the den that night. And then I saw her . . .'

Eli stuck out a boot and nudged a log back into the fire with his heel.

'She was being held captive by a kith named Absolom Shale, an evil cuss with a black-braided beard and a belly-band studded with throwing knives. He'd strung her up for all to admire, and was boasting to anyone who'd listen—and I'm ashamed to confess that there were a fair few kith

101

who did—that he'd slain the great wyrme she'd ridden, and that this wyrmekin now rightly belonged to him. I reckon he had it in mind to make a slave of her.' He shook his head. 'Or worse . . .

'He had this great cumbersome sidewinder propped up at his feet, primed and loaded with a triple-barbed bolt, and it was with this fearsome weapon he claimed to have done the deed. Not that I believed him. Not for a moment. See, lad, wyrmekin ain't like us kith folks here in the weald. They're special. Chosen. They live with the wyrmes they ride in a unique communion, and the mysteries of their kinship is something we kith can only guess at.

'For instance, you saw that suit Jura wears?'

Micah nodded.

'All kin wear such attire. Soulskin, they call it. It is the slough of their wyrmes, shed at the time of their kinning, and worn by them ever after. Powerful strong it is, beyond all reckoning. Why, I've seen soulskin deflect a spitbolt from ten yards and leave no impression on the wearer. Proof against the harshest of weather, to hear Jura speak of it. And for as long as I've known her, I ain't never seen her wearing anything but.' Eli smiled ruefully.

'And then there's that shard of a lance she carries—that's what was left of her kinlance after Absolom Shale took her. All wyrmekin are armed with kinlances. For the most part, they're fashioned from the black spruce that grow deep in the valley country. Or sometimes from methusalah pine, lone trees only found at the top of the highest, hardest to reach crags.

102

'The great wyrmes select the straightest branches for their chosen kin. They season and temper them on the tree with their fiery breath, or so it's said, before cutting them down. Then they strip the bark and sharpen the wood with their claws, and coat the point in a venom from their fangs that causes slowdeath in those the lance wounds. Kith has no cure for it. Only another kinlance, heated whitehot in wyrmebreath, can draw the poison out and cauterize the wound . . .'

Eli looked up. 'A mighty painful business, as you learned to your cost, lad.' He stared deep into the glow at the heart of the fire. 'A great wyrme and its kin are just about the deadliest combination there is in all the weald. Ain't the wyrmekith been born that can match them, and to my mind, there was no way a petty thug like Absolom Shale could have pulled off such a feat without some skulduggery or other . . .

'So I called Absolom Shale a liar to his face, and he rose to the bait, going for that big old sidewinder at his feet. But my spitbolt was lighter and swifter, and I shot him through the eye before he had the chance to aim, let alone fire. The scrim den erupted in uproar, and in the confusion that followed, I was able to get Jura away.

'Like I said, I'd been trying my luck as a falls fisher at that time, and I knew just the spot where the two of us could hole up while the rumpus calmed down. So I took her to that cave behind the waterfall in the green haven, away from the trails most kith tread. I nursed her back to health there, and her beauty and spirit took such a firm hold upon my heart that they ain't never let go, not from that day to this. Of course, she was grateful to me

103

for my kindness and returned my affection . . .' He sighed. 'As far as she was able . . .

'You see, Micah, she's wyrmekin, and there'll always be a part of her that a kith like me can never reach. Though I ain't never stopped trying . . .

'It was during this time in the cave that I learned the truth of what had befallen her and Asra. They had encountered Absolom Shale in the valley country they were protecting. Apparently, he was out hunting lakewyrme with that monstrous sidewinder of his. She'd disarmed him easily enough, and had him pleading for his miserable life at the point of her kinlance.

'But then . . . though she regretted it ever afterwards . . . and against Asra's will . . . she let Absolom Shale go. Jura always maintained she lacked that instinct to kill that makes wyrmekin so formidable. Perhaps that's what makes her so fine a healer,' he mused. 'Anyway, she spared his life on the condition that he quit the high country and return to the plains. For ever. It was a promise he did not keep.

'Instead, he ventured into the caverns deep beneath the mountains. He did a deal down there with a moonshiner, one of the keld . . .'

Eli saw the puzzled frown that crossed Micah's brow.

'Keld's them that have taken to dark places, the better to hide their evil-doings,' he told him. 'They're monstrous and depraved. Yet they're cunning. Clever. They're skilled at extracting the riches of them dark places—precious metals, priceless gemstones—and they use such riches to lure kith underground, like manderwyrmes to a sweet-bait trap.' He shuddered. 'But it's a fearful

MANDERWYRME

price the keld exact, down in them evil subterranean places, with their stunted wyrmes and all . . .'

He frowned. 'Why, but Micah, you've gone mighty pale. Here, lad, take a swig of this liquor,' he said, pulling his flask from his belt and handing it out.

'N . . . no, I'm fine,' said Micah.

Eli shrugged and took a swig himself, then tossed another log onto the fire and poked at it till the flames crackled and sparks flew.

'Anyways, whatever Absolom Shale traded—and I shudder to think what it might have been—he came away with a flagon of the poisonous oil that keld use to stunt their wyrmes. They call it quench. And Shale used this quench to poison the waters of Asra's home tarn. When wyrme and kin got sick, he moved in and wreaked his revenge, bringing Asra down, capturing Jura . . .'

Eli's voice faltered. 'Jura never spoke of what she suffered at Absolom Shale's hands before I rescued her, but she swore that she would never allow kith to take her alive a second time . . .

'She wept bitter tears for Asra, convinced that he was dead. But then one night, a few weeks later, Asra found her. Don't ask me how he did it. Even now, I can scarce credit it myself, but then great wyrmes are truly the most extraordinary creatures that ever inhabited this world—strange, powerful and with an intelligence that far outstrips that of our kind . . .

'He was grievously wounded and feversick from the quench, but somehow he had managed to drag himself down into the green haven and through the waterfall into the cave. He crawled to the back of the cave and laid himself down.' Eli looked up, and wiped a sleeve across his brow. 'Where he has remained to this very day.

'As for Jura, she has a talent for healing. She distils cures and creates potions for those few—kin, and some kith like me—that she trusts enough to know her whereabouts. She cares for Asra, and welcomes any wyrmes that choose to roost in her cave.' He nodded gravely. 'And it is my sincere belief, Micah, that she won't never leave that cave, not so long as there is breath in that great wyrme's body, for when wyrme and kin have joined in kinship, there ain't nothing that can break it.'

Eli reached forward and took the liquor flask. He raised it to his lips and took a swig.

'And that, Micah—that is the story of how Jura and I first met.' He smiled. 'Now get some sleep, lad. We've got a hard trail ahead of us.'

TWENTY-ONE

They stopped at the edge of an overhang
of black rock and looked down. It had
been raining hard since they'd set off that
morning, yet not even the rippling sheets
of rain could obscure the magnificence of
the landscape that lay before them. The
high country was studded with floodlakes
that gleamed like opals, while the
surrounding mountains looked to be
threaded with silver as cascades of rainspill
coursed down their sides.

'The scrimshaw den's down there a
ways,' Eli said. 'Behind that tall stack. The
one shaped like a rooster.'

Micah squinted, but was none too sure
which stack the cragclimber meant. He
reached for the brass and copper spyglass
hanging on a chain round his neck and
raised it to his eye. He focused on the low
crags in the distance, one by one.

'Rooster?' he said.

When Micah lowered the spyglass, Eli
had already set off, and was striding down
the scree- strewn slope at the steady pace
Micah had got to know so well. With a
weary sigh, he let go of the spyglass and set
off after the cragclimber. The sun was low
in the sky by the time they reached the
valley floor and the light faded as they
made their way between clusters of
crouched boulders until a tall rockstack

rose up before them.

'The rooster rock,' Eli announced. He raised a hand. 'There's its long neck and crested head, its beak jabbing to south. It's just about as rooster-like as a rock can be, I'd say.' He turned to Micah, who was frowning, perplexed. 'When you've walked the wyrmeweald as long as I have, boy,' he said, 'you too will see all manner of likenesses in the rocks, and learn to navigate your way by such.'

Micah nodded. 'And the scrimshaw den?'

'For that,' Eli said, 'we need to step between the rooster's legs.'

He took Micah by the arm and led him through the great stone arch below the rooster rock, into the narrow canyon on the other side. At the far end was the entrance to a cave.

'Stick with me when we get inside,' said Eli.

'I shall,' said Micah, reaching up and removing his hat.

Eli frowned. 'The scrimshaw den ain't no prayer-house or temple, Micah,' he observed.

'I know it,' said Micah. He had taken off his hat and was concentrating on removing one of the sharp three-pronged birdhooks attached to the hatband without cutting his fingers. When it came free, he dropped it into his pocket and started on its neighbour.

Eli watched, intrigued, as Micah's fingers teased and worried at the hook. 'What you doing, boy?'

Micah looked up. 'Any filchthief'll get more than he bargained for should he try dipping into my pockets.'

Eli nodded slowly. 'Give me a couple of them things,' he said, and when Micah had unhooked two more, he dropped them into his own jacket pockets.

They entered the low-ceilinged cavern and through a haze of aromatic oil-lamp smoke, Micah saw that the scrimshaw den was filled with people. At least two dozen by his quick reckoning. They were crouched down in pairs and small clusters, and the cavern was filled with the low thrum of their confidential conversations.

'A raincloak! For this wyrmepelt?' he heard an outraged voice protest. 'I'd want more into the bargain for it to stick . . .'

A squat wyrmekith with a broad nose and slits for eyes was shaking his head so hard the cluster of fishing-weights attached to his lobstertail cap jangled. Hanging by the neck from his bunched fist was the eviscerated body of a green fisherwyrme, its once magnificent purple crest limp as damp cloth.

'But it'll keep you good and dry for many seasons,' his companion drawled, and the heavy oilskin cape he was holding out shimmered like a curtain of water. 'And I'll throw in a clutch of deadbait to seal the bargain . . .'

'Those boots are past mending, but I've got a new pair if you're interested . . .'

'I'll give you a pot of wyrmefat—good for greasing and for burning . . .'

'Bone-handled staffs? That all you got? . . .'

'Five wingbones and two teeth. That's my final offer . . .'

Eli made his way over to a rotund kith with salt-and-pepper stubble who was sitting with his back against the cave wall, chewing slowly and open-mouthed. Two tiny lamps were clamped to the brim of his hat, one on either side of his head, the flickering flames making it look as though his ears were on fire. On the floor around him were bottles, jars and amphoras of various sizes. The air smelled oily and sickly sweet.

Eli leaned forwards. 'Fixing to get me some wyrmeoil,' he said.

The oil renderer nodded. 'Come to the right person, friend.' He pushed himself away from the rock wall, tugged at the leather braces that held his capacious breeches up and leaned forward. 'What have you got?'

Eli unstrapped his rucksack, swung it from his shoulders and set it down on the ground. He unbuckled the top and pulled the bundle of wyrmebones from inside. He laid them out on the cavern floor. The man viewed them with disdain.

'That it?'

'Fine mistwyrme bones, most of 'em,' said Eli.

The man shrugged. Eli picked up one of the bones and turned it over in his hand.

'Make buttons, toggles. Fancy bits of scrim-shaw . . .

'Mistwyrme, you say?' the man interrupted.

'Skinned and boned it myself,' Eli told him.

The man picked up one of the bones, sniffed it, then ran the tip of his tongue along its length. 'You got the pelt too?'

'I do,' Eli said. He stooped down and rummaged in the bag, before pulling the wyrmeskin out with a flourish and holding it up. The patina of skin swirled like liquid silver in the flickering lamplight atop the oil renderer's hat as he reached forward. He nodded appreciatively.

'I'll give you a quart for the pelt and the bones.'

'Two quarts.'

111

The man's eyes narrowed. His chewing eased. 'One quart,' he repeated slowly, his voice thoughtful and soft.

'Two quarts,' said Eli firmly.

The man took the wyrmeskin and rubbed it up and down a stubbled cheek.

'Two quarts it is, friend,' he said, looping two fingers through the ring-handle of a stubby earthenware pot and hefting it up into the air.

He held it out, but Eli did not take it. Instead, the cragclimber stared back at the oil renderer, his blue eyes narrowed and unblinking. The man held his gaze for a moment, before smiling slyly.

'*Two* quarts,' he said, replacing the pot and picking up one twice its size. He turned it over in his hands, then held it out to Eli, who took it and got to his feet.

As Micah followed Eli further into the cavern, he saw two wyrmekith huddled over a small pit dug into the cave floor, from which sulphurous coils of smoke wisped.

'Wyve collectors,' muttered Eli to Micah as they passed.

A score or more of newly hatched wyrmes, fragments of wyveshell still clinging to their heads and backs, squirmed about and clambered over one another at the bottom of the pit, as two wyrmekith prodded them with gloved hands and haggled.

'Feed 'em right and they'll be pelt-ready in a season.'

'Too small—and they look to be sickly. Got anything bigger?'

Eli stopped. In front of him was a wyrmekith in a stained apron and a thick belt bedecked in knives. He crouched down again. Strung to a large backpack behind the wyrmekith were the preserved entrails of wyrmes—lungs, kidneys, gizzards, dried twists of bowel and twinelengths threaded with shrivelled objects that Micah realized, with a start, were eyeballs.

'I have something that might interest you,' Eli said, bringing forth the jar containing the scentsac from his pack and setting it down on the ground.

The gutsman said nothing, but Micah noticed the involuntary twitch of interest that plucked at the pock-marked skin of his hollow cheeks. The man pushed back his hat, strands of lank hair flopping across his forehead, leaned forwards and placed his hands upon the jar.

'May I?' he asked.

'Be my guest,' Eli told him.

The man unplugged the top of the jar, breathed in, then noisily exhaled, smacking his tongue against the roof of his mouth as he did so.

'Quality stuff,' he said, his voice nasal and harsh. 'And excellently preserved.'

Eli accepted the compliment with the briefest inclination of his head.

'I guess you know the worth of such a thing.'

'I guess I do,' said Eli, and allowed himself a small smile. 'I'm aiming to stock up.'

The man nodded. 'You stock up with everything you need,' he told him, 'and I'll keep a tally. Tell you when we're getting close to barterbalance.'

Eli nodded. 'I need wyrmesalt,' he said. 'And scalemilt . . .'

'Wyrmesalt,' said the man, picking up a cloth bag beside him. 'Scalemilt . . .' He measured out a ladleful of brown granules from a copper jar, poured it into a square of waxed paper, which he gathered at the points, twisted round and tied it off with a length of string.

'Chokesalve, bladderlye,' Eli continued. 'And if you have some of them bone-needles, I'll take a dozen—and a spool of gut-thread . . .'

Just then, a small plaintive cry sounded from behind Micah, and he turned to see one of the tiny mottled wyrmes from the pit standing at his feet. He crouched down and, as the creature cocked its head to one side and looked at him askance, Micah mirrored its inquisitive posture.

'Ek-ek-ek-ek,' the wyrme cried, the muscles in its sinuous neck pulsing.

'Ek-ek-ek,' Micah echoed.

The wyrme blinked twice. There was a thin leather leash around its neck.

'Cute little critter, ain't he?' came a voice from behind him, and Micah looked up to see the leash was held by one of the wyve collectors, a lean powerfully built man with slick black hair and beady deepset eyes. ' 'Course, they get vicious when they get older. And strong with it.'

The little creature looked up at Micah and cocked its head.

'Ek-ek . . .'

'It's almost like it knows we're talking about it,' said Micah.

'I'm sure it does,' said the man. 'They're smart, stormwyrmes. Not as smart as a great whitewyrme, mind, but then nothing else is . . .' He thrust out a hand. 'Name's Cleave.'

Micah seized the hand, and shuddered. It was cold and moist as toadskin, but the grip was strong.

'I . . . I'm Micah,' he said.

114

'Micah,' said Cleave, smiling. 'That's a good name. Got a cousin by the name of Micah,' he added. 'I shall take that as an omen.' He clapped an arm around Micah's shoulder, and Micah found himself being steered towards the back of the cavern. 'And tell me, Micah, boy, got anything you're fixing to trade?'

Micah smiled uneasily, and glanced back over his shoulder. Eli was still deep in business with the gutsman. Cleave's grip on his shoulder increased, and he felt the man's nails dig into his skin.

'N . . . No, sir,' he said.

'Those are mighty fine boots you have on,' Cleave commented.

Micah looked down, and nodded.

'Fact is, a lot of folks neglect good boots,' Cleave continued, 'and that can be their undoing. You need good equipment to survive up here.' He paused and turned, and his dark deepset eyes bored into Micah's. 'You got good equipment to survive up here?'

'I . . . I got stuff,' Micah said uncertainly.

'Stuff,' the man repeated, and his lip curled so that Micah caught a glimpse of the green hue to his scant collection of uneven teeth. He pushed his face close. 'What stuff you got, boy?'

Micah glanced round, his heart beginning to protest loudly inside his chest. The lamplight was dim back here and the air was shot with shadow. A little way off, other wyrmekith were huddled over their trades, backs turned, and he could no longer see Eli at all.

'I got a hackdagger,' he said, patting the knife at his belt as he backed away. 'Some birdhooks. Arrowheads. A tin of bollcotton for making

115

fires . . .'

Cleave nodded, but Micah had the feeling he wasn't listening. He felt the cavern wall at his back. The sour odour of the man's breath was in his face. Cleave reached up and pressed his left hand flat against the rock, just above Micah's shoulder, and plucked at the chain around Micah's neck with the other. Micah froze, shivers tingling at his chest as the smooth metal slid up over the skin. He glanced down to see his spyglass appear at the neck of his jacket.

'Now that *is* a good piece of equipment,' said Cleave. He pulled it free and cupped it in his hand. His eyes narrowed.

'Thing is, I lost a spyglass just like this one,' he said, his voice lazyslow. 'Happen this is *my* spyglass.' His eyebrows flicked upwards. 'What do you say?'

Micah shook his head jerkily. 'No,' he said, 'it . . . it's mine.'

'I don't think you understand me right, boy,' Cleave said. 'This is *my spyglass*.'

Micah tried to pull away, but the man had a tight hold on the chain, and he could barely move. The breath in his face was gagging rank.

'I . . . I found it,' he gasped.

'See?' said Cleave. 'That's the issue. I lost it. You found it. But if you were now to return it to me, its rightful owner, I should consider the matter closed.'

Micah swallowed hard, the chain grazing his Adam's apple as he did so.

'You all right, Micah, lad?' came a gruff voice, and Cleave and Micah looked round to see Eli standing behind them both, his arms folded.

116

'He's fine,' said Cleave, taking a step back. 'Ain't you, Micah?'

'I was asking the boy,' said Eli evenly. He unfolded his arms, and unsheathed the knife at his belt with his right hand.

'Micah here was just showing me his spyglass,' Cleave said uncertainly. 'I believed it to be the one I had lost . . .'

Eli slowly twitched the knife.

'Though now I look at it more closely, I see I was wrong,' Cleave admitted and raised his hands, palms up, unthreatening. His green teeth flashed a quick smile. 'No hard feelings, eh, Micah, boy?' He stuck his hand out to Eli. 'Name's Cleave.'

Eli stared at the hand, then turned to Micah. 'Come on, lad,' he said. 'Our business here is concluded.'

Micah stepped away from the wall and followed Eli, who had turned and was walking away. He glanced at Cleave as he walked past. The smile had gone, and those deepset eyes of his were glaring at him, hard and vengeful.

'I'm sorry, Eli,' said Micah, as he fell into step beside the cragclimber. 'I got distracted . . .'

Eli shrugged. 'Stuff happens in scrimshaw dens,' he said, and paused. 'Even to an old hand like me.'

'You?'

'That's right, Micah. I too have learned a lesson,' he said. 'I fell prey to a filchthief . . .'

'You did?' said Micah. 'What did he steal?'

Eli smiled. 'Nothing.'

'Nothing?'

'That birdhook of yours nigh on sliced his thieving thumb off in the endeavour.'

TWENTY-TWO

The wyrmeling was hungry. That much it knew. Its empty belly was writhing.

It had to escape. That much it also knew. It had to break out.

It wriggled and squirmed, but in vain. Its legs were folded back on themselves, and its wings were crumpled and pinned to its sides.

All at once, there came a soft cracking noise and a fragment of light penetrated the darkness.

Its claws scraped frantically at the shell, which splintered and cracked, until one foreleg broke through, followed a moment later by the other. Grunting with effort, it butted forward with its head and kicked back with its hindlegs, and the whole wyve split apart.

With a thin mewling cry, it straightened up as best it could and gulped at the air.

The world smelled good.

The wyrmeling blinked away the skin of rheumy mucus which slithered down its eyeballs, till its yellow eyes were left shiny bright and gleaming. It tipped its head back, and the rain washed away the wyvedregs both from the corners of its eyes where it had gathered, and from every other part of its fresh-hatched scaly body; and the shards of shell still clinging to its head and shoulders were dislodged and fell away.

It belched, and a twist of smoke coiled from its angular nostrils.

The smoke seemed to take it by surprise. It snapped its mouth shut and swivelled its head round, watching as the smoke drifted and dissolved.

It shook its head, then raised its hindlegs, but too vigorously. It pitched forward and landed hard on its chin with a small cry and more coils of smoke.

Then it tried again.

This time it raised itself up on its forelegs, slowly, deliberately. When the front legs had stopped wobbling, it pushed up on its back legs and its body rose. It stood for a moment, its neck rigid. Then, head held high, it took a tentative step. Then another. And another . . .

It scritched gingerly over the speckled rock, leaving the fragments of broken wyveshell behind it.

Its gaze fell upon darting movement, and the wyrmeling jumped, pushing off the rock with its hindlegs and snapping with needlefang jaws. It flapped its wings, but seemed unable to flap and snatch at the air at the same time, and collapsed in a heap.

It turned its head and its gaze fell upon a firebug, motionless in the air before it. It took a cautious step forward, head raised and nostrils breathing in the tempting sweet succulent fragrance.

Food.

Its neck lunged forward, and it seized the morsel in its mouth and started chewing, its eyes opening and closing with each movement of its jaw.

The kingirl held out a second firebug, and the tiny wyrmeling snatched it from her fingertips and gulped it down. Then another, and a couple more, before the wyrmeling turned away and scuttled towards a smoking crevice in the surface of the speckled stack.

It paused, raised a back leg and scratched its neck with its claws. Then it lowered its head and scritched down the crevice towards the redglow warmth inside.

The kingirl stood up and pulled her heavy hood over her head, casting her face into shadow. Above her, a great whitewyrme circled in the rain-filled sky.

TWENTY-THREE

Micah's backpack lay at his feet, bulging like a truffle-stuffed hog.

'Doesn't do to rush a good pack,' Eli commented gruffly, wrapping up a hunk of sechement in oilskin and carefully stowing it in his own rucksack, 'for what starts as a burden becomes a necessity on the trail.'

Micah frowned. Eli had given him half of everything, which suggested that this was to be a parting of the ways. His gaze fell upon Eli's empty canteen, and he jumped to his feet.

'I'll get us some water,' he said eagerly.

He gathered up the canteen and his own watergourd, and before Eli had a chance to decline his offer, set off headstooped across the cavern. The murmur of bartering voices was absent now. Instead, it was regular breathing and the rumble of snores that filled the lampshot air. Micah picked his way carefully through the sleeping bodies and stepped outside.

The early light was gruel-grey. The rainfall had eased up some, but was still falling steadily. He shucked his collar and tugged his hat down low over his head, and proceeded along the canyon. A few twists and turns later, Micah stopped. He unstoppered Eli's canteen and held it beneath a glistening rope of water that trickled down the canyon wall.

121

'Micah, Micah.' The voice was low and almost weary-sounding.

Micah turned to find himself staring into a pair of dark deepset eyes. The taut brown skin grew tauter still as green-tinged teeth flashed; but the eyes were not smiling. It was the wyve collector.

'Leaving already?'

Micah nodded. 'I have all the provisions I require,' he said, and nodded towards the canteen. 'I was just getting some water.'

'Business concluded in the scrimshaw den,' said Cleave, nodding thoughtfully. He reached up and dragged filthy fingernails through his slick black hair. The teeth flashed again, and Micah caught a whiff of the man's rank breath. 'Yet I would say *our* business remains unfinished.' His eyes narrowed. 'Wouldn't you agree?'

Micah reached up and felt the spyglass through the folds of his jacket. His brow furrowed and his legs began to shake. He glanced round over his shoulder, and Cleave laughed unpleasantly, a hic-hic of sneering amusement.

'Ain't no one gonna come to your aid this time round, boy,' he said. 'It's just you and me.' He stepped forward, seized the front of Micah's jacket and wrenched him closer. And as Micah stumbled forward, he felt the sharp point of a knifeblade press at his belly. 'You and me.'

Micah swallowed. 'But I thought . . . '

'Don't think, boy,' Cleave butted in sharply. 'It ain't good for you.' He pushed his face into Micah's, his taut features twitching with wry satisfaction. Micah felt the knife jab harder. 'Thinking can lead to a slit belly and spilt guts,' he leered. 'Just hand over the spyglass . . . '

122

The canteen struck the side of Cleave's head hard, slamming against his jaw with a hollow crunch. Cleave staggered backwards, a look of dazed surprise in his deepset eyes. A hand went to his jaw.

Micah swung the canteen again, but Cleave was alert now. He caught it by the strap and wrenched Micah toward him. The blade flashed. Micah let go the canteen, and jumped to the side as Cleave stumbled backwards, and the slashing blade sliced the air harmlessly, inches from his chest.

With Cleave wrong-footed, Micah lunged at him, his jaws clenched and blue eyes blazing. His left fist landed hard in Cleave's belly. Cleave grunted and bent double, and Micah's right fist cracked solid against his chin as it came down. The knife dropped from Cleave's hand and skuttered across the canyon floor. Micah hit him again, once, twice, three times, the blows thumping into his chest and head. Cleave staggered backwards, tripped and fell heavily to the ground.

Micah checked his attack. He stood before the man, legs braced and fists clenched ready, just in case Cleave was not as defeated as he appeared to be.

'You all done?' he said, and the gruffness to his voice sounded unfamiliar to him.

The wyve collector looked up. There was blood trickling from one side of his mouth, and his left eye was already beginning to close, the eyelids top and bottom taking on the appearance of two redripe plums. He clutched at his stomach, his face grimace-twisted with pain.

'Enough . . .' he panted. 'Y'beat me fair and square, boy.' Another spasm racked his features.

'Happen you might've snapped a rib or two . . .'

Micah's eyes widened. His fists unclenched.

Head down and eyes lowered, Cleave reached out a hand towards him. It flapped weakly. Micah hesitated. Cleave groaned, and Micah gripped the hand and pulled the wyve collector to his feet . . .

The impact of Cleave's bony forehead cracking against the top of his nose stunned and blinded Micah. Cleave's knee jerked up and slammed into his groin, and his knotted hands shoved him hard in the chest and sent him toppling backwards. He fell heavily to the ground, striking his head on the canyon wall behind him. His head filled with stars, and there was a ringing in his ears.

Moments later, Micah became aware of something tugging at his boot. He opened his eyes slitwide. Cleave was crouched forward, his knife gripped between green teeth, frowning with concentration as he pulled at Micah's boot. It came free with a jolt, and Cleave set to work on the second boot, the heel gripped in both hands, yanking hard.

Fool! Micah chided himself angrily. To fall for a coward's head-butt.

The boot came free. Cleave pulled the knife from between his teeth and, before Micah could react, dropped down heavily onto his chest, his sharp knees bruising Micah's ribs and forcing the air from his lungs. He slashed upwards with the knife, cutting through Micah's jacket and shirt in one fluid movement, and placed the sharp edge of the blade to Micah's exposed neck.

'I was of a mind to let you live, boy. Till you antagonized me so,' he growled. The cold metal slid slowly across the skin at the base of Micah's throat, and Cleave sneered at Micah's terror. 'Now you have only yourself to blame for what's coming to you . . .'

Cleave's leering face registered a momentary look of startled surprise, before he was whisked away backwards with a violent lurch, and the weight on Micah's chest was abruptly lifted.

Micah pulled himself up onto his elbows. A tall man with dark eyes and a shaved head, beaded with rain, had the back of Cleave's collar bunched up in a large hard fist. Cleave screeched with rage, and swivelling round, brought his arm down, the point of the knife aiming for his assailant's eye.

But the man was too quick and too strong. He seized Cleave by the forearm, which he brought down sharply as he raised his leg, and there was a splintering crack as he snapped the bone over his knee. Then the man pulled his own knife from his belt and plunged it deep into Cleave's chest. Blood welled up in an instant, dark and thick and pumping down Cleave's front. He staggered backwards for a moment, one arm clutching at the wound, the other dangling limp at his side, and Micah saw the spark of life in those deepset eyes disappear as he keeled forward and fell face down in the mud of the canyon floor.

The man looked at him, a dark eyebrow raised. He re-sheathed his knife, then raised a hand and scratched his head.

'Odd way to greet a stranger,' he mused calmly, his voice gravel-dry but not unkindly. He tapped at the dead body with the toe of his boot. 'A little friendly conversation might have helped the situation proceed in a more civilized manner. Still.' He shrugged, then turned to Micah, a pleasant look upon his face. 'What's your story, son?'

Micah climbed to his feet shakily. Blood stained the mud he stood in. Bile rose up at the back of his throat.

'He . . . he attacked me,' he said. His voice was cracked. 'Tried to rob me of my stuff.'

The man nodded, and his amiable expression puckered with concern. 'Shook you up, eh, son?'

Micah nodded, blinking rain and tears from his eyes. He was cold and shivery. His fair hair was dark with mud and wetness, and he shuffled awkwardly from foot to bare foot, his fingers flexing and bony shoulders dipping from side to side. The man bent down, picked up the tooled boots, and Micah watched him as he turned them over in his large powerful hands.

He had a broad even-featured face; strong, possibly even brutal, if it hadn't been for his smile and the amiable gleam in his dark eyes. His jaw was blue-black with stubble, and his tapering nose turned up slightly at the end, which seemed to add a youthful, almost boyish, look to his otherwise rugged features.

Micah had seen at once that he was wearing the long overcoat of a seasoned wealdwalker, festooned with carefully maintained equipment. His rucksack, casually slipped from his shoulder in readiness for the fight, lay at his feet. It was as well-packed and tightly strapped as Eli's.

The man looked up. 'Quality workmanship,' he commented, and held the boots out. 'Put 'em back on, son, then we can see to your assailant.'

Micah took them and, leaning back against the rock, pulled the boots onto his feet, one after the other. He leaned down, tugged the bindings and

126

knotted them securely. When he looked up, the man was crouched down next to Cleave's body, rifling through his pockets. He pulled the familiar hackdagger out first, followed by the copper and brass spyglass, then glanced back over his shoulder at Micah.

'These yours?'

'They are, sir,' Micah replied, impressed despite himself at Cleave's evident ability to strip him of his valuables with such speed and precision. He took possession of the proffered objects. He returned the knife to his belt; he put the chain over his head and let the spyglass dangle at his front.

'Anything else?'

Micah patted his pockets. 'My bollcotton tin,' he said.

The man reached into Cleave's pocket and rummaged about inside.

'Is this it?' he said a moment later, and returned the tin to Micah. He winked. 'What say we take a look at what else he's got?'

Micah nodded, picked up his hat and pulled it back down on his head, then watched dumbly as the man upended the backpack and tipped out its contents. Three more spyglasses and half a dozen knives tumbled out, together with a few grubby undergarments, some meagre provisions and, from the bottom of the rucksack, carefully wrapped and preserved, a frayed huskdry corn dolly of woven straw.

With a sudden pang of sadness, Micah recognized the straw figure as one made at harvest time on the plains, and exchanged by sweethearts beneath a golden harvest moon. This hard-faced brutal wyve collector lying dead in the mud, must have once been a ploughhand, just like him; young, hopeful and in love . . .

'Looks like you weren't the first person he waylaid,' the man said, glancing round at Micah. He snorted. 'But I reckon you'll be the last . . . Anything you can use, son?'

'I'll take this,' said Micah, picking up the corn doll and wrapping it carefully.

The man frowned. 'What's that there?'

He wasn't looking at the corn doll, but instead at Micah's chest, and Micah looked down to find his leather jacket and calico shirt had been sliced open by Cleave's knife. The man climbed to his feet and stepped forward. His eyes narrowed as he looked closely at the nubbed red scar at Micah's chest.

'That's a mighty impressive wound for a recent departer,' he observed quietly. 'How did you come by it, son?'

'Wyrmekin, I was told,' Micah replied, 'though I don't remember much about it.'

The man nodded thoughtfully. 'I'd say that whoever did the telling got it right,' he said. 'What *do* you remember?'

Micah shrugged. 'Something came at me out of the mist. I didn't see it, nor hear it—not till it was upon me.'

The man nodded. 'Sounds like kin all right,' he said. 'And where exactly was this?'

'Beyond the mountain range yonder,' Micah told him. 'Four days distance or thereabouts. There's a craghut on a jutting mound of rock, and some way below it'—he shuddered—'was where I got this.' He pulled the jacket together at his neck. 'Beneath a rockstack.'

'Rockstack?' said the man.

128

'Tall and sheer, and angled at the middle like an elbow. And speckled,' Micah added.

'Speckled.'

'Hard black rock, it's made of,' said Micah, 'and speckled with lumps of grey-white . . .'

'A speckled stack,' the man mused.

Just then, there was the sound of heavy tramping boots, and the pair of them turned to see two men come marching round the end of the canyon. Both were dressed in long leather capes that grazed the muddy ground, and carrying bulky well-strapped backpacks. They noticed the body lying on the ground; they looked at Micah, and the one on the right—the more heavyset of the two—reached inside his cape.

' 'S all right, Esau,' the man told him. He turned to Micah. 'This here's . . .' He paused and his dark eyes widened. He chuckled. 'In all the excitement, I done forgot to ask you your name, son.' He held out his hand. 'Mine's Solomon. Solomon Tallow.' He swept his arm round towards the others. 'And these here are my colleagues, Esau and Jesse.'

Micah seized the outstretched hand and shook it firmly. 'I'm Micah.'

'Micah,' Solomon repeated, and turned back to the others. 'Micah here fell foul to a no-good trailthief.' He grinned, and Micah noted the two rows of even white teeth. 'Taught him a lesson he won't need learning twice.'

The three men chuckled. Jesse stepped forward and shook Micah's hand, followed by Esau. They were big and powerfully built, with youthful faces begrimed and bewhiskered by long weeks on the trail. Their ready smiles and easy friendliness filled Micah with a warm feeling, and he realized how much he'd missed the company of others. Solomon turned to him.

'You could join us, if you had a mind to,' he said. ''S all right with you boys, ain't it?' he added, turning to the others, who nodded their assent. 'The wyrmeweald's a dangerous place for lone travellers,' he told Micah, and his white teeth flashed, 'as you've already discovered for yourself. Far better to travel with company. Trusted company . . .'

'Safety in numbers,' said Esau, nodding sagely.

'I'm assuming you *are* travelling alone,' said Solomon.

Micah frowned as he caught sight of Eli's canteen lying in the mud next to his gourd and waterflask.

'I . . . I'm not sure.'

'Well, either you are or you ain't,' said Solomon, smiling broadly to his companions.

Micah picked up the canteen, gourd and waterflask and began filling them.

'This cragclimber,' he said, as Solomon and his companions watched him. 'He saved my life back there when I got hurt, and we sort of fell in together on the same trail . . .'

'And now *I* just saved your life, Micah, and have offered to share my trail with you,' said Solomon. He stroked the dark stubble on his chin. 'Seems to me you've got a choice to make.'

Micah nodded.

He could go back to the scrimshaw den, give Eli his canteen, retrieve his backpack and leave to join Solomon Tallow and his companions. They were seasoned wyrmekith by the look of them, well-equipped and provisioned. Perhaps he could pick up a thing or two from them; learn their trade, become a seasoned wyrmekith himself. A trapper. A hunter . . .

A killer of wyrmes.

Jura the wyrmekin's words that he'd overheard, spoken to Eli Halfwinter in that strange cavern behind the waterfall, came back to him. *You should teach him, Eli Halfwinter. If you do not, then someone else will, only they will not teach him what he should know. Only bad things . . .*

Micah returned Solomon's smile. 'Thank you for saving my life,' he said, as he stoppered the full canteen, 'but if you'll excuse me, I need to get this back to Eli Halfwinter.'

TWENTY-FOUR

The wyrmeling wriggled up through the narrow fissure, its foreclaws scrabbling at the pitted rock and hindlegs kicking at nothing. It emerged panting from the crevice onto the flat rock at the top of the speckled stack.

It was cold and windy, but not wet, the broad expanse of sky streaked pink and orange to one side; indigo-dark and shot with the pinpoint twinkle of stars to the other. The wyrmeling raised its snout and sniffed at the turbulent air, its eyes glowing flame-yellow and bright.

The creature was no longer rib-thin and fresh- hatch weak. Ten days in the furnace heat of the crevice had given it time to grow. Its snout had lengthened, lost its snubbed and stumped appearance, and was now slender and ridged and tapered to a whisker-fringed nub. Its long sinuous neck had become strong enough to support its head without dipping and swaying, while taut muscles flexed and rippled beneath its silver-white skin as it trotted across the rock on strong legs, the thin arrowhead tail swishing powerfully behind it.

The wind grew stronger. It plucked at its scales and ruffled the still tightly furled wings at its back. At the edge of the speckled stack, the wyrmeling halted and stretched its neck out over the howling void.

Below, the rugged brown slopes spread off towards the craglined horizon in all directions. In the sky, the stars went out, one by one, as the indigo faded, and all at once, with a dazzling flash, spoked sunlight topped the distant mountaintops and spread across the horizon.

It fell on the tall bent speckled stack, and on the small creature crouched at its top.

The wyrmeling braced itself as the wind blew into its face. Dark clouds were rolling in. With a small grunt of effort, the wyrmeling tensed the powerful muscles at its shoulders, sending rippling shudders through its sinuous body. It arched its back, and its tightly furled wings began to unfold, white and gampish. They extended far beyond its body, the scalloped edges quivering as its pounding heart sent blood pumping through the delicate network of veins.

Its shoulders tensed and the wings braced. Its foreclaws gripped the edge of the rock. Its eyes grew wide.

Then, as the sun rose, red and gelatinous, a heavy gust of wind swept the wyrmeling off its feet and sent it tumbling back across the flat top of the rockstack and off the edge at the far side. It tumbled down, screeching and squawking in a flurry of wings, claws and a desperate flailing of its whiplash tail, until another sudden gust took it again.

The wind plumped its outstretched wings from beneath, and it soared upwards, scoring a line across the blue and grey. Then the wind eased for a second, and it flapped its wings down, then up, then down again, holding them steady and

133

adjusting to the gusts and squalls it detected with its barbelled snout.

It dived down, neck dipped and ruddered by its tail. It skimmed the lower peaks, then soared back upwards, clamping its wings to its side and speeding like an arrow for a moment, before slowing back down on raised windcatch wings. It side-slipped and rolled, it glided and wheeled, then flew back high into the sky once more, and circled round the speckled stack.

And, as its long shadow lapped the rockstack below, it swooped down lower, its powerfully beating wings silhouette-black, and a jet of white flame blazing before it.

TWENTY-FIVE

Eli hadn't uttered a single word all day.

After hours of hard climbing, they'd come at last to a high ridge that wound its way along a range of jagged mountain peaks, heading north. Eli reached behind him as he crested the mount, and pulled his walking staff from the straps at the back of his rucksack—and Micah did the same. A rhythmic clacking started up, the two sticks shifting in and out of time with one another.

The landscape opened up. There were crags and peaks on either side of them, dark with wet and blurred by falling rain. With his head down, Eli didn't seem to notice, but Micah studied the looming forms. To his eyes, the crags seemed indistinguishable one from the other, with none possessing the distinctive features that might help him memorize them as signposts, or even tell them apart.

'Twelve,' he announced a while later.

Eli paused and turned. 'Twelve?'

'Them crags,' said Micah, pointing. 'We've passed twelve of them, eight to the east of us and four to the west. Before we changed direction . . .'

Eli nodded, smiled. 'You're learning,' he said, turning away and striding on.

Micah followed happily, as grateful for the scrap of praise as a farmyard dog

135

tossed an oxbone.

They headed down a ravine to the west, which was lowforested with small scrubby thornbushes, the prickly branches grazing and scraping at their shins as they picked their way between them. Eli stopped and prodded about in the undergrowth just ahead with his walking staff, before continuing. Soon after, he stopped and prodded the bushes in front of him again. When he stopped a third time, Micah couldn't help himself.

'What are you looking for?' he said.

Eli replied without looking round, and Micah had to strain to hear the words above the driving rain and windhiss of the thornbushes. 'We're not the first to have trod this trail,' he said, probing at a dense thicket with his stick. 'A trapper's been through here . . .'

There was a sharp crack, like the snapping of a twig, and Eli's walking staff jumped in his hand. He raised it and held the tip out towards Micah. Wrapped around the end of the staff was a twisted loop of oiled wire.

'A choke-snare,' Eli observed. 'Harder the wyrme struggles, the tighter the noose gets.'

Eli tugged hard at the wire, till the end that had anchored it to the base of the thornbush came free. He tossed it aside.

By the time they reached the end of the scrubby ravine, and the trail started to rise once again, half a dozen more snares had been tripped by the cragclimber. Micah was bracing himself for another arduous climb when he heard a sound. He paused and listened.

There it was again. Weak pitiful whimpering . . .

'Eli!' Micah shouted. 'Eli, over here!'

136

The wyrme was lying flat on its belly, legs splayed and chin resting in the mud. It was the size of a pack-mule, pale blue in colour, with an orange crest that ran from the top of its head to the tip of its tail, and dark velvety black wings at its shoulders, half unfurled and twitching. One of its back legs was caught in the snare. The wire had cut through the skin and bitten deep into the bone. Its eyes were clouded over. Its tongue lolled out of its head . . .

Eli stopped beside him and looked down. 'Been trapped for days by the look of it,' he opined through gritted teeth. 'See them wounds there?' he said, nodding at the trapped limb. 'Got so desperate it tried to bite off its own leg.' He crouched down. 'I don't hold with trapping wyrmes,' he said. 'Kin got that one right. There's plenty of natural death to profit by without the need to cause suffering such as this.'

Thick yellow pus oozed from the wounds as Eli freed its leg. The wyrme didn't stir.

Micah watched the cragclimber closely as he stooped low and rubbed the back of his powerful fingers slowly up and down the wyrme's throat, before placing an ear to its chest.

Eli straightened up. 'Only one kindness we can do for this poor creature.'

He gripped its head tightly with both hands and placed a boot on its back. Then, with a sudden jerk, he tugged the head upwards, twisting it at the same time. There was a muffled crack from inside the wyrme's slender neck, and when Eli let go, the creature slumped to the ground, dead.

Micah swallowed. 'Shall we gut and skin it?' he asked quietly. 'Honour it by using to the full what it has to offer?'

Eli smiled at the sound of the familiar words. 'Not this time, Micah, lad,' he said. 'Putting the poor creature out of its misery is one thing, but thieving from a snare is quite another.'

He shifted the heavy pack on his shoulders.

'No, much as it galls me, we must leave this wyrme to the kith that laid the snare—unless carrionwyrmes rob him of his prize, as I fervently hope will be the case.'

Setting off again, they crested a series of barren hills, and arrived at a steep cliff-face shortly before nightfall. It looked like a stack of griddlecakes heaped up one on top of the other, the rock soft and yellow-brown, and with thin shadow-filled crevices between each of the cliff's individual layers. Micah's heart fell. It would have been a challenging ascent at the start of the day. Now he was footsore and boneweary, and the steep climb looked all but insurmountable. But when Eli started climbing, Micah bit his tongue.

A dozen or so feet up, Eli stepped into a shallow crevice. It didn't look like much. It offered little protection from the driving rain and was scarcely more than a ledge with an overhang of rock, so low that Micah had to bend double to fit under it. He glanced at Eli, who was crouched down, his hands grasping a slab of rock that was wedged into the cliff-face.

With a low grunt, Eli braced hard and shoved. There was a grinding of rock on rock and the slab shifted to one side, revealing a small opening in the crevice wall. Without looking back or saying a word, Eli unshouldered his rucksack and pushed it through the opening. Then he thrust his head and shoulders into the gap and disappeared from view.

'Come on,' his echoey voice floated back.

Micah pushed his own backpack into the dark opening and scrambled inside. In the darkness, he felt Eli reach past him and heard the rockslab scrape back into place across the entrance. There was a spark of light, then a glow, as Eli lit a lantern and held it up.

Micah's jaw dropped.

The cave was small and round and completely sealed. On all sides, in carefully ordered piles, bundles and neat stacks, were provisions. Dried fish hung in clusters from hooks in the cave's roof, a scuffed liquor barrel was wedged in one corner next to several sacks of grain and packs of carefully wrapped dried meat. Pots and vials of medicaments took up one side of the cave, stacked one on top of another. A shallow dip in the rockfloor, with a heap of blankets laid out inside it, occupied the rear wall.

Eli unfastened the top of his rucksack and began sorting through its contents.

'The high country's a harsh and unforgiving place,' he said in in a low voice, as he stored his newly acquired provisions away. 'But I venture you know that already.'

Micah nodded, mesmerized by the abundance all around him in this tiny cave.

'Here in the wyrmeweald, there are six seasons that you'd do well to note,' Eli continued. 'First there's halfsummer, time of green shoots and growth, and then there's the bloom of summer, time to gather. Then comes the dry season, harsh and thirsty, followed by the rain season—through which we've lately travelled . . .'

Micah opened his own rucksack and tentatively reached inside.

'Soon,' Eli continued 'it will get colder. The rain will freeze and the rivers stiffen with ice—halfwinter—a time to take stock of provisions and make plans . . .' He swept an arm round the cave, indicating the riches it contained. 'In preparation for the harshest and most unforgiving time of all. Winter in the wyrmeweald. Fullwinter.'

Micah nodded, taking his provisions out of his rucksack, one by one, and placing them on the floor in front of him.

'Many recent departers perish in their first fullwinter in the weald,' said Eli. 'I've seen it happen. Those who survive do so by falling in with any company that'll take them—often of the worst sort, and learning from and outdoing their misguided teachers . . .'

Micah flinched as first Cleave's, then Solomon Tallow's brutal faces flashed into his mind.

'It would be a shame if that happened to you, Micah . . .'

'Is that why you've brought me here?' said Micah. 'Shown me all this?'

Eli nodded. 'This is my winter den. It's kept me alive for many a year, and could do the same for you. You see, Micah, there is a way to live in the wyrmeweald without thieving, killing and despoiling. A way I can teach you if you wish it.'

Micah emptied the rest of the contents from his backpack and pushed them over to Eli.

'I wish it,' he replied.

Eli gathered up the provisions, then glanced up at Micah. 'By the way, do you want to tell me what happened to that jacket of yours?' he asked.

Micah looked down and plucked at the tear in the leather, and at the calico beneath. 'I didn't think you'd noticed.'

Eli grunted. 'There's needles and gut-thread in that box over there if you want to make some repairs,' he told him.

'Thanks,' said Micah, then added, 'I didn't want to bother you with what happened. It was back at the scrimshaw den. That wyve collector, Cleave, waylaid me as I was filling the water containers. He had a knife . . .'

He watched as Eli methodically added the provisions to the store, not looking at him. But his casual indifference no longer fooled Micah. The cragclimber was listening intently.

'I beat him, though. I beat him good.' His face dropped. 'But then he tricked me with a coward's head-butt. I was down and defenceless . . .'

Eli grunted again. His top teeth grazed his lower lip as he concentrated on stacking the pots of salve on top of one another in the corner.

'Then some kith came along. Solomon Tallow and two friends of his—Jesse and Esau, I think they were called.'

He paused and looked at the cragclimber. Eli's face registered nothing.

'I guess that had they not, then Cleave would have killed me. He'd already sliced open my jacket and shirt with his skinning knife, and was fixing to cut my throat when Solomon stopped him dead. Dealt with him, he did. Then recovered the things that Cleave had filched, which was when he noticed the scar, unless he'd seen it before . . .'

Micah was aware of babbling now, the words tumbling out under Eli's impassive gaze.

'He saw the scar?' Eli said quietly.

'Through the split leather,' Micah said, nodding.

'Scar like that, Micah, there's only one way you might have come by it.' He frowned. 'And wyrmekith like this Tallow of yours would know that well. Did he enquire as to where you came by it?'

'He . . . he did,' said Micah, 'and I told him.' A strange sense of unease gripped him. 'Did I do something wrong, Eli?'

'Let me put it this way,' said Eli, shaking his head thoughtfully. 'A wyrmekin is protecting a wyve up on that speckled stack. That much is clear. And now that Tallow and his gang know about it, they'll go after the wyve for themselves, which means there's going to be a fight.'

A sly look crossed the cragclimber's weatherbeaten face, an expression of cunning in those clear blue eyes that Micah had not seen before.

'Which gives me an idea . . .'

TWENTY-SIX

The most ancient of the great whitewyrmes inclined his head. His scales were ash-tinged and his powerful wings were moss-spotted and bore the scars of many matings. A whispering sigh rose from deep in his throat, followed by the suggestion of a growl, low and almost imperceptible.

As with all great wyrmekind, his speech was lilting and minutely cadenced. Its upper and lower registers were undetectable to the ears of the two-hides, while the sounds between were sonorous as distant thunder and subtle as softly falling rain.

His companion—a younger wyrme, bright-scaled and pearly white—turned, the barbels on either side of his angular mouth flexing as he did so. A series of clicks and gentle flowing rasps sounded as he opened his jaws. The old wyrme arched his sinuous neck and whistled drily. In reply, the younger wyrme inhaled and vibrated the muscles at the base of his tongue, creating a resonant drone.

The pupils in the old wyrme's eyes widened, and white smoke plumed from his nostrils as the clicks in his throat rose to a reverberating rumble. The younger wyrme stepped back and bowed his head in supplication.

143

The two wyrmes surveyed the cliffs around them, where the vast colony roosted. It was an ancient wyrme gallery. The soft stone of the yellow-grey cliffs had been tunnelled into by generations of great wyrmes, until the very core of the massive rock seemed to have been hollowed out, to be replaced by a labyrinth of winding tunnels and exquisitely chiselled fluted columns. Now, the wind that blew through the galleries added a plaintive whistling accompaniment to the wyrmes' conversation.

The old wyrme's nose quivered. He turned his head and sniffed the breeze. His scaly lips drew back in a snarl as he detected the unmistakeable taint in the air. He turned back and looked down from the high boulder on which he was perched at the peaceful colony below him.

The caverns were alive with whitewyrmes of all ages. Precious hatchlings flittered in and out of the lower galleries, the flares of their exuberant wyrmebreath causing the caverns to twinkle like windguttered lanterns. In the galleries above, older wyrmes rested. Each of them was curled round their own stone pillar, and it was the rub of countless wyrmes' scales over the centuries that had caused the characteristic fluting to the columns, just as the claws of their tunnelling ancestors had added swirling grooves and striations to the cavern walls.

He was old, even for the great wyrmes who measured their lives in rockweathering and riverflow. The eldest in the colony by far, he remembered when the valley country had yet to suffer the taint of the two-hides. But that time, when the newcomers had first set foot in the weald, was now long past. They had taken hold and spread like contagion, and now, if the younger wyrme's report was correct, they were far beyond the highstacks and festercrags where the great whitewyrmes had once laid their eggs, and now threatened the ancient galleries themselves. And still they came on.

Just then, the gentle hum of the colony was shattered by a long keening howl. The two wyrmes looked down, their yellow eyes fixing on a magnificent whitewyrme female standing on a jutting outcrop a little way below them. Her wings were raised, and her neck arched as she stared out towards the darkening horizon.

The old wyrme glanced at his companion and shook his head, the crest rippling at his neck. His anguine tail switched from side to side. The younger wyrme replied with a soft rippling sigh.

The impassioned call sounded again from the great whitewyrme on the rocky outcrop below. She pitched and gyred and flapped her wings in a frenzy of movement. Her neck was raised and her dark-red eyes sparkled like gemstones.

Then, clapping her wings, the whitewyrme leaped from the outcrop, spiralling as she rose. The sun struck her body, flashing across her wings and scales, and glinting on clawtips and fangs as she swooped round the colony in a low arc, her jaws open wide. There was a blast of yellow flame. Then another. And then, as the fire died away, the air echoed with a roaring call of unbridled longing as she beat her wings and flew off towards the rising sun and the distant highstacks.

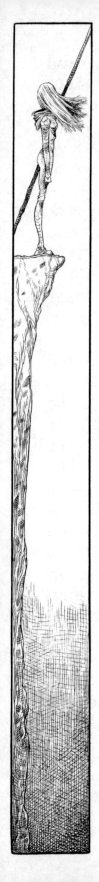

TWENTY-SEVEN

A keening cry echoed across the void. The kingirl turned her head.

She was standing at the edge of the tall speckled stack, one hand on her tilted hip, the other gripping the savage-looking kinlance at her side. The pearl-white suit of soulskin hugged her slim body and was beaded with drizzle and opalescent. As she craned her neck back, the wind blew her long straight hair across her face. Golden-grey, the colour of weathered pine, her hair shimmered in the rainy light as she turned her hauntingly beautiful face to the sky.

Her gaze fell upon the small wyrmeling, and she watched it wheel round in the wet air, its broad wings dipped to one side. It was learning.

Each evening now, when the wyrmeling emerged from the fiery vent and took to the air, its flight was longer than the one before and performed with more grace and precision. It flapped languidly, then dipped the other way, and came swooping round in a smooth broad arc. Fire roared from its gaping jaws, then went out, then roared a second time as its whiskered snout led it into an upcurrent of air that sent it soaring ever higher in a rising spiral.

The girl turned to the great whitewyrme behind her and looked deep into his eyes.

146

The whitewyrme inclined his great head, arching his long sinuous neck with its jagged black scar, until their foreheads were almost touching.

Overhead, the wyrmeling approached the top of the stack, flexing its wings, twisting them back, and beating down hard, its four taloned feet braced for landing. It came down lightly, its legs giving, then straightening up, but not losing their footing as it folded its wings and came to a halt.

The wyrmeling looked round, its head cocked to the side. It surveyed the girl and the whitewyrme through one eye, the vertical slit of pupil pulsing wider for an instant. Then it dipped its head abruptly and skittered off towards the narrow crevice and scritched down into the warmth of the fiery vent.

The kingirl continued to look deep into the whitewyrme's eyes. Their familiar golden yellow had grown darker and was now a deep amber, the black pupils dilated and wide.

Just then, the distant cry reached them again on the drizzling wind. It was a plangent wail of emotion, wild and impassioned and edged with menace. The whitewyrme broke the girl's gaze. His long serpentine neck quivered and turned sharply as he stared off in the direction of the cry.

The girl reached up and placed the flat of her hand against the creature's tremulous neck. Her lips tightened, blanched.

The call came again. Louder. Closer.

The great wyrme skittered about agitatedly on the tips of his claws. He opened wide his mouth in a silent roar, and white smoke and flashes of yellow flame poured forth. His mighty wings flexed and bunched; his thick tail swished from side to side, sending loose stones tumbling down over the edge of the rockstack as he craned his long neck towards the sky.

'Aseel, Aseel,' the girl breathed, and bit into her lip as her fingers traced the length of the zigzag scar while tremors coursed through the whitewyrme's neck.

She closed her eyes and pressed her face against his breast. She could feel his heart beating fast; she could hear her own heart thumping faster still.

Again, the keening wail echoed across the sky, urgent and imploring.

The whitewyrme tilted back his head and a low rumbling growl reverberated at the back of his throat. It grew to a soft hissing sigh as his jaws parted.

'Ay . . . ell . . . saaaah . . .'

Smoke plumed from his mouth and flames lapped at the wet air, turning the droplets of rain to steam. The creature's shoulder muscles tensed and contracted, and his vast white wings unfolded and flapped, raising him up from the speckled rock and pitching him into the air.

The kingirl's arm fell to her side as she watched the great whitewyrme rise up into the sky without her and move off with slow rhythmic beats of his mighty wings. She stood rigid, and she clenched her fists so tight her nails punctured the skin. She watched until he had disappeared from view into the rain-filled duskdark sky.

A drop of blood fell from her bunched fist and plashed on the wet rock below. The girl lowered her head, the golden-grey hair falling like a shroud over her face. A stifled sob shuddered through her soulskinned body.

━✛━

TWENTY-EIGHT

'Remind me what it is we're looking out for,' said Esau, the barrel-chested wyrmekith, scratching at the matted clump of blond beard at his chin.

He was a huge man, with a head shaped like a block of stone; a square jaw, a flat forehead, and a nose that was also flat—a decade of brawling and brutal fist-fights had seen to that.

'That would be the third time of reminding,' Solomon Tallow laughed, his even teeth flashing white against the blue-black stubble of his jaw. 'And I reckon three times is too much, even for a big dumb lug like you, Esau. Ain't that right, Jesse?'

Behind them, Jesse snorted with amusement. Further down the trail, the two women, Bethesda and Leah, who were striding alongside one another, exchanged glances.

'Just tell me, Sol,' Esau entreated.

'Hell's teeth, Esau,' said Solomon, shaking his head, 'I swear if your brawn took to matching your brains, you'd shrivel up before my very eyes. You big dumb lug.'

Esau's face creased up as though he was in pain. 'You know I don't appreciate that, Sol,' he said. 'I don't appreciate you calling me a big dumb lug the whole time.'

Bethesda caught him up, slipped her

small hand into Esau's great paw and squeezed it reassuringly. Beside the others she looked short and slight, her small heart-shaped face set beneath a tangle of stringy ash-brown hair. With her sharp nose, beady eyes and thin top lip which barely covered her prominent front teeth, she looked like an inquisitive rat.

'The speckled stack,' she whispered.

'The speckled stack,' Esau repeated. 'I'm obliged to you, Bethesda.'

'That's right,' Solomon nodded. 'Say it again, now.'

Esau shrugged.

'Indulge me, Esau. Let me hear them words.'

'The speckled stack,' he mumbled.

Solomon's even white teeth flashed in a smile. 'Let it sink in. You big dumb lug.'

Jesse snorted again.

'That boy reckoned the stack was four days away,' said Solomon. 'And if this rain—and your endless jawing—keep up, it's gonna take us longer than that.'

He turned away and set off along the trail, the hard soles of his boots setting up a thudding rhythm that the others were obliged to follow, consciously or no. There was a spring to his step despite the rucksack on his shoulders, which was heavy with provisions acquired at the scrimshaw den and the stout crossbow strapped to its side.

Hurrying to catch up, Leah fell into step beside him. She slipped her arm through his, and looked up at him. She had almond-shaped eyes of lake green that looked deep enough to drown in, high jutting cheek-bones, flawless skin and full lips above a delicately tapered chin. Her brown sunflecked hair was swept back from her face. Solomon returned her gaze, an easy smile on his face, but the eyes beneath his heavy brows remained impassive.

Behind them, taking care not to be observed, Jesse eyed Solomon's girl and licked his lips.

He was the tallest of the five wyrmekith, though his stooped shoulders and loping gait made him look shorter than he actually was. His hair was black and tied back with a thong, and his beard was greasy and flecked with bits of food. He had a hooked nose and hooded eyelids, and his top lip seemed permanently curled into a sceptical sneer. His cold grey eyes missed nothing.

No one spoke as they tramped through the afternoon across the boulder-studded plateau. The sky was darkening and the rain getting up once more when words at last cut through the sound of thudding boots and creaking leather.

'Happen we should find a place to rest up for the night.'

It was Solomon. He'd been looking out for likely places of shelter for the previous hour, and now made towards a mess of tumbled slabs that looked like it might serve the purpose well.

Esau set down his backpack, by far the biggest of the lot. Strapped to it was a variety of equipment: nets, coils of rope, serrated spear tips, heavy canteens and padded bedrolls. He selected a hatchet and two of the canteens, and went off in search of wood and water. Leah slipped her small compact rucksack from her shoulders and let it drop. The rock-spikes, rope-irons, twists of wire and scores of snaptrap springs hanging from it jangled as it hit the ground. Crouching down, she

151

arranged the rocks at her feet into a circle. Esau returned with the wood and Leah soon had a fire blazing. Beside her, Bethesda unhooked the deep cooking pot from her belt and set it over the flames. She chopped and diced the dried meat and roots she'd removed from her own pack, threw them into the pot, and the smoky air was soon filled with the scent of cooking stew.

'Made good progress today, I reckon,' said Solomon an hour or so later. He spooned up a mouthful of stew from the cooking pot. 'Might make it there in less time than we'd anticipated,' he mumbled as he chewed.

'Less time,' Esau repeated, plunging the ladle down into the steaming pot.

'Three days maybe,' said Solomon. 'Daresay we can manage it quicker than some greenhorn stripling.'

Solomon was perched on a low boulder in front of the bubbling cooking pot, his legs splayed. Leah sat between them, her back against the rock. Esau and Bethesda were opposite them; Esau with his massive legs pulled up, hugging his knees with one arm, and Bethesda beside him, her legs folded beneath her. Jesse was standing back a ways, the flickering light from the fire playing on his mean features.

'Though it ain't going to be easy once we reach there,' Solomon added. 'The wyve is defended—I saw the scar the boy bore.'

'Wyrmekin,' Leah bristled, her green eyes flashing. 'Vicious, unnatural wyrmehags . . . Ain't no reasoning with them.'

Solomon nodded. 'Which is why we're gonna have to employ all our skills of stealth and concealment,' he said, looking around at his companions. 'Like I say, it ain't going to be easy.'

'We'll need to approach downwind and scent-masked,' said Bethesda, wiping a splash of stew from her pointed chin.

'And climb the stack under cover of darkness,' said Leah. 'Before dawn's best, when the wyrme and its kin are off hunting for food . . .'

'Snare-nets, harpoons,' said Esau, looking up eagerly. 'Rock-pins, deadbait, and skinning knives, good and sharp, just in case . . .'

Jesse snorted. 'They won't save us if the wyrmekin catches us,' he observed darkly. 'Nothing will.'

'If we do this right, we won't be caught,' said Solomon. 'Trust me.' He reached forward and ruffled Leah's hair affectionately. 'And just think of it. The wyve of a great whitewyrme! The wealth it'll bring us!' He turned to Jesse. 'For such returner's wealth, isn't it worth risking everything?'

Leah pressed back against Solomon's fingers, almost purring with delight. Esau chuckled, spat a lump of gristle into the fire, which hissed and sputtered, and lay back on the rock. He laid his head down on a rounded rock, tipped his hat forward and placed both hands flat upon his belly. Bethesda curled up beside him, and he shifted one arm and wrapped it round her and squeezed.

'Maybe,' said Jesse, his lidded eyes black and unreadable in the flickering firelight. 'If you say so.'

TWENTY-NINE

The kingirl sat motionless at the top of the speckled rockstack, silhouetted against the daybreak sky. The air was nightcrisp, but her body was warm from the fiery heat that billowed up from the smoking vent beside her. Her eyes, darkringed from lack of sleep, were fixed on the lightening sky ahead. The slender lance rested across her lap.

Two days and two nights, and Aseel had still not returned. Two empty days. Two long sleepless nights . . .

A scratching sound came from deep inside the rock. The wyrmeling was slowly waking from sleep. Soon it would emerge for its morning flight.

The wyrmeling had grown fast during its fiery incubation, and soon would be too big to take refuge in the crevice at the top of the speckled stack. Then it would spread its wings and venture out into the vastness of the weald to join with its own kind . . .

The girl scanned the horizon. Aseel, Aseel. Why had he not returned?

A distant speck of movement, dark against the grey sky, set her heart pounding. But it was just a carrionwyrme. Its tattered wings fluttered as it scoured the rocky terrain beneath, then tilted back as it spiralled down for the dead creature it must have spotted.

The girl sighed, then tensed, her body stonerigid. She tipped her head to one side and listened. Her eyes narrowed.

She was not alone.

Gripping the lance tightly, she rose to her feet in one graceful movement. The tip of the lance glinted as she turned slowly around, hips swivelling and eyes boring into the gloom. She raised her head and sniffed.

There was nothing to be seen. Or smelled. Or heard—yet the absence did nothing to ease her mind, for she could sense a presence; the silent presence of someone or something watching her . . .

All at once a figure rose up from the edge of the rock on the west side of the stack. The blush of morning gleamed on a shaven scalp. White teeth grinned from blue-black jaws. The blade of the knife gripped in a powerful fist flashed.

The kingirl sprang at the intruder, her lance lowered and aimed at his chest. The man did not flinch. There was a sudden whirring sound, head height and behind her, and the girl was enveloped in a wyrmenet, tight-meshed and rock-weighted. She fell heavily to the speckled ground, writhing and squirming in its grip.

The man strode towards her, the knife still raised. His boots thudded against the rock.

'Well, well, well,' he drawled, and rubbed a heavy hand over the fine dusting of black stubble on his scalp. 'A wyrmekin without her wyrme . . .'

A woman with long hair and buck teeth appeared behind him, a second wyrmenet in her hands, followed by a hook-nosed man gripping a vicious-looking cleaver. He stepped forward and kicked the girl squarely in the ribs, before ripping

155

the lance from her grasp and handing it to his shaven-headed companion. The kingirl looked up, her beautiful face impassive and mask-like through the checkered mesh of the wyrmenet.

'Where's her wyrme? Why isn't she with her wyrme?'

There were two more of them coming from the other side of the stack. A tall woman with sunflecked hair and green eyes, and a great hulk of a man with a newgrowth beard and a heavy cape, his slit eyes questioning. He strode towards the netted girl, fists clenched.

'Easy there, Esau,' said the shaven-headed man. 'First things first.' His face hardened as he flipped the lance round in his hands and pressed the sharp point hard against the centre of the girl's chest. 'Where's the wyve?'

She glared back at him. 'Kill me,' she breathed.

The weak sun gleamed on tossed hair as the taller of the two woman tutted with her tongue and teeth, and turned away.

The shaved skull loomed closer. Teeth flashed. 'Where's the wyve?' he repeated, dark menace in his tone.

'Kill me,' the kingirl said again.

Behind the man with the gleaming skull, the hook-nosed man raked his long hair and snorted. 'We done this little routine already,' he said gruffly. 'We been lucky so far. Her wyrme ride's not here, but I wouldn't want to press that luck too much further.'

'Kill me, kill me,' the kingirl murmured softly, the words clicking at the back of her throat.

'Not till we get to the bottom of this mystery,' the shaven-headed man told her lightly. He leaned down on the lance, pressing hard into the soulskin, and the girl stifled a cry of pain. The white teeth clenched, and he spoke through them. 'Where's the goddamn wyve?'

Suddenly her words came in a torrent. 'Aseel will come. Soon he will come, with wrath and revenge, and he will cut you down and slaughter you all, and—'

The hard crack to the side of her head silenced her. She flinched, then glared back defiantly as the hook-nosed man stepped forward, a strand of thick black hair dangling down over a heavy-lidded eye. A calloused thumb delicately stroked the blade of the cleaver.

'You're a pretty little thing,' he began, 'but I have a mind to change that, and grievously . . .'

'There ain't no wyve,' the smaller woman hissed from over by the smoking vent.

The shaven-headed man looked across the stack. 'No wyve?'

The woman turned, and pushed back her straggle hair. She shook her head. 'It's hatched,' she whispered, pointing into the crevice and placing a finger to her lips.

The shaven-headed man nodded and whispered to his companion. 'Keep her quiet.'

'It would be my true pleasure,' the hook-nosed man purred.

He crouched down next to her, flicked back the strand of hair behind his ear, and his sneering mouth twisted into what passed for a smile. What teeth he had were large and yellow. He placed the cleaver aside, leaned forwards and clamped a hard bony hand across her mouth, then placed his other hand on top of that. He swung his knee over her body, straddling her, then with his shoulders bunched up at the side of his head, pushed down hard.

Beneath him, the girl arched her neck back and tried desperately to see what was happening at the vent. The shaven-headed man was crouched down over it, wreathed in yellow smoke and gesturing to the other wyrmekith who had silently gathered round him, nets and ropes in their hands.

'Mighty pretty,' the hook-nosed man whispered into the girl's ear. 'Happen I might keep you just for myself.'

The girl twisted back. Her eyes were fired with fury. With one hand still gripping her mouth, the man was pawing at her with the other.

'Just for myself,' he repeated.

He leaned back and pulled a filthy rag from a pocket in his jacket. He thrust it through a hole in the net. Beneath his hand, he could feel her mouth clamp shut, and he gripped her nose and held it tight until she snatched a breath, when he pushed the rag inside her mouth and pressed his hand back down over it. His fingertips gripped vicious hard at her jaws and cheekbones.

Fury turned to fear in the girl's eyes.

He leaned back a second time and reached for the edge of the net. He pulled it up over her legs, her belly and breasts. He flicked it back over her head, clamping her arms to her sides with his folded legs. His head came down towards her.

He stank, this kith. He stank of wyrmeflesh and wyrmeblood. Wyrmebone. Wyrmeheart . . . And her body juddered as she heaved, the rag in her mouth stifling her protests.

She broke free of the fingertips for a moment.

158

Her body flexed and her head thrashed from side to side. The man grinned, his top lip twisted on one side into a gleeful sneer.

'You keep writhing like that,' he whispered, pressing his hooknose close to her face, his dark eyes intense behind their fleshy lids, 'and my cleaver might have to teach you the error of such action.'

She fell still. He pressed his hand back over her mouth, shoving the rag in deeper.

The kingirl braced her neck and her eyes swivelled back in her head as far as they would go. The wyrmekith were poised round the crevice, stonestill and ready to strike.

The wyrmeling's head appeared out of the narrow crack in the rock. Its yellow eyes blinked twice. It scrabbled out onto the flat speckled rock, paused, and its wings ruffled and started to unfurl.

The nets came down.

The wyrmeling squawked with alarm and tried to flap, but its wings became entangled in the thick mesh. Quickly and expertly, the wyrmekith set to work. Ropes looped the netted body. One was pulled tight, trapping its wings to its back; the other brought its legs together till they could no longer move. A sack descended over it, and the wyrmeling was in darkness and swinging upside down.

The kingirl let out a muffled groan and her body went limp. The man looked back down at her. He reached to his side, grabbed one of her arms by the wrist, dragged it across her body and gripped the other wrist, then with both of them clamped in one hand, drew her arms back and pressed them down hard against the rock above her head. The soulskin stretched as her body tensed. With his free hand, he traced a filthy taloned finger slowly down her cheek.

'C'mon, Jesse,' said the shaven-headed man. 'Finish her off before her wyrme shows up.'

The hook-nosed man turned momentarily as he reached for the cleaver at his side. It was enough. The kingirl wrenched a hand free and slashed at his face, her nails slicing the skin at his forehead, across his eyeball and down his cheek.

The man hollered, and his hands shot to his face. Blood dripped through the fingers.

The kin brought a knee up hard between his legs, and squirmed out from under him. His fingers grazed the back of her leg as she scrambled to her feet and ran.

'I'll get you, wyrmehag!'

They were the last words she heard as she reached the edge of the speckled stack and dropped down into the empty void below.

THIRTY

They set off at first light. The wind howled like a plains wolf, chivvying the clouds across the sky in scudding flocks and chilling Micah to the bone.

'Happen there's time for one more foray before the first snows,' Eli said as he set a steady, even pace. 'And what you told me last night set a notion in my head from which we may profit.'

Micah was intrigued, but when he asked what Eli's idea was, all the cragclimber would say was, 'Wait and see.'

After a hard day's tramp and a long cold night spent shivering half awake, half asleep beneath the starfleck black, a shallow ravine they'd been taking opened up to sprawling saltscree slopes, the white rocks fuzzed with green buckwheat.

'Two weeks hence,' Eli said, 'none of this will be here no more. It'll die back as the frosts set in. But for now . . .' He broke off a seedhead and chewed it. 'Sweetest thing y'ever tasted,' he said. 'And distills down to a mighty powerful brew.'

Micah surveyed the buckwheat. It swayed luminous green in the wind, rippling like the surface of a lake.

'You want I should gather some up?'

Eli nodded. He unshouldered his rucksack, stood it upright, open-topped. 'Go ahead, son,' he said. 'There ain't

161

nothing like a shot of green liquor to ward off the bite of fullwinter.' He pulled two empty flour sacks from the rucksack and handed one to Micah. 'If we fill these, we'll have enough for a two-quart batch at least.'

Side by side, they commenced stepping through the screefields, plucking the tops of the buckwheat and dropping the green seedheads inside the sacks. After an hour or so the sacks were full and, stowing them carefully in their packs, they moved on.

They rested up that night beside a stream that was swift and, though barely a stride across, thick with plump fish. They ate well and slept early. The wind had dropped and the thin yellow hook of a waxing moon hung over the jagged silhouettes of the distant crags.

They added sugarcones and blackroots to the green buckwheat the next day, and Eli gathered a cluster of yellow stones he told Micah he would grind to a powder that killed scabies and lice. The day after that they spent some time up on a sandstone bluff, uprooting plant after prickly plant, to reveal the woody gulchroot that Eli was so partial to chewing.

On the fourth day, after a night spent in the wyrmescent warmth of a shallow rockcave, they swung west and took a narrow track scratched into the base of high cliffs. It was like a graveyard, the ground littered with the corpses of wyrmes, some freshdead, others stripped and bleached: jackwyrmes and mistwyrmes that had missed their footing on the steep rocksides, pitchwyrmes that had been driven into the wall of rock by violent storms, and the occasional larger wyrme—greys, buffs and blue ridgebacks—that had stumbled over

162

the cliff edge and plummeted to their death.

Eli garnered what there was to garner. Bones for scrimshaw. Needlefang teeth. Skins. Claws. Some meat he considered fresh enough to salt. But the real prize was the flameoil.

They stumbled across the body of a lanternwyrme late in the afternoon, its body lying beside a small tarn—the Claw Lake, as Eli called it, on account of its shape. The dead creature was big and old, its pelt too pitted and scarred to be of any value, its meat too tough to eat.

'Yet it might still reward us,' Eli said.

He drew his skinning knife from his belt, and Micah watched closely as the cragclimber cut a slit in the creature's extended throat. Then, using a hooked finger, he pulled out the knot of fibrous nodules and held it up, triumph in his pale eyes.

'This is what gives the lanternwyrme its fiery breath,' Eli said, as he decanted it into a glass jar. 'Hottest and fiercest flame of all the lesser wyrmes.'

With the jar carefully wrapped and stored in his rucksack, Eli set off again, heading south.

They tramped on into the hours of darkness that evening, Eli only stopping when they had crested a sharp rise, and dropped down into the windlee on the other side. They set their packs down in deep hollows, ate sechemeat, drank loamy water and fell asleep without setting a fire. The sky was overcast. There was no moon.

The sun broke into Micah's deep sleep as it rose above the distant mountains and he awoke to find himself alone. He sat up, rubbing his eyes in surprise. Before him, some half a mile yonder, stood a bunch of stacks, one of them speckled white and smoking.

'Eli?' he said anxiously. 'Eli?'

He scanned the wide open sky.

'Eli?'

The cragclimber appeared from a behind a low ridge and strode towards him, his expression dark.

'Hush up, boy,' he told him.

Micah swallowed and felt foolish. Eli hunkered down next to him and nodded back the way he'd come. 'There's tracks back a ways,' he said. 'Recent tracks, of five travellers. Kith. Three men, I reckon, two women.'

He pulled his spyglass from inside his jacket, put it to his eye and trained it on the speckled stack ahead. Micah did the same. As he focused in, the blur sharpened and the tall rock stood out in stark relief against the sky; dark basalt patched with speckles of milky white.

At the top, thin twists of yellow smoke plaited themselves together as they rose into the early-morning sky. Halfway down, the stack bent back on itself in a series of rocky ledges, like a pile of carelessly stacked books. The lower slopes were screeflecked and boulderstrewn, and as Micah's gaze fell upon the clastic brown bedrock, his hands began to shake.

He lowered his spyglass and reached inside his shirt to touch the scar at his chest, which had started throbbing.

'Thing is,' Eli said, his gaze still upon the stack, 'we know that a wyrme and its kin were up there at the top. We know they killed two kith, and all but sent you off to the next world too . . .' He rubbed a dry hand over a stubbled jaw. 'That told me they were protecting a wyve.'

164

Micah turned to look at Eli. The cragclimber's blue eyes were unblinking.

'See, whitewyrme wyves ain't like no other wyves, Micah,' Eli went on, his words ponderous slow. 'They don't like to be rushed. Some say they can lie hidden for years before they have a mind to hatch out. Yet once a hatching gets going, it happens fast. A light starts to glow inside the wyve, a faint glimmer first off, but intensifying as the days pass. *That's* what alerts the wyrmekin,' he added, 'to watch over them. Then, week or so later, ofttimes during the rain season, the wyve hatches.' He smiled. 'Tiny little critters, fresh-hatch wyrmelings. But they grow powerful fast, whitewyrmes, nourished by the fires that burn deep inside such rocks.' He nodded to the speckled stack. 'And the wyrme and its kin, they protect the wyrmeling until it's old enough to fly.'

'And you think that's what's happened?'

Eli shrugged. 'Maybe,' he said, and looked at the boy. 'When was it you were attacked, Micah? Three weeks back? Maybe the wyve has hatched and the wyrmeling flown.' He scratched at the back of his neck. 'I sure can't see no sign of wyrmekin now.'

Micah put his spyglass to his eye again and scanned the stack, the magnified image flitting over the rock surface, hovering over cracks and crevices, clumps of hagweed, screespill . . .

'Nor kith,' said Eli. He lowered his arms, shook his head. 'So much for my great idea. I didn't want to trouble you with it before we got here, Micah—seeing as this is where you came by your wound.'

Micah turned, waited.

'I had a notion there would be a fight, boy, a

165

skirmish—and I was betting on the wyrmekin to win that fight. I expected them five kith to wind up dead, their equipment and supplies just lying there waiting to be picked over . . .'

'Like by carrionwyrmes,' said Micah quietly.

'That's the way it is here in the weald, son,' said Eli, glancing down at the fine spyglass in Micah's hand. 'It don't do to get too squeamish.'

Micah nodded. 'So where might they be?' he asked.

'That, Micah, is the question.'

Eli snapped the spyglass shut, pushed it back out of sight in the folds of his jacket and clambered to his feet. He held out a hand and pulled Micah up.

'Come on, lad, let us take a closer look. That accursed curiosity of mine won't diminish till it's been satisfied once and for all.'

They headed down the steep slope, keeping downwind. Micah struggled to keep up, scanning the sky, peering behind rocks, for dangerous kin, dangerous kith. The land levelled out. They approached the deserted speckled stack, stopped at its base and looked up.

'Happen they must have arrived here, found as little as we have, and left empty-handed . . .' said Eli. 'Been and gone.' He tugged the brim of his hat and tipped it forward. 'We might as well head back to the winter den, Micah. There's nothing for us here.'

He turned away, and Micah was about to follow when something caught his gaze.

'What's that?' he breathed.

THIRTY-ONE

Aseel saw the whitewyrme in the distance, climbing towards the heavens, and quickened the beat of his wings. He opened his jaws wide and from deep in his chest there came a booming call.

'Ay . . . ell . . . saaah . . .'

As he rose to meet her, the whitewyrme inclined her head and replied, her call as soft and susurrating as a wyrmecomb breeze.

'Aah . . . zheeeell . . .'

Aseel folded his wings and swooped down through the air towards her.

Facing each other now, their bellies almost touching, the two whitewyrmes flew upwards in a near vertical ascent. Aseel looked into the whitewyrme's eyes and saw a dark-red passion that mirrored his own.

This was the whitewyrme who had been calling to him; the whitewyrme he'd known since their fledging in the colony. This was Aylsa.

The clicking sounds in the back of her throat were almost lost in the windrush as they soared ever higher, but Aseel saw her neck tense and her nostrils flare. She could smell the taint of his kin, Thrace, upon him. Yet she did not break away.

'Ay . . . ell . . . saah . . .'

Her name, like a sigh, escaped from Aseel's mouth, with a wisp of smoke that

167

was snatched away on the wind. His gaze strayed along the length of her body.

Like his own, it had darkened, the white skin suffused with a pearl-grey sheen that swirled with evershifting colours—gold and magenta, vibrant blues and greens—like oil on water. Her raised scales gleamed as if freshly burnished, and her fiery breath was silver-white and powerful and smelled of an intoxicating musk that drew him ever closer to her.

'Aah . . . zheeell . . .' The sound quavered at the back of Aylsa's throat and set her tongue flickering.

A great plume of breath billowed out of Aseel's nostrils into the icy air, and suddenly the two wyrmes were spiralling together like a length of twisting twine in a fury of neckwinding and wingcaress. Then they were falling; tumbling down, down, their sinuous bodies locked together as they clawed and grasped at each other in a cloud of smoke and flame.

The jagged mountain peaks came rushing up to meet them until, with a judder of ecstasy, they separated at the very last moment and rose once more on scorched wings to repeat the process again and again and again . . .

They landed at last on two high crags and stood looking at each other with yellow eyes, dimmed with exhaustion. They both bore the marks of their mating—backs criss-crossed with clawmarks, wings scratched and chafed and fire-charred. Yet the pain they felt was deeper.

Aylsa looked into Aseel's eyes. She could still smell the taint upon him, and knew he would now return to his kin, wherever she was.

Aseel nodded.

Aylsa launched herself from the crag and rose up into the air. Slowly, deliberately, with steady wingbeats, she headed towards the setting sun.

She did not look back.

THIRTY-TWO

It was a girl.

She was lying face down at the foot of the speckled stack. Her head was turned away, and long hair, the colour of ashflecked corn, hung down over the rock. The silver grey, Micah now saw, was wyrmeskin of some sort, but finer and more silken than any he'd ever seen. A limp arm dangled forward at an angle that did not look natural.

He stepped closer and crouched down by her side, his mouth dry and heart hammering in his chest. The gossamer-like covering encased her slim body like a second skin, the sheen gleaming at her elbows, her backbone; tight over the contour of her hip and curve of her thigh.

She was still alive. Just. He could hear her low faltering breath, and watched as her slender back moved gently up and down.

Behind him, Eli sucked in air between his teeth with a wet click. Micah tore his gaze away from the girl, and looked at him.

'Wyrmekin,' he said, 'and she looks to be in a bad way. We're gonna have to sort out that dislocated shoulder.'

Micah turned back to the fallen girl, and his gaze fell upon the top of her back, where the bladebone was pressing up through the silver-grey wyrmeskin, sharp

170

and angular.

'Just as well she's not conscious,' Eli murmured. 'For this will surely hurt.' He cleared his throat and stepped forward. 'I'm gonna need your help, son. I want you to do exactly what I tell you.'

Micah nodded grimly.

'We'll have to turn her over onto her back, real gentle. You ready?'

Micah nodded. Blood rushed in his ears, like wind through thornscrub. The muscles in his jaw tensed as he reached forward and placed trembling hands upon the girl's skinclad body, at the top and bottom of her back. The wyrmeskin—or soulskin as Eli had called it—was smooth and soft, and he could feel the gentle rise and fall of her breathing beneath his fingertips.

'Easy now,' Eli said, taking a hold of the dangling arm and supporting it between the elbow and the wrist. 'That's it. Now, push.'

Carefully, tenderly, they turned the girl over. She wasn't heavy. She rolled onto her side with a soft gasping sigh, and Micah leaned across her, his hand cupped at the back of her neck. Her long ash-yellow hair lay across her face like a veil. Micah could smell its musky smoke-tinged scent as he laid her head gently down on the rock and straightened up.

'Take a hold of her shoulder,' Eli was saying, 'but don't exert any pressure. When I say so, press that jutting bone, kind of smoothing it. Firmly,' he added. 'But gentle. Don't force it none.'

Guided by Eli, Micah placed one hand at the top of her shoulder and the other just below the protruding shoulder blade, and winced as he felt the obvious dislocation of the joint. His gaze slid down her body; over the breasts that quivered with every faltering breath, across her flat stomach and down her slim legs. Slight, delicate and broken she might be, but there was also a sinuous strength in this girl—toned muscle beneath the soulskin, firm and hard beneath his fingers.

'You all set?' said Eli.

Micah gave the slightest of nods. The cragclimber was stooping down, pulling off a boot, which he kicked aside. He placed his bare foot carefully in the girl's armpit against her chest wall. Then, leaning forward, he shifted his grip, using both hands to hold her arm, above and below the elbow, and levered it steadily backwards. He increased his grip and twisted the arm slightly.

The girl stirred, muttering softly, but did not wake up. Micah swallowed.

Eli exerted more pressure, grunting with the effort of it. 'Now, Micah,' he said. 'Nice and smooth . . .'

Micah pressed down firmly on the protruding bone and endeavoured to ease his hand forward. His fingers shook; sweat beaded his forehead and ran down into his eyes, making them sting.

Eli pulled the arm a mite harder. 'Gentle but firm,' he breathed.

Micah felt a soft grinding sensation in his fingertips as the ball of the upper arm bone slipped back into its socket, and a low gasp of pain escaped from the girl as her body flinched, and then relaxed. Micah's heart cramped up inside his chest, leaving him aching and breathless. He reached forward and gently parted the curtain of hair that obscured the girl's face, and bit into his lower lip as a yawning hollow seemed to open up in the pit of his stomach.

She was beautiful, so beautiful; but it was a strange and wild beauty. Her nose was slender and slightly upturned, yet the flare of the nostrils suggested strong passion, and a hint of disdain. Her pale lips were full and sensuous, with the faintest traces of lines at their corners; lines that spoke of determination, of wilfulness. The slight cleft in her chin looked so sweet and delicate that Micah found himself drawn to touch it tenderly with his fingertips.

He leaned forward. Her breath was warm and aromatic, though laced with something sour. Her eyes were closed, and he longed for them to open and return his gaze. As for her skin, it was pale, translucent and flawless and, just looking at it, Micah felt the yearning to reach out and caress it swell inside his chest.

The rushing noise in his ears intensified. He felt hot and shivery. Transfixed, he stared at her face, open-mouthed and perfectly still, then gasped sharply as he remembered to breathe.

He reached forward and brushed gently at particles of red dust that clung to her quivering eyelashes. He traced his fingertips round the dark semi-circles that saucered her eyes and looked like bruises, but were not, and over the real bruise, black and mottled, that smudged her high cheekbone. The skin was so soft it felt like buttered silk . . .

He noticed a thread at the corner of her mouth, and his fingers closed upon it. He pulled. The thread lengthened, but then stopped. He crouched forward. He parted her lips.

There was something there—a corner of dirty

cloth, which he eased out, slowly and gently from her mouth. The cloth snagged for a moment on sharp teeth, then gave, and he found himself staring down at a crumpled square of filthy rag that glistened in the palm of his shaking hand.

He turned to Eli. 'We can't leave her here,' he said.

THIRTY-THREE

The girl's head swam and her body felt bruised and sore, and when she tried to move, a blade of pain stabbed at her shoulder. She winced, and froze, and waited for the sharp pain to subside.

Her nostrils flared as she sniffed at the air. It smelled spicy and dustdry. Peatmoss, she identified, and valley bracken, and her fingertips confirmed that she was lying on a soft mattress of their dried filaments and fronds. She detected another smell besides, sweet yet acrid, that she recognized as the odour of burning wood. Spit-hickory. And when she listened she heard the hissing crackle of a fire; that, and the creak and rustle of someone moving somewhere close by, trying to be quiet. The creeping footfalls sounded heavy and the breathing was low. This was a man—a young man, she judged, by the sound he made when he cleared his throat.

Where was she?

Tentatively the girl parted her eyelids till there was a thin crack between them. She saw walls—thick oppressive walls, constructed from large slabs of rock that had been painstakingly placed together, one on top of the other, and appeared mortared by the darkness of night that seeped between them.

She knew she must be inside one of the

craghuts that she had seen many times, but never ventured into.

It was windowless. There was a closed door to her left that offered no way out, and a hole at the centre of the low flat ceiling above that might. Brownstain smoke was twisting up through it. There was a sturdy table, with a bench on either side. By the side wall was some kind of dip in the floor, shallow and curved, and she was lying in it.

And there was the man.

He was crouching down in near darkness at the far side of the room, turned half away and hunched over. Something was glugging. Flameglow flickered on his back, and on the side of his face. She smelled the leafcrush odour of fresh sweat, then caught a whiff of oil.

Wyrmeoil.

The man was filling a lantern, his breath coming in short jerks as he poured the wyrmeoil carefully from a large earthenware pot and into the small copper reserve. When he splashed some, he chided himself. The girl saw his jaw flex and his Adam's apple move as he swallowed.

She eased herself round, screwing up her face as the blade of pain twisted at her shoulder once again. She leaned up on one elbow.

A pang of separation, acute and charged with longing, juddered through her body as she thought of Aseel. She wanted to be with him, not holed up in this craghut. He was out there somewhere, and if he had returned to the speckled stack already, then he would be looking for her . . .

Where was the craghut? And who was this man?

Was he kith? He sure looked like kith, with his heavy jacket and thick breeches, and the calflength

176

boots of tanned skin. Wyrmeskin. And he smelled like kith, too—woodsmoke and damp, and a faint oily odour, which was the smell of the grease they rubbed into their boots.

Her lip curled, and a shudder passed through her slender body.

Kith had come, she recalled. Five of them. They had taken the wyrmeling. Two women, three men. One with broad shoulders and slit eyes; one with his head shaven, and one with a hook nose and gap teeth and foul breath, and the long greasy black hair that had dangled down over her as he'd crushed her beneath his stinking weight and run his filthy hands over her body . . .

The man in front of her was none of these. But he was kith, and that was enough.

She tilted her head round to one side. Her shoulder cramped and she had to stifle the yelps of pain that gathered in her throat.

Her gaze fell upon the knife. It was lying on a wooden board at the far end of the table. She could see it gleaming. She needed to get out. To escape. The knife would make that possible.

The glugging stopped and she heard a cork stopper being pushed back into the neck of the earthenware pot with a squeak, and a thud as the kith hammered down on it with the heel of his hand. She sat up. The knife was so close. If it wasn't for her shoulder, she would already have retrieved it and had it in her hand.

There was a sharp scratching noise, and a flash of white light, and she saw a wooden match clamped between the kith's forefinger and thumb as he reached out and held the flame to the wick. His fingers were long and slender. The mantle

177

clattered softly when he lowered it, and the walls and ceiling of the rock chamber were abruptly bathed in honeyed light. He picked up the lantern from the bench, and turned.

The blade glinted. It might as well have been a thousand miles away now. Suddenly it was also too late for her to lay herself back down unnoticed . . .

'You've woke up,' the man said—except he wasn't a man at all, she saw, but a boy.

He was gangly and wide-eyed, and had nothing in the way of beard or moustache save for a downy fuzz on his top lip that glistened in the light, and wiry hairs on his chin, so sparse it looked like you could count them off one by one. He smiled. She stared back impassively. It was a kithsmile, and not to be trusted.

The smile faltered, and the boy swallowed. 'Y'all right there? How's that shoulder of yours doing?'

The girl's eyes flicked wider for an instant. This kith knew her shoulder was injured, and she wondered what else he knew.

'You took a bad tumble,' he said, nodding, and his brow furrowed. 'Heaven alone knows how far you fell, but so far as Eli could determine, you suffered nothing worse than an arm that had jumped its socket. At the shoulder. Eli set it back into place,' he added. 'I helped.'

She flicked back her long hair with her fingers and looked round the craghut. There was no one else there that she could see. When her gaze fell back on the boy, he swallowed again. He swallowed a lot, she observed, that jutting Adam's apple of his jerking up, then down. It looked like he did it when he was nervous, or made to feel uncertain of himself, and she was gratified that she could instil

178

such feelings in him. It was an advantage.

If she could just get hold of the knife . . .

'Eli's a cragclimber,' he said, talking again. 'Him and me's partners, leastways, that's the way I figure it, though Eli's not one for open declaration.'

He talked more than he swallowed, and possibly for the same reasons, the words tumbling out in a rapid jittered gush. It was difficult for her to keep up. She hadn't had a conversation for so long, longer than she could remember—and she missed it not one little bit. Aseel and she had no need of words to understand one another. The arch of his body, the tilt of his neck, the length of a stare from his pale ambercolour eyes was more eloquent than any of the guttural sounds that spewed from the mouth of this kith. And Aseel understood her just as well.

He would know what she was thinking now. He would have noticed the knife.

'We found you at the bottom of a stack,' the boy was saying.

This kith could never understand her, no matter how many words he used.

'A speckled stack, it was. You were lying on a ledge down near the base, but like I say, we couldn't tell how far you'd fell . . .' He paused, his brow creased and the corners of his mouth turning down. 'You got bruises,' he said. 'There's a bad one on your cheek . . .'

Her hand shot to her face, and she probed gingerly at the skin, grimacing as her fingers found the injury.

'So you *can* understand me,' she heard him say quietly. 'I was beginning to wonder, on account of you not speaking and all . . .'

Her gaze flicked back to his face, and she gave him the trace of a nod. The smile came back to the boy's face, brightening it up like sunshine.

He was thick-necked, she observed, long-limbed and broad-shouldered. His fair hair was cropped short and stood in spikes, like candle wicks; his cheekbones were wide and prominent. He shambled awkwardly where he stood, his boots scuffing the stone floor.

The girl raised a hand and raked the fingers down through her thick hair, teasing at the tangles, her head cocked slightly to one side.

He was, she allowed, pleasant looking. His features were open, unthreatening, and his ready smile disarmed her. There was no trace of the scorn, or revulsion, or dark intent that the sneering faces of those kith up on the speckled stack had betrayed. And his voice, which babbled on incessantly, was oddly soothing.

Yet he was kith, for all that. She would kill him.

She watched his smiling blue eyes narrow and cloud over. 'Would you like some water?' he asked, and nodded as if answering his own question. 'Let me get you some water.'

He turned and his boots thudded on the stone floor as he crossed the craghut and stooped over a backpack leaning against the far wall. The girl heard a stopper popping and water trickle. His back was towards her.

With her gaze fixed on his broad back as it tilted to one side, she clamped her left hand to her right shoulder, and climbed smoothly to her feet. She stepped from the sleeping groove. The peatmoss and valley bracken crackled and sighed, but the boy didn't notice. She darted to the table, seized

180

the knife and slipped it up her sleeve, before darting back to the bed.

The boy turned back, a metal cup clasped in his hand. He swallowed, and approached her.

'Here,' he said. He held out a tin cup. 'Here's your water.'

The girl raised the cup to her lips and sipped, peering up at him from beneath lowered lids. He was much taller than her and, though thin, he looked strong, this kith.

'I can get you something to eat as well if you're hungry.' The boy was still filling the silence with words. 'There's some smoked fish and stuff. Eli's just off fetching us some extra wood.'

The girl felt the knife pressing into the soft skin of her inner arm. She knew she'd get only the one chance to use it.

'Eli is what you might call my mentor,' the boy was telling her. 'See, I'm fresh to the weald, and I am grateful to Eli for taking it upon himself to teach me its ways.' He sighed. 'Though I sure ain't finding it easy. 'Course, there's some I've encountered whose ways I don't care for. Wyrmekith. Bad wyrmekith. Wyrmekith that trap and snare and kill . . .' He shook his head. 'But not Eli. That's not *his* way. Eli does not hold with trapping wyrmes, or making them suffer. "Kin got that one right", that's what Eli reckons . . .' He hesitated. 'You're kin, ain't ya?'

The girl took another sip of water, then lowered the cup. She stared back at him.

Just the one chance, she reminded herself. She would have to be clever.

'I'm Micah, by the way,' he told her, and frowned. 'I guess you have a name too.'

She nodded, smiled. 'I have a name,' she said, and the unfamiliar husky voice sounded strange to her ears. She cleared her throat, placed the cup down and rose to her feet, lithe and unhurried, her hand behind her back. 'Thrace.'

'Thrace,' Micah repeated. 'That is a strong and beautiful name,' he declared solemnly. 'Thrace.'

The girl flinched. She didn't know whether it was strong or beautiful; it was her name. She'd forgotten how it sounded on someone else's lips. Her hand gripped the haft of the knife and she forced herself to keep smiling as she came close to the kith, her other hand smoothing down the crumpled soulskin at her hips, then reaching out towards him.

All at once, there was a grinding of wood on stone, and both of them turned to see the door of the craghut swing open. Micah grinned.

'Eli!' he exclaimed. 'You're back.' He nodded to the wyrmekin. 'This here is—'

'Step away from her, Micah,' Eli interrupted grimly.

'But—'

Eli's face hardened. He dropped the armful of wood at his feet. '*Now*, Micah.'

Micah frowned, but did as he was told. The cragclimber strode forwards, his pale eyes metalcold. He reached out with his hand, palm up.

'Hand it over,' he said, his voice little more than a whisper. 'And don't try nothing smart.'

The girl stared back at him defiantly. This second kith was tall and rangy, with taut muscles that were like knotted wood. He looked tough and hard. She would not stand a chance against such a man. Of course, if Aseel was here; if she had her lance gripped in her hands . . .

Eyes blazing, she brought her arm slowly around from behind her back and opened her clenched fist. The knife clattered to the stone floor.

Micah stared down at his hackdagger, his scalp prickling, then back at the wyrmekin's beautiful face. Her dark eyes did not blink, and were unreadable. He swallowed hard.

'This here is Thrace,' he said.

THIRTY-FOUR

The boy, Micah, was looking across the room at her from the table.

Thrace set the empty bowl aside, licking the fishoil from her fingers, and flinched at the pain that gripped her shoulder. She was seated on the floor in the corner of the craghut, her knees drawn up to her chest.

The boy swallowed the mouthful of smoked fish and rootmash he'd been chewing, then looked down at the table. But he couldn't seem to keep his eyes off her for more than a moment, for he looked up again almost immediately.

'You had enough?' he enquired.

She looked back at him. There was mistrust in his eyes.

The food and drink had done her good, bringing a shine to her dark eyes and a blush of colour to her cheeks. She'd intended to kill him, and he was in no doubt of it, for she saw him check for the knife at his belt. It was where it should be.

Thrace could feel his gaze still upon her. Her shoulder hurt and she grimaced.

The cragclimber tutted softly. He was seated on the bench next to the boy.

'Seems to me you're gonna need that shoulder of yours seen to,' he observed. 'I could get you to someone who might be able to fix it up, had you such an interest.'

Thrace turned to him. His pale-blue

eyes looked disquieted.

'Fact is,' Eli went on, laying down his spoon, 'an injury like that, if you're not careful, you could end up losing the use of your arm.'

The words made her stomach cramp and her head whirl. Her eyes welled up till the two faces before her blurred.

'It's a wyrmekin of Eli's acquaintance,' the boy said quietly. His eyes scanned her face. 'Jura. She can work miracles—though it could hurt some . . .'

Thrace looked at the boy, then at the cragclimber. She'd heard tales of kin being taken by kith and sold on as slaves. Aseel would have known whether or not they were lying; whether there wasn't something underhand at play. But Aseel was not there with her and she had to make her own judgement.

Neither of them looked deceitful so far as she could determine. And though the boy's blue eyes, that seemed so drawn to her, gave nothing away, the cragclimber's words sounded sincere. Yet they were wyrmekith, both of them. That fact remained. They'd ministered to her injuries; they'd fed her and eased her thirst with honeywater. But they *were* kith . . .

She shook her head.

'As you please,' said Eli gruffly. 'The offer's there, but it makes no odds to me. I'm not your keeper.' He climbed to his feet, then nodded towards the door. 'You're free to do whatever you choose.'

Thrace took a deep breath. Her shoulder jarred as she pulled herself to her feet, and when she went to take a step, her head spun and the walls of the craghut seemed to turn and smudge. She stumbled forward, reaching out to balance herself, and the shoulder jarred again, so badly that her legs crumpled and she sat back down heavily on the floor. She pressed a hand tenderly to the throbbing pain. Even through the soulskin, she could feel how hot her shoulder had become.

'We could be there before nightfall,' the cragclimber said, glancing up through the hole in the roof. The first glimmer of the new day was flushed across the sky. 'Assuming you're up to walking that long,' he added.

Thrace nodded, and before her, the two kith faces blurred again. There was nothing for it but to accept.

*   *   *

As the sun rose, she set off with them, the walking staff that Eli had whittled her gripped in the hand of her good arm, her right arm, and clacking on the rock as she used it to steady herself. The boy was on one side of her, the cragclimber on the other. She was discomforted by their close presence. The sound of their breathing curdled in her ears; their smell all but made her gag.

Yet when they reached the top of the rockstrewn slope, and the colour abruptly drained from the landscape, and her head swam and the end of the walking staff slid across the rock, she was grateful for the hands that reached out and grabbed her and stopped her crashing to the ground in a dead faint. And when she felt well enough to continue, revived by cold water, a spoonful of the honey that Eli kept in his rucksack, and a while spent sitting with her head between her knees, she was grateful

186

again for the arms that supported her.

The boy kept looking round at her, the muscles in his jaw tensing and untensing. There was concern behind the mistrust, and she wasn't sure what made her quake beneath his gaze.

'We can stop any time you like,' he told her. 'You get too weary, or giddy, or you want to stop for something more to drink, then you just tell me.'

Thrace rubbed at her left hand, which was feeling numb, and felt her cheeks flush red and hot in the face of his kindness.

It was dusk by the time they reached the edge of the yawning ravine.

'This is the place,' said Micah, looking at Thrace.

The wyrmekin stared ahead. She knew the green haven, of course. It was one of two dozen or so that she and Aseel would fly over. Many times they had dived down into this very one—at sun-up and sundown—and skewered the plump damsel flies that danced in the rainbow spray of the waterfall. This would be the first time she had ventured into the ravine on foot, and she peered down warily. Rain had started falling mid afternoon and, though it had eased off, the soft grey sheets of rainfall misted her view, and she heard the distant waterfall pouring from the rock-cleft far to her left before she saw it.

The boy must have noticed where she was looking. 'That's where Jura lives,' he told her. 'She's kin, like you.'

Thrace stared at the smudge of falling water. She'd been so close to it, so many times, without ever suspecting that there might be wyrmekin living there. There was Riga and Arram at the black pinnacles, Zaia and Aluciel who roamed the saltflats far to the west, and there were others she knew of in the yellow peaks beyond, but whose names she had never learned. But Jura. Why had she never seen this Jura and her whitewyrme here in the green haven, so close to the highstacks she and Aseel watched over?

She looked back at the boy, Micah, and he looked at her. She leaned heavily on his arm.

*   *   *

Micah felt the warmth of the girl's body close beside him. When the descending trail became too narrow to walk three abreast, Eli strode ahead while Micah remained at the girl's side. He walked on the outside of her, one hand on his hackdagger, the other gripping her good arm firmly. He stole glances at her as often as he dared, then some more.

Her features were so delicate, yet her expression so strong. Her skin was the most flawless he had ever seen, and her dark eyes seemed to hold mysteries he could scarce but guess at. Time and again he felt his gaze drawn to them.

She glanced up at the sky, as she had throughout the journey, looking—Micah surmised—for her companion, the great whitewyrme. A shiver of apprehension ran through him. This was no farmgirl from the plains walking next to him. This beautiful girl with the milk-white skin and pooldeep eyes was wild, dangerous, unknowable . . .

Not for the first time, Thrace caught him staring at her. She raised a hand and folded it over her shoulder, and her eyes winced as she gently

188

squeezed it.

Micah winced, too. 'That shoulder of yours is still hurting you some, ain't it?' he said softly.

They continued in silence, and were walking sideways on, when Eli stopped. The jutting slab of rock was just ahead of them. The sky was purple grey with imminent night. The cragclimber reached down awkwardly on the narrow ledge and picked some thing up.

Micah watched him, then leaned forward and thrust a rigid arm out at Thrace's side, that she could grip a hold of and not slip.

'What you found there, Eli?' he asked.

Eli looked back, his finger and thumb raised and a look on his face that Micah could not determine.

'A wyrmehook,' he said. 'Kith wyrmehook.' He shrugged and pushed the five-pronged hook into a pocket, and continued.

Thrace followed, with Micah's arm still outstretched protectively at her side. One by one, they slipped behind the falling water and into the concealed cavern. A darkness filled with flitting and skittering folded itself around them.

Something was wrong.

Eli took the lantern that hung from a hook-like spur at the side of the entrance. He struck a match, lit the wick and pushed the mantle down into place. A sputtering glow filled the cavern. He raised the lantern and swung it from side to side . . .

Thrace let out a high-pitched scream.

THIRTY-FIVE

The kingirl was on her knees, rocking to and fro, her mouth open and her eyes rolling back in her head, glistening and marble white. She reached up and tore at her hair, dragging it down over her face, then out at the sides, her fingers clenched and buried in the tangled strands. She started moaning, softly at first, something that Micah couldn't understand, then getting louder till a single word was echoing round the cavern.

'Kith . . . Kith . . . Kith . . . Kith . . .'

Micah stared about him, bewildered.

The neat order of stacked boxes and lines of urns had been ransacked, reduced to splintered boards and broken shards, while their contents lay every-which-way; shrivelled roots and coarse powders, and dried leaves that covered everything, turning the cavern ground to a forest floor in late halfwinter. Cracked red earthenware pots dripped yellow ointment like pus seeping from ruptured boils. Dead wyrmes littered the ground, with the living—some injured, some not—picking their way between them, their eyes ablaze and stomachs bloated.

'What . . . what's happened?' Micah said, his voice a faltering whisper.

Thrace howled.

Micah went towards her. He put his

hand on her shoulder. She shot backwards, violently shaking it off and turned on him. Micah recoiled at the sight of the savage eyes that glared back at him through hanks of wild and matted hair. She was breathing hard through flared nostrils, while her lips had peeled back in a snarl, and the small pointed teeth gleamed. A low rasping hiss emerged from her throat.

'There!' she cried.

Micah followed the line of her pointing finger into the flickering shadows at the back of the cavern.

The great whitewyrme lay in a lifeless coil, its head to one side and long arrowtip tail looping back the other way. It had been kithstripped. Pliers had wrenched the claws from its feet and the teeth from its jaws, leaving the mouth bloodgummed and slack. Its stout ivory horn had been torn out by the roots, leaving a gaping hole at the centre of its long snout. The wings had been crudely hacked off. The valuable bones had been harvested; the valueless strips of skin discarded, and now lay in a tattered heap amid blood and half-digested food, for the creature had been eviscerated. The kidneys and liver were gone, and the heart. And there was a ragged incision at the base of the wyrme's neck, where its flameoil sac had been ripped out.

Thrace sprang to her feet, her limber body flexed and agile. With no trace of the injured shoulder now, she ran across the cavern floor and fell again to her knees, in front of the dead wyrme. Head down, her face shrouded by her corn-white hair, the wyrmekin girl reached out and ran her fingers over the bloody wounds on the whitewyrme's head. Micah hurried across to her,

191

stepping over the dead and dying smaller wyrmes in his path.

'Thrace,' he whispered, and she looked up at him. There was cold hatred in her eyes.

Kith had done this. And he was kith.

Just then, the light dimmed. Micah looked round to see Eli down on his knees by the wall on the far side of the cavern. His body was hunched forward, a flickering halo of lantern light around him.

Micah crossed the cavern floor towards him. Eli must have heard his footsteps, for he glanced back over his shoulder, his face haunted and drawn, then turned away again. Micah came to a halt just behind Eli, and peered over the cragclimber's shoulder.

The body was on its back, the arms angled like broken wings and the legs apart. There were clumps of hair beneath broken fingernails, and dried blood. The head was lying on its side and tilted at an improbable angle.

'Jura,' Micah whispered.

The kin's silver-grey suit of soulskin had been slashed open down the front, leaving the slender body exposed, and none too fastidiously, for there was a long thin line scoring the skin from the base of her neck to the top of her thigh; a scratch in some parts, deep in others. The blood had congealed, but Micah could see that, in places, it had been smeared by roving hands, by probing fingers.

He turned away, bent double and vomited; vomited till his stomach was empty and his heaving dry. Then he straightened up, wiped his mouth, wiped his eyes. Thrace had emerged from the shadows and was standing next to him. There was blood down the front of her soulskin. She was looking down at Eli, watching the cragclimber's every movement intently. Micah turned back.

With taut delicacy, Eli cupped the dead kin's head in both hands and turned her face to his. There was a deep gash in her neck. Red-black blood had gathered in a pool and soaked into her ashen hair. Her eyes were open and filled with defiance. The mouth was open too, the lips parted to reveal the dark empty hole inside, where the tongue had been cut out.

'Why . . . why would they do that?' Micah groaned.

'Because she refused to speak to them,' said Eli, his voice toneless. 'Kith do this. Do this to kin who won't answer them.'

Micah shook uncontrollably. He heaved emptily and tears sprang to his eyes.

Eli reached out a hand towards the dead kin. Gently, tenderly, he passed a finger and thumb over her eyelids, closing her eyes. His hand moved to her mouth, and he closed that too. Then, reaching further forward, he bent down, and pressed his lips to hers.

'Rest peaceful, Jura,' he whispered softly as he pulled away.

He climbed to his feet, his gaze still resting upon Jura's face. Then he turned. He looked at Thrace, then at Micah. His expression was grim and so hard it looked as though those pale-blue eyes of his were staring out of a wooden mask.

Beside him, Micah heard Thrace softly hiss. Her fists were clenching and unclenching.

'There were five of them,' Eli said, his voice flat

and emotionless. 'Them five kith I expected to find dead at the speckled stack.' He sighed. 'Most likely they spotted that this green haven had been visited—maybe even followed tracks we left behind.' He surveyed the mess of spilled remedies and herbs. 'Couldn't believe their luck, finding such a place . . . Jura would have sensed their coming, but she wouldn't have run, not with Asra back there, sick and defenceless . . .'

Micah glanced at Thrace. She was nodding slowly. Her face was composed once more, her mouth set and her eyes wide. She was beautiful.

'Judging by the marks here, and the blood spatters, and the hair and skin beneath her nails, she fought powerful hard,' Eli was saying. 'It must have taken all five of them in the end. The women pinned her down at first, but she was too strong for them. She lashed out, wounding at least one of them by the look of it. Then the men came to help out. If I know Jura, she'd have held out as long as she could, not said a word in the hopes that she'd keep their full attention; that they wouldn't venture into the back of the cavern.' He hesitated. 'Then they slit her throat.'

'They will pay,' Thrace said darkly. 'For the whitewyrme. For the kin. For the wyrmeling they stole. I will hunt them down. I will make them pay.'

Eli nodded, his expression unchanging. 'Yes,' he said. His voice was low and measured, and colder than Micah had ever heard it. 'And I shall help you in the endeavour.'

THIRTY-SIX

It was hot and cramped. The wyrmeling's eyes were wide open, but it couldn't see anything. Its heart hammered inside its chest.

This darkness, that swayed and bounced, was oppressive. It was suffocating and dense. It stank like death. It seemed without end.

The wyrmeling tried to blink the darkness away, but it could not. The same matt night remained. It was as if it had been returned to the wyve that it had struggled so hard to break out of.

It strained to flex its wings; it tensed its legs. It had to escape. It had to hatch a second time. One hindleg broke free and its claws scratched desperately against the soft walls that flexed yet would not yield. It would have breathed fire had it been able, but its nostrils were blocked and its jaws would not open.

Something struck it hard on the shoulder.

It fell still.

The swaying jolting darkness returned.

When, a time later, the wyrmeling came down heavily on its haunches, it let out a muffled cry of alarm. The rocky ground was hard, and it jarred. Above its head, it heard scraping and scratching, and dazzling light abruptly flooded in.

195

Its eyes snapped shut. It felt something cold drop down over its head and tighten round its neck. It blinked, once, twice. It looked up.

A gaunt hook-nosed figure loomed over the wyrmeling. Dark hair hung down to his shoulders and was thick on his face. One eye was concealed by a dirty bandage; the other, deepset and hooded, flashed as fleshy lips parted and guttural sounds emerged. A woman beside him nodded her head. There were half-healed scratches down one of her cheeks. She grunted softly as she pulled a rucksack from her shoulder, then rummaged inside and retrieved a package that unfolded to reveal thin brown strips.

The strips smelled good. They smelled like food, and the wyrmeling's belly rumbled.

The wyrmeling went to lurch forward, but the noose round its neck held it back. The woman pushed her hair out of her face and reached out a hand, a single strip of meat dangling from her fingers. The meat grazed the wyrmeling's snout, but still it could not open its jaws.

The guttural noises started up all over. First from one mouth, then the other. Then from the first again, but louder.

The woman shrugged. She picked up a stick and cut a snick in its end. She rolled up the strip of meat and wedged it into the split wood. Then she held the stick to the wyrmeling's snout and pushed the skewered meat between its tightly bound jaws and into its mouth.

It swallowed. It wanted more, and more came. It came until the wyrmeling could eat no more and, sated, turned its head away.

It saw the other three. They were close by, two

196

of them standing. One had a gleaming hairless head. One was broad as a boulder. The third was small and hooded and sat hunched up on the ground, her face pinched and hands clasped at a hip. Noises were coming from each of their mouths; guttural, nasal, sibilant . . .

The one with the hairless head was loudest. His noise was like a roar. He kept pointing off into the far distance, following the line of his outstretched finger with his eyes, then looking back at the others. He stared at the seated woman, then shrugged and raised his hands. She shook her head from side to side. Her eyes were wet, and her face creased up as she stroked tenderly at her hip, then pulled aside blood-soaked material to reveal a wound that had barely started to heal. There was ragged skin and clotted blood, and dark raw flesh. The broad man crouched down next to her and wrapped a large arm around her shoulders. He looked up at the one with the hairless head, and jabbed a finger towards him.

Suddenly, everyone was making noises at the same time. All five of them. They pointed and gestured; they put their hands on their hips, then flapped them about. They shifted their bodies, they shuffled their feet. Heads jutted forwards, jaws set. They growled and whined and snorted and sighed as lips moved, tongues darted and teeth flashed in and out of view. It got louder, faster, then stopped as abruptly as it had started.

The wyrmeling cocked its head to one side. Its eyes widened as its gaze darted from one to the other.

The one with the gleaming hairless head had his hands raised. He alone was making noises. Soft and soothing now, and much slower. The others sat in silence. Three of them were looking at him, nodding occasionally; but the one with the hood was still. Her head was lowered and she was staring down at the ground. The broad man was watching her intently, soft cooing sounds coming from his rounded thin lips.

Then she nodded.

The next moment, there was more guttural noise, quick movements and bustling activity. The tight noose at the wyrmeling's neck was released, and the suffocating darkness suddenly returned. A lurch made the wyrmeling gasp, and the darkness began to sway and judder.

It squirmed and struggled for a moment. Then, anticipating a blow, it fell still.

THIRTY-SEVEN

'You are kith,' said Thrace. 'I am kin.' She glared at the cragclimber. 'This is kin business.'

'That may be so,' Eli said evenly, 'but your great whitewyrme is not with you at present, Thrace, to speed you across the weald skies in pursuit.' He met her gaze. 'You'll need my help to track them on the ground.'

He looked down at Jura's broken body at his feet, anger and pain clouding his eyes.

'And I have my own score to settle with them wyve collectors,' he said grimly. 'And that is kith business.'

Thrace gave a curt nod, but said nothing. Eli turned away and knelt beside Jura. He slapped away a small wyrme with a jagged crest that was sniffing at the wound in her neck, sending it skittering away, squeaking with indignation. He pulled off his rucksack, undid the straps and reached inside.

'Keep your backpack on, Micah,' he said. 'We'll be moving out directly.'

Micah frowned and glanced behind him at the rushing curtain of water. The lantern light picked out glittering streaks in its shifting surface, like rock shot with silver or gold, but beyond it was black with nighttime.

'We're leaving?'

Eli spoke without looking round. 'You may have a yearning to spend the night in this charnel-cave, boy, but I surely do not.'

Eli pulled a rolled wyrmeskin Micah had not seen before from the depths of his rucksack. He unfurled the gleaming coppercolour skin and laid it over Jura's body.

'Been saving this fine skin for a winter cloak,' he muttered gruffly. 'But Jura deserves the best. Now, Micah, lad,' he said, gently turning the body over and gathering the wyrmeskin into a bundle. 'There's some salve over there.' His shoulders flexed as he nodded towards the mess of shattered urns and broken boxes by the wall. 'At the far end. Look for a pot that has a circle with a cross through it on the front. And see if you can't find me an unbroken one.'

Micah did as he was told. Leaving Thrace standing over Eli and watching his every action intently, he crossed the cavern.

There were more pots that had escaped destruction than he had at first thought. They'd been upended and lay on the ground, but many were still stoppered up, their contents intact. He located one with the markings that Eli had described, and pulled the stopper. Pungent odours wafted up. Pine oil, camphor . . .

Micah returned to Eli with the pot. The cragclimber was still on his knees, but now cradled the rolled wyrmeskin containing Jura's body in his arms.

'Is this it?' he said, showing the pot to Eli.

'It is,' Eli confirmed. 'Give it to Thrace.'

Micah held the pot out to the girl, who was still

staring at Eli and the bundle in his arms.

'Jura would have given you this herself, had she been able,' Eli said quietly, climbing to his feet. 'Rub it into that shoulder of yours, and it'll take the fire from the joint.'

Turning to Micah, Thrace took the pot from his hand. She sniffed at it suspiciously, then nodded. She reached for the soulskin at her neck and pulled it down, revealing her collarbone. Then, wincing with pain, she carefully eased the pale clinging slough of the great whitewyrme, her Aseel, down off one shoulder. The pliant soulskin peeled from her smooth white skin as she turned her back on Eli and Micah.

'You will have to help me,' she said in a quiet faltering voice.

'That means you, boy,' said Eli, as he carried the wyrmeskin bundle towards the wall of water. 'And bind it tight with whatever comes to hand—but don't take too long about it.'

Her back to him, Thrace held up the pot with a steady hand. Micah reached into it and withdrew three fingers coated in pungent yellow ointment. In contrast to Thrace's, his own hand was trembling, and he had to grip his wrist with the other to steady it.

Her shoulder blade was dark with a mottled bruise, stark and ugly against the whiteness of her skin. Micah reached out and touched it. The skin felt hot beneath his fingertips, and silken smooth. Slowly he traced circles across the bruise until the cooling ointment had gone from his fingertips, and only its heady intoxicating smell remained.

Thrace gave a soft sigh, and Micah saw her fingers go white as she gripped the pot.

201

'Am I hurting you?' he asked, reaching for more ointment and smoothing it over her shoulder as gently as he could.

Thrace shook her head. 'Not hurt,' she said, and she did not wince as she looked back at Micah. Her fierce dark-eyed stare was vulnerable yet defiant. 'Your touch is gentle.'

'You two done yet?' called Eli from the entrance to the cavern.

'Nearly,' Micah called back, flustered and fumbling beneath Thrace's gaze.

He reached round and grasped his tattered cloak and took hold of its hem in his teeth. Quickly and savagely, he tore a strip of cloth from it. Then, with clumsy awkward fingers, he wrapped the strip of cloth under her arm and over her shoulder. His fingers brushed lightly against her skin as he repeated the manoeuvre three more times.

'It's not too tight, is it?' he asked.

She shook her head.

'I . . . I'll just tie it off then,' he told her.

He brought his head down close to her shoulder, and slit the end of the cloth in two with his teeth. He could feel the warmth of her body on his face. He could smell its sweet musky scent. He stooped forward, knotted the two frayed lengths of material together, then straightened up.

'That should do it,' he said, his attempt at confidence undercut by the catch in his throat.

Thrace eased her soulskin back over her shoulder, and Micah helped her, his touch lingering longer than was necessary for the task.

'All set?' said Eli, from the cavern entrance.

The pair of them nodded.

'They went that way,' he said when they joined

him at the cave entrance. He indicated a couple of bloody bootprints leading off along the ledge and out from behind the waterfall. His jaw clenched. 'And so do we.'

He set off. His walking staff was attached to the back of his rucksack, the wyrmeskin bundle cradled tenderly in his arms. Thrace followed him, with Micah close on her heels.

'What'll happen to Jura's great whitewyrme?' he asked her.

'The smaller wyrmes will pick it clean.' She shrugged. 'Wyrme to wyrme. Kinwise.'

They left the cavern behind the waterfall and stepped out onto the narrow ledge. Outside, the sky was overcast, but the full moon behind the thin blanket of cloud lightened the grey sky. It looked like soured milk.

'Watch your footing,' Eli's voice floated back.

It was sound advice. This track was steeper than the one on the other side of the waterfall that they'd taken before. It zigzagged up the sheer rockface, so narrow in parts that Micah was forced to rely on no more than the toes of his boots and the tips of his fingers to keep from toppling backwards. He was soon panting hard. He looked up.

Thrace was just ahead of him. She too was using her hands for support, but despite her injured shoulder, she displayed a remarkable grace and agility in every movement she took. Aware of the danger in being distracted, Micah forced himself to look away from her slender soulskin-clad body and concentrate on his own progress.

Glancing up a little while later, Micah saw that Eli was now some way ahead of them, sure-footed and tireless despite his precious burden.

As they reached the top of the green haven, the cloud thinned out completely, and the fat moon sent down bright shafts of light that turned the crags silver. Before them lay a flat stretch of pitted rock, yet Eli kept climbing up the rough surface of a solitary outcrop. Micah was about to follow, but Thrace stilled him with a hand placed on his arm.

She placed a slender finger to her lips, and looked up. Micah tipped his head back and craned his neck.

The cragclimber had reached the top of the crag. The moonlight glowed on one side of his face, one shoulder, one arm—and on the gleaming wyrmeskin bundle that he laid reverently on the rock. He knelt down and unwrapped the wyrmeskin.

Micah caught a glimpse of Jura's hair. It looked like spun silver. Eli arranged the body on the draped wyrmeskin with tender care, straightening the legs and shoulders and crossing the arms over the chest, then climbed slowly to his feet.

He looked down at Jura, up at the moon, then turned away. His pale-blue eyes gleamed wet.

He clambered purposefully back down the side of the crag and rejoined them on the pitted rock. Micah continued to stare at him, but the cragclimber made no response to his questioning gaze. Instead, he crouched down. He peered closely at a squirl of mud; he touched a small pebble, knocked loose in its own depression like a tooth about to come out. His arm rose and he pointed off across the rock slope.

'That was the way they went.'

Thrace's dark eyes narrowed as she looked

204

ahead. 'They'll follow this shelf, then drop down through the crevices beyond those peaks,' she said.

Eli nodded. 'Reckon you're right on that score,' he said, setting off across the rock. 'You take the wyrme's-eye view, Thrace, and I'll keep my kith eyes on the ground at our feet. They'll not escape us.'

Not for the first time, Micah saw the girl hesitate and look up expectantly at the skies for a moment, before following in Eli's footsteps. She didn't look back and, with a shrug, Micah brought up the rear, his tattered cloak flapping forlornly behind him.

They walked through the night. It was a relentless tramp. The only breaks Eli and Thrace allowed themselves were those foisted upon them by the thickening cloud. Whenever it grew too dark to see by, Eli would hold up and wait for the moon to reappear, to confirm they were still following the tracks, before continuing. He would not strike a match. Behind him, Thrace kept her eyes resolutely on the horizon—when she wasn't scanning the skies overhead.

As for Micah, even when the sky was swept cloudclear and the moonlight illuminated every single grain of sand, he was unable to spot the signs that the cragclimber saw so effortlessly. A bruised leaf. A tousled tuft of grass. Displaced dust . . .

They continued, with Eli stooping and squinting at nothing that Micah could see, then striding on; and Thrace always close behind. The sky ahead was flushed with dawn when Micah's gaze fell upon a telltale sign there was no mistaking. Blood. There were spots of the stuff lying on the trail in a red constellation, and a larger puddle that had gathered on a squat rock and tippled down one side.

Eli caught Micah's eye and nodded thoughtfully. 'That's right, lad,' he said. 'One of them's hurt. And hurt bad.'

He straightened up and pulled the length of gulchroot he'd been chewing from the corner of his mouth. Beside him, Thrace surveyed the landscape; up ahead, and back the way they'd come.

'Stopped here recent,' Eli noted. 'The fourth place they've stopped since the head of the ravine.'

'And the trail ahead gets no easier,' Thrace added.

Eli pushed the root back between his teeth and nodded. 'They're slowing up.'

He tipped his leather hat back and scratched thoughtfully at his scalp. He squinted up at the sky. The clouds were melting away, snatched off by a rising wind that had a chill about it and nipped at the skin.

'Happen we could rest up ourselves a while,' Eli announced.

The words made Micah realize just how weary he had become, and he moved on past the bloodstained rock, swung his backpack to the ground and sat himself down heavily beside it. His legs were aching. His belly growled. The others sat down on either side of him.

They ate in silence. They did not set a fire, despite the cold.

Thrace seemed unaware of the drop in temperature. She sat still, one hand wrapped round her raised legs, the other plucking now and then at the dried meat in her hand. She looked up at the sky, her eyes wide with expectation as she

206

scanned the darkness overhead.

'What's your wyrme called, Thrace?' said Eli, his brow creased and voice gentle. He was still chewing on the same wad of sechemeat that Micah had seen him put in his mouth five minutes earlier. It was like he'd forgotten how to swallow.

'Aseel,' Thrace replied, and her voice was filled with pride and longing.

'Aseel,' Eli repeated. He shifted the sechemeat from one side of his mouth to the other.

Thrace bit into her lower lip, and Micah saw her eyes moist over. Eli turned towards her.

'Been called?'

Thrace nodded.

'It's hard to resist the call of your own kind. Leastways, that's what Jura always maintained of Asra.' He frowned. 'How long's Aseel been gone?'

'This is the fourth day.'

'And you feel like you have been cleft in twain,' said Eli softly. 'That was how Jura described it when she and Asra got parted.' He shrugged. 'But they found one another again. It's a mighty powerful thing, kinship . . .'

Micah frowned. He was staring down at the ground, tracing circles and crosses with a fingertip.

'You and Aseel been kinned for long?' Eli went on.

Thrace nodded, her lips pressed hard together. The pair of them fell still. Micah raised his head and looked at Thrace.

'How do you get to become kin with a greatwyrme?' he asked, his question breaking into the silence.

He saw Eli and Thrace exchange looks. Thrace's eyebrows flicked up. He'd said something foolish,

207

he knew it, and he swallowed uneasily.

Eli turned to him. 'Kinship's a deep matter,' he told him gravely. 'Not easily spoken of . . .'

He fell still again and stared off to the left, as though he was turning something over in his mind. Then he swallowed the sechemeat and cleared his throat.

'Jura once told me of her kinship with Asra,' he began. 'She spoke of it unbidden by me, but I was honoured by the hearing of it.'

Micah drew his legs up to his chest and rested his chin upon his knees. He glanced at Eli, who was tugging thoughtfully at an earlobe.

'Jura told me she found kinship when she was but a slip of a thing, no more than seven years old . . .'

Micah frowned. Beside him, he heard Thrace's soft intake of breath.

'She was wealdborn, a child of the high country . . . Her mother died at the moment of giving her life, or as soon after as makes little difference. She was raised by a gutsman who may or may not have been her father. Jura had no way of knowing. She was set to work by him as soon as she was able.' He shook his head gravely. 'Like I told you, Micah, the weald's a harsh enough place for those of us that are fully grown and can choose our trail, let alone for the young ones who have no say in the matter.'

He fell still and looked down at the ground. Micah watched him for a moment, then turned to Thrace. Her lips were tight, and she was smoothing a hand slowly across her bandaged shoulder, over and over.

'Way Jura told it to me,' Eli continued, 'the gutsman left her in a craghut and didn't return.

Four days and four nights she waited, through a duststorm in the middle of the dry season, as she remembered it.' He turned to Micah. 'You ain't yet experienced true dry season in the weald, have you, lad?'

Micah shook his head.

'It can be a ferocious time, 'specially when them winds get up. They can drive in duststorms from the east so bad you can't see your hands before your face. Gets into your mouth, your eyes, your nose, and it stings like the forkprod of the devil hisself.' He nodded. 'Jura reckoned it was the worst duststorm she had ever seen. Maintained it went on for the four days and nights, and on into a fifth, though I'll allow it was a long time after the events that she did the maintaining. And she was but a child . . .

'Anyway, she told me how, on that fifth day, she gathered what little courage she possessed and went out into the storm in search of her maybe father. How she searched for him, staggering blindly, her hands grasping at the dark swirl, finding no one; her voice screaming out for him as loud as the choking dust would allow . . .'

He shook his head. When he spoke again, his voice was calmer, more measured. His eyes were wider than Micah had ever seen them.

'Said she lay herself down when she could go no further, and then slept.' He sighed. 'Apparently the duststorm had passed when she awakened.' A smile tugged at one side of his mouth. 'She said the whole world looked like it had been dusted with oatmeal flour.' He frowned. 'She was lying at the top of a white crag, and . . .'

Micah stared at the cragclimber. The fine hairs

209

CARRIONWYRME

at the back of his neck stood on end in the chill wind. He did not raise his collar.

'And?' he breathed.

'And there was a whitewyrme coiled up about her,' Eli said. 'It was protecting her. Keeping her safe and warming her with its embered breath.'

'Asra,' said Micah.

'Asra,' said Eli. '*He* found *her*. For that is the way with kinship. Wyrmes find their kin, and sacrifice everything for the communion they undertake.'

Micah frowned. 'Sacrifice?' he said.

'There ain't no other word to describe it, Micah, for by helping a lost kith child in that way, a great wyrme is tainted, and that taint won't never leave. They're shunned by others of their kind, for ever; excluded from the fellowship of the wyrmeclan that they lived among since their hatching.' He shrugged. 'I'd call that a sacrifice, wouldn't you?'

Micah nodded.

'It was a sacrifice that Asra saw fit to make. And that's how their kinship began. Leastways, that was what Jura told me years later—when I'd gained her trust and friendship,' he added. He glanced across at Thrace. 'But I guess each kin has their own tale to tell.'

Thrace was half turned away and looking back into the distance from where they'd come. Micah followed her gaze.

There was no sign of Aseel, yet the sky was not empty. Far behind them, black specks, like scraps of charred paper, were fluttering down towards the top of a glistening white crag.

Carrionwyrmes, Micah realized. They had found Jura's body.

He turned back to Eli, but the cragclimber's

211

eyes were shut. Something else in the sky caught Micah's attention.

'Eli,' he said.

The cragclimber made no reply.

'Eli,' he said, more urgently.

'I seen 'em, Micah,' Eli told him quietly. 'That's the way kin are honoured up here in the weald . . .'

'No, not Jura,' said Micah softly. 'Look.'

Eli opened his eyes.

Micah was up on his knees, his arm pointing at the trail ahead of them. Thrace was now looking the same way. Slowly, Eli turned, and all three of them stared at the thin twist of grey-yellow smoke that rose up into the sky and flexed in the chilled breeze. Eli's lips curled to reveal the stained teeth behind them.

'Well spotted, Micah, lad.' He looked back at Thrace, his pale eyes ice-hard. 'Seems like we're closer than any of us anticipated.'

THIRTY-EIGHT

'And you're sure he'll hold to his promise?' Bethesda persisted.

Esau rubbed a hand over his cropped hair. 'He'll do right by us, Bethesda,' he said, his deep voice sounding almost plaintive. 'Solomon ain't never let me down.'

Bethesda nodded, but the scepticism remained in her beady eyes. The pain at her hip wasn't helping her temper. She was loath to call it intolerable, because that would have meant admitting defeat. But in truth, that was what it was. Intolerable. She skitched round awkwardly on the rock, trying to ease the searing darts of pain that ran up and down her leg. She grimaced.

Esau grimaced with her. 'If I could take your pain upon myself, you know I surely would, Bethesda.'

She nodded. She knew he would too. 'You can't,' she said bluntly.

She was angry. Angry they'd got left behind, and angrier still that she'd been careless enough to fall victim to that kin creature in the cavern. It was an old one, but stronger than it looked, and as slippery and hard to pin down as all of its kind. And vicious deadly. She hadn't seen the spike of the lance until it was embedded in the top of her leg and being twisted, in that

213

way kin do when they skewer their victims.

Her howls of pain had brought Esau and Jesse skittering over, and they had dealt with the creature. Jesse had taken pains and time over its torment, as was his habit, while Esau had turned away and tried, with caring intent and clumsy fingers, to tend to Bethesda's wound.

It was bad. All kin wounds were bad. Deep-lingering and painful slow to heal. Bethesda had done her best to keep up, but on the third day had been forced to concede defeat. Solomon had gathered them round the fire, and they'd all said their piece. The matter was decided. Leah and Solomon would take care of the wyrmeling deal. Jesse would travel separate, and find the highest bidder for the spoils of the whitewyrme. She and Esau were to go to the winter den, where they would wait for the others to join them.

That was the plan. But her doubts kept on niggling. 'I mean, what's to stop them splitting the riches between the three of them and heading back to the plains without us?'

'Solomon wouldn't do that,' said Esau stubbornly. He crouched down in front of the shivering kith woman and took a hold of her small cold hands. 'He just wouldn't, Bethesda, believe me.' He frowned, and his eyes narrowed from thin slits to two dark lines. 'I ever tell you 'bout the time back in the northern scrim, couple of years gone, when he confronted three gutsmen in my defence? Or how he rescued me from that swallow hole down snake falls? He took me on when I was a greenhorn departer, with no seasons in the high country under my belt, and he taught me everything I know. Trapping, skinning, bartering,

214

scamming. I tell you, Bethesda, we go back some, Solomon and me. I would entrust my life to him.' He squeezed her hands warmly. 'He will see us right.'

Bethesda nodded, the expression on her small face taut and bleak.

Esau smiled. 'You'll see,' he said, reaching up and straightening her hood. 'He'll meet up with us at our winter den, just like he promised.' His smile grew broader. 'Besides, Leah'd have something to say to him if he did not.'

Bethesda nodded again. Her eyes glittered. 'And Jesse?'

Esau shrugged, then turned away. The fire gleamed on his broad sweaty face. He tossed a couple of trimmed sticks from the meagre woodstack into the flames. They hissed and spat, and the fire gave off writhing coils of smoke. It wrapped itself round the deep cooking pot, which was beginning to steam.

'I trust Jesse no further than I can spit,' Bethesda was telling him. 'And that missing eye ain't gonna make his temper no sweeter. You know what he's like.'

'Jesse'll do what he's told,' said Esau grimly. He was crouched down, his hunched back turned to Bethesda. She was right, of course, and his thin lips tensed and all but disappeared as he recalled what Jesse had done to that kin woman in the cavern, and what he'd intended to do to the kingirl on top of the speckled stack. The wind shifted, and he screwed his eyes up as the acrid yellow-grey smoke blew into his face. 'He knows better than to cross Solomon.'

'You could have gone with them, left me

215

behind,' Bethesda muttered, and she saw how Esau's back flinched as though struck.

'That's foolish talk, Beth, and I will not hear it,' he said softly.

Bethesda continued to stare at his back. She liked its reassuring bulk. She liked his broad powerful shoulders, and the thick neck that was wider than his head. She liked the hacked hair that had no vanity in it. He was big and he was dumb, and he would walk barefoot across bladesharp flints for her if she desired it. She knew that. He'd have liked nothing better than to press on, she knew that too, yet he had stayed with her, for he was smitten and thoughtful and loyal—as loyal to her as he maintained Solomon was to himself. And Bethesda hoped he was right on that account.

She watched Esau reach down, remove a pouch from a pocket of his jacket and drop pinches of dried yarrow leaves into the mugs that sat side by side next to the fire, his big broad fingers looking incongruous at such a delicate task. She plucked at the wyrmepelt that he'd laid down for her to sit upon.

He'd chosen their rest-up spot well. Just about as kithwise well as a big dumb lug like Esau could manage, Bethesda thought affectionately.

They were settled in the bowl of a shallow depression in the rock. It offered some shelter from the winter-laced wind, while still affording an unbroken view across the broad expanse of flat rock all around them.

There were three large boulders in a loose cluster on the rim of the dip. Two were tall and leaned together conspiratorially, whispering in the wind. While opposite them, the third was broad and grey and shaped like a wedge.

Esau had placed their rucksacks one on top of the other between the two leaning boulders, to form a windbreak that eased the lighting of the fire he'd set on the flat sandy rock in their lee. A gnarled and stunted tree grew out of a crevice in the lip of the depression. Esau had snapped off its dead branches and broken them up for firewood, and when that had dwindled, he'd taken his black and gold handled skinning knife to the living branches, hacking them off, stripping them of their furled leaves and cutting them to length.

The fire smoked and crackled as Bethesda huddled close to it for warmth. She'd grown cold since they'd stopped marching, and she raised her hands to the shimmering heat. The fire was warm and welcome. She would have liked to turn round and feel the heat on her back, but the pain seemed to have dulled for the moment, and she was in no mind to put an edge back on it. She gripped the thick heavy cape—Esau's cape, that he had wrapped around her shoulders—and gathered it tightly to her chest, but her hip hurt her anyhow.

Esau heard the soft gasp that escaped from her lips, and turned.

'You all right?' he said, and smiled when she nodded bravely back at him. 'Like I keep on saying, Bethesda,' he told her, nodding with furrow-browed sincerity, 'you are gonna be just fine.'

He raised his arm and clapped the flat of his hand to one eye and looked back at her. Bethesda's smile widened into something more genuine, and her two protruding front teeth grazed her lower lip.

'What're you doing now?'

217

Esau twisted his head and looked off into the distance; then up at the sky, the hand still clamped over the eye. Then he turned back to Bethesda.

'Esau!' she laughed.

Esau grinned. 'I was just seeing how Jesse must now be viewing the world.' He pulled his hand away, to reveal his eye beneath all screwed up and the side of his face twisted round and slumped into a disfigured grimace. 'And how the world must be viewing Jesse,' he laughed.

Bethesda's face straightened. 'Jesse got off lightly, by my reckoning,' she snarled, and flinched at the pain that stabbed at her hip. 'What's more, he had precious little sympathy for my hurt. You heard him at that fireside parley, Esau. He could not wait to leave me behind . . .'

Esau reached forward, cupped his hands around hers and squeezed them briefly, then climbed to his feet. He turned and stooped down, grabbed the sides of the pot, using his sleeves to protect his fingertips from the hot metal rim, and tipped water into the cups. He stirred honey into Bethesda's cup, then turned and held it out it to her.

'Drink that,' he told her. 'It'll make you feel better.'

The chattering call of a snatterjab wyrme cut through the hiss of the cold wind. It was answered, moments later, by the warbled cry of its mate.

Esau looked down at Bethesda's hip, and his eyelids flickered tenderly. 'Then I'll see about changing them dressings and . . .'

The sound of footfalls made him glance up. A figure was approaching over the expanse of flat rock in front of them. It was a youth. He was tall and gangly, his face broad and guileless and

218

stained red at the cheeks. His eyes flittered from one to the other of them, and he swallowed, a tentative smile tugging at his mouth.

'G . . . Greetings,' he said.

Esau got to his feet and stood braced, his trunk-like legs apart and powerful arms folded, the black and gold handle of his knife gleaming at his belt. The woman's small eyes glittered with suspicion.

'Where in hell's name did you spring from?' she demanded, rat-like inquisitive with her long front teeth and sharp twitching nose.

'I saw your smoke,' said Micah amiably, nodding to the fire. 'I have a fresh-trapped wyrme here in my pack.' He jerked a thumb back over his shoulder. 'Thought I might share it in return for a place by your fire . . .'

'I know you, don't I?' Esau broke in, his brow like crumpled brown paper.

'The scrimshaw den, Esau,' Micah told him. 'You were with a man called Jesse. And Solomon Tallow . . .'

'That's right,' said Esau, nodding, his clouded face brightening. He unfolded his arms and turned to the woman. 'It's that greenhorn departer who told Solomon about the speckled stack, Bethesda.' He looked back at Micah. 'Matthew, ain't it?'

'Micah,' said Micah.

'Micah,' Esau repeated slowly. 'That sounds about right. Solomon had just saved your skin as I recollect . . .'

'From a trapper,' said Micah, nodding grimly. 'He'd have robbed me and left me for dead if it hadn't been for Solomon Tallow.'

Esau turned and gave Bethesda a knowing look. She ignored it, her black beady eyes glaring at

Micah fiercely.

'Fact is, it was Solomon I was hoping to encounter,' Micah went on lightly. 'He made me an offer that I was too foolish not to accept at the time of his offering. He said I might join you.'

Esau nodded. 'He did,' he said. 'I recall that.' He swung a great arm in an broad arc. 'But as you can see, friend Micah, Solomon Tallow is not here at present.'

Micah winced. 'Well, that vexes me,' he said, 'for I was hoping to take him up on his offer now that I've become more acquainted with the dangers the wyrmeweald holds for a lone traveller . . .'

'I thought you was travelling with some cragclimber,' Bethesda cut in sharply. 'Isn't that what Solomon said, Esau?' Her gaze remained on Micah.

Esau nodded.

'I was,' Micah mumbled, and shrugged. 'We went our separate ways.'

'And so you followed us.' Bethesda's face was cramped up and sour.

'I saw your smoke,' said Micah, 'like I said.'

'Not from seven days off, you didn't,' said Bethesda. She turned to Esau. 'He followed us all the way here.'

'I . . . I guessed where you might be heading,' said Micah, turning from Esau to Bethesda, and back again. His eyes widened, as if seeking confirmation. 'For that speckled stack I told Solomon Tallow about, and that he took such an interest in. I was hoping I might meet up with you, all of you . . .'

'I don't trust him,' Bethesda hissed. 'What you really after, boy?'

'After?' said Micah. 'Like . . . like I said, I should like to take Solomon up on his kind offer.' He hesitated. 'Did he and the others go on ahead?'

Bethesda snorted. She pushed a strand of stringy hair inside the hood. 'I don't like the idea of being tracked.'

'No more do I, Bethesda,' said Esau grimly. 'Even if he is just a greenhorn departer.'

'Reckon Solomon would slit his throat for such an impertinence.'

Esau smiled, and Micah glimpsed the spittle on his tarnished teeth. The kith reached for his knife.

'I think I might spare him that inconvenience, Bethesda,' he said, and nodded towards the backpack at Micah's shoulders. 'And relieve him of that burdensome load . . .'

'Drop the knife!'

Bethesda swivelled round. Esau turned his head. A rangy cragclimber was standing at the top of the depression behind them. The crossbow gripped in his hands was aimed at the centre of Esau's chest. At the same moment, from the opposite side of the rock depression, a wyrmekin girl stepped from behind the second slanting boulder; in her hands, a walking staff whittled to sharp points at both ends.

Micah watched Thrace as she moved slowly, sinuously round the rim of the depression, her head held high, her dark eyes on the wyrmekith woman and her corn-silver hair swept back behind her ears. He saw how the flameflicker touched her, making her soulskin shine, and her eyes blaze.

'I don't aim to tell you twice,' Eli said softly, walking slowly forward.

Esau stared back into the hard emotionless face of the cragclimber, with his skin like tanned hide and pale-blue eyes unblinking. His gaze flicked to the crossbow, and the cragclimber's steady finger held lightly to the trigger. It was a recurve bow. Powerful. The tips of the crossed-D curved towards him, designed to crank up the draw-weight of the string to maximum. It was old, not much used by the look of it; no scratches, no stains, but no less deadly for that.

Micah saw a flash of metal as the knife dropped to the ground. It landed with a soft clatter.

'Pick it up, Micah,' said Eli.

He stooped down. He snatched it from the rock. It was bigger and heavier than it had appeared in Esau's hand. He looked up to see Bethesda staring at the wyrmekin before her. There was a sneer on her lips, even as she eyed the makeshift lance gripped in her hands.

'Filthy kin,' she growled, her voice low and beady eyes harsh with hatred. She sneered. 'Jesse should have finished you off at the stack.'

Thrace stared back down at her, and Micah saw not a trace of emotion in her face. Then one eyebrow slowly arched, and the point of the lance jumped as her grip tightened and her arms flexed.

Eli jerked his crossbow at Esau. 'Where's Solomon Tallow?' he said. 'And the other two?'

Bethesda answered for him. 'We don't know where they are. Stinking kinlover,' she added, her lip curling.

Eli nodded slowly. 'Well, that is a surely a shame and a great disappointment,' he drawled. 'For you see, I have business to conclude with Solomon Tallow.' He frowned. 'But if he is not to be found, you two will have to answer for his misdeeds.'

Esau blinked, then turned to Bethesda. She

spoke, her gaze fixed on Thrace. 'It's Solomon or us?' she said.

Eli's mouth twisted into a smile, though his eyes did not move. 'That's about the long and short of it.'

'I swear,' Bethesda hissed, her two buck teeth grazing her lower lip, 'I ain't gonna get stuck by no kin creature a second time . . .'

Bethesda's hand darted inside the folds of her cape, withdrew a spitbolt and took aim. She squeezed the trigger. Thrace flexed her left leg and lurched to the right, twisting her body round as the tip of the bolt struck her glistening soulskin-clad body and glanced harmlessly off.

With a low hiss, Thrace threw herself at Bethesda, coming down heavily on her chest. The kith's head slammed back against the rock.

'Beth!' Esau bellowed, lunging towards the two of them—only for Eli to step forward and fire his crossbow.

The bolt buried itself in Esau's leg. With a howl of rage, the wyrmekith lashed out at the cragclimber, his massive fist connecting with Eli's chest. Eli flew back and landed heavily on the rock. The crossbow went skittering off across the rocks.

Esau dropped down on top of him, his knees forcing the air from his lungs, and he punched him hard in the face, once, twice, and a third time, the blows landing on his jaw, his nose. Then he gripped the dazed cragclimber by the neck with both massive hands and began to squeeze.

Esau's jacket was stretched taut across his broad shoulders, which heaved with exertion. His knuckles were white. Beneath them, Eli's face was blotchy and purple and his pale eyes stared back at

223

him, bulging and bloodshot. Micah sprang forward, Esau's skinning knife in his hand. Eli's throat looked so vulnerable in Esau's strangling grip and Micah knew that, with one jerk, the kith could snap it like a hickory twig.

'L . . . let him go,' he shouted.

Esau glanced up, a scornful twist to his top lip. 'You don't have the guts, boy.'

The colour drained from Micah's lips and his muscles seemed charged with something hot and strong. He gritted his teeth as he half turned away, then drew back his foot and kicked Esau in the jaw with all the power that he could muster. There was a splintered crack, and Esau's head shot backwards, his hands torn away from Eli's neck as his body arched back. At the same moment, Micah lunged forward, and thrust the knife hard upwards into the kithman's exposed chest.

Esau's expression flinched with surprise. He grasped towards Micah but, white-faced with shock, Micah stepped back. Esau looked down and pressed a hand gently to the black and gold haft of the knife that stuck out from his chest. Blood was welling up around it. He looked back at Micah's horrified face, his eyes growing wider and wider till the narrow slits were large and round, and Micah saw with a sudden terrible pang of pity and remorse that they were a dusty shade of green, like moss.

Esau's mouth opened to speak, but he could not. A soft rasping breath clicked in his throat, and his body slumped sideways, twisting round on itself as Eli scrambled free, and landed heavily, front down, on the ground.

Micah staggered backwards, staring at the body

224

of the man. The dead man. The man he had killed.

He swallowed and looked at Eli, his eyes pleading. Eli held his gaze as he pulled himself up onto his elbows. One hand rubbed at his chafe-red neck.

'It was him or me,' he said simply.

Micah looked back down at the body that lay there on the ground like a fourth boulder. He saw the patch of blood grow larger at the centre of Esau's back. It spread across the rough leather, thick and red, like sunrise spilling across the sky.

Behind him, he heard words cut through the cold sniffling wind.

'Tell me where, and the pain will stop.'

Thrace. It was Thrace . . .

Micah spun round to see the kin hunkered down over Bethesda, her legs crooked, her back bowed and one hand resting against the rock. Her head was lowered, and she was whispering into the kith's ear.

Blood was trickling down the wedge-shaped rock from the wound at the kithwoman's hip. More blood spilled down from her neck, and Micah flinched as he saw the red tip of the makeshift lance protruding from the skin, just below her ear.

The whispering continued, and was followed by an anguished scream as Thrace twisted the lance in the wound. She cocked her head, and pushed her ear closer to the kithwoman's mouth . . .

Then the kith juddered and slumped, her mouth dropped open and her beady eyes stared ahead of her, as blind and lifeless as a doll's glass gaze. Thrace sat back. She pulled the lance out of the woman's neck and wiped it on the cloak. Some of the blood smeared her fingers.

225

She turned to the others, as if as an afterthought. Her eyes were rapacious and smoulderdark.

'She would not say where the two kith have taken the wyrmeling,' she said. The impassive mask of her face betrayed nothing. 'But the third of them, Jesse, has gone to the gutting tarn, by clear lake.'

THIRTY-NINE

'Micah?'

'Yes?'

'Are you all right?'

'I . . . I don't know . . .'

'You never killed before?'

'No, Thrace, I have not.'

'Aseel and I have killed.'

'I know it.'

'We have killed wyrmekith, though only when we had to . . .'

'Had to?'

'When they came hunting. When they threatened us and our kind.'

'. . . And you took no joy in it?'

'What do you mean?'

'I'd better tend to that fire. Eli will have need of it when he wakes. I'll rouse him at sun-up I reckon.'

'Micah, what do you mean?'

'I saw you, Thrace. I saw you kill that wyrmekith back there. I saw the look in your eyes. You relished the killing . . .'

'I had good reason.'

'What did those wyrmekith do to you at the speckled stack?'

*   *   *

'Micah?'

'Yes?'

'Why do you watch me? You think I

227

haven't noticed, but I have. In the craghut, on the trail, by the campfire . . . Now, in the middle of the night. You watch me. Your eyes never leave my face . . . Why do you watch me?'

'You interest me.'

'Because I kill and relish the killing?'

'No . . . not just because of that.'

'Then why?'

'There was a girl . . . Back on the plains. Her name was Seraphita . . . She was rich and I was poor . . .'

'What has that got to do with me?'

'I came to the wyrmeweald to make my fortune so I could return to her . . .'

'And yet you watch *me*.'

'I can't help it . . .'

*   *   *

'Thrace?'

'Yes?'

'When you fell from the stack . . . You were gagged. You had cloth stuffed into your mouth. I removed it . . .'

'I didn't fall. I jumped.'

'What *did* happen?'

'The wyrmekith they called Jesse. He had a knife. A sharp knife—soulskin sharp. You saw what they did to Jura, well, Jesse was going to do the same to me . . . So I jumped.'

'And Eli and I found you.'

'Yes, you found me.'

228

FORTY

Eli hunkered down next to the fire, poking at the glowing embers with a green stick and sending sparks soaring up to the arched roof of the cave, where they clung to the rock, glowing like red stars for a moment, before flickering and dying. He held a spoon, its bowl thick with pale clag.

'Either of you two care for any more?'

Micah stared down at his bowl. It was still half full, and he shook his head. The rootmash held no appeal, despite the saltmeat that flavoured it.

'Don't seem to have much of an appetite,' Eli observed. He turned to Thrace, who was crouched by the cave entrance, staring out. 'Either of you.'

She didn't turn at the sound of his voice, and Eli saw that the bowl that he had set beside her was untouched. He climbed to his feet and kicked sand and dust over the shimmering orange-blue embers, taking care not to allow his boots to smoulder. He clapped his hands together.

'Reckon we should be moving on out,' he said.

Micah and Thrace looked up at him, and it was clear to them both that this was not the first time he'd made the suggestion, though it was the first time either of them had heard it. Micah

229

climbed to his feet. Thrace pulled herself up onto her knees, flicked her hair behind her ears and handed her bowl to Micah.

Eli sluiced out the cooking pot and tipped the dregs away. He wiped it clean with a soft rag, which he dropped onto the remains of the fire, where it flared for a moment, turned black as it curled, and collapsed into ash.

Micah cleaned his own bowl, and Thrace's, and stowed them both away in his backpack, which bulged taut with the gleaned possessions of the two dead kith—saltmeat, drying-cloths, bone-spikes and crampwedges; a coiled length of gutrope; a heavy knife with a serrated blade and a black and gold haft . . .

He heaved the pack onto his back, and felt the tremor of the slim spitbolt strapped to its side. Small knots of muscle flexed in his jaw and his face grew hot, and he glanced round at Thrace, to find that the kingirl was staring at him intently—though her gaze slid away as their eyes met.

She picked up the long black lance that had been strapped to Esau's backpack and gripped it fiercely. It was her kinlance; the lance she'd left behind at the top of the speckled stack when she'd jumped, and that Esau had kept as a trophy. At the sight of it in Thrace's hands, Micah's shoulder gave a small but uncomfortable twinge.

With the fire out, the cave was soon chilled. Micah could see his breath, and when he inhaled his eyes watered with the sharp coldness of the air. There was a smell to it too that he couldn't identify. Like ink. Or potato peelings . . .

'This cave's afforded us good shelter,' said Eli. His mouth turned down and his bruised neck creased into thin ridges as he inspected and adjusted one of the chest buckles of his rucksack. 'I shall endeavour to remember it for future use.'

He went out through the cave entrance with Thrace by his side, and Micah followed. As he stepped outside, Micah's boot-heel skidded, and his eyes were filled with dazzling brightness. It was snow. That was what he'd been able to smell, the cold harsh earthy tang of snow that had fallen through the night while they had been sheltering in the cave. It wasn't thick, just a light dusting, yet it had transformed the landscape, draining it of colour and softening its sharp edges. It clung to the windward sides of boulders, crags and rockscree, leaving them white and sparkling in the low pale sun, while the leeward sides were bare and dark, and stood out in stark relief.

'First snow of halfwinter. And mighty early by my reckoning,' Eli commented as he examined the mistspun sun and the length of the shadows it was casting. He looked at Micah, who was raising his collar and pulling his cuffs down over his clenched hands. 'You watch your step, boy,' he said. 'Frailcover such as this can be irksome.'

Micah nodded back at him, then saw how the cragclimber's gaze strayed to Thrace. She had her back to them and was standing rigid still, her head raised as she surveyed the pale sky ahead. Eli raised an arm and scratched gingerly at the side of his neck.

'Happen I owe you thanks, Thrace,' he said slowly. 'If you hadn't forced the woman to speak . . . Back there. Well . . .' He breathed in noisily and exhaled through his nostrils, the two plumes of breath white and fragile. 'With this unseasonable

231

snowfall we would have surely lost track of Solomon and the other kith.' He jerked his chin far ahead. 'Their traces are concealed and will be washed away utterly when the snow melts. Had it not been for her information we might never . . .'

Thrace turned. 'I don't know this . . . this gutting tarn she spoke of. This clear lake . . .'

'I do,' Eli told her. 'Clear lake is just that, diamond-clear and bottomless deep. It nestles far yonder, at the western end of a winding range of mountains that are striped orange and ochre brown. Like a manderwyrme,' he added, and flapped a hand at the horizon. 'The gutting tarn is close by it. Gutsmen gather there—have done for as long as I can remember—and the water has been tainted by their visceral trade . . .'

'Ah.' Thrace nodded gravely. 'Redwater. This I know.'

She returned her attention to the landscape before her, then raised her lance and aimed it towards the point on the horizon that Eli had indicated, before swinging it further south. She jabbed at the air. Eli frowned.

'That's some distance out of our way, Thrace,' he observed.

'But the pass is lower,' she countered. 'Easier. And on the far side, the rockface is stepped and quick to climb, and leads down to a gulch that will take us most of the way there . . .'

'Now that the floodwaters have gone,' Eli said, nodding. He rubbed his stubbled chin. 'How long do you reckon it'd take us?'

'To redwater?' She paused and squinted into the distance. 'Two days by my trail. Three or more by yours.'

232

Eli nodded. 'Happen you're right,' he said, and added with a tight smile, 'I shall defer to your superior knowledge. We'll follow your trail.'

They set off, the low sun to one side and their elongated shadows gliding along over the uneven surface to the other. Despite his talk of following, Eli walked alongside Thrace, with Micah walking behind.

He observed the laboured rolling gait of the rugged cragclimber, and the spring in the wyrmekin's step. She seemed to want to pull ahead, which caused Eli to lengthen his stride, and Micah watched his exhaled breath flap at the sides of his head like fine white hair. Then Micah skidded, jarring his knee, and felt foolish under Eli's knowing backward glance. He continued more cautiously, placing his boots flat on the ground with each step, rather than heel to toe, just as the cragclimber was doing.

He listened to the soft crunch of their footsteps, and noted the light impressions left in the snow where the kith and kin, walking side by side, had passed. The ridges on the soles of Eli's boots shifted the snow, exposing bare rock, whereas Thrace's step left the covering unbroken, and her slough boots were so fine that the arch of the foot they encased could be seen with every step. Micah glanced back the way they'd come and saw how similar his own footprints were to Eli's.

He turned back and looked at Thrace. This wyrmekin, she was strange and savage and wild, but so beautiful that Micah struggled to take his eyes off her. She was deadly too. But last night, in the glow of the firelight, Micah felt they'd made a connection. The unpredictable cruel girl had understood his shock and pain at taking Esau's life, and had shown him pity. And he had shown her that he wasn't like the kith she hated.

He'd wanted to reach out and touch that extraordinary soulskin of hers, seemingly so soft and pliable, yet strong enough to deflect a crossbow bolt. He'd wanted to run his fingers through her pale hair and breathe in its smoky musk. Most of all, he'd wanted to feel the fierce crush of her beautiful disdainful lips against his, to hold this delicate dangerous girl close to him in that cold dark cave and feel their heat mingle . . .

But his courage had failed him, and now, as he tramped along behind her, all he could feel was a heavy ache of longing in his chest, as burdensome as the guilt he carried in his laden backpack.

The sun rose, and the breath that billowed from their mouths grew wispy, then disappeared completely. Beneath their feet, their footprints became wet. The sheet of snow thinned to finest lace, then gossamer filaments, like a covering of spiderweb, before melting to nothing, leaving the ground softer than it had been, and glistening. The wind bit though, and far ahead, beyond the pale blue above their heads, the sky was yellow-grey and threatening, and seemed laden with heavier falls of snow to come.

It was midday when Micah noticed the speck in the sky, far to the east, like a smut of soot on a freshly laundered shirt. Thrace and Eli tramped on ahead, both lost in thoughts of their own, but it wouldn't be long before they also noticed the speck in the sky.

Micah looked back at the ground, then up at the mountain range that towered ahead. The morning's climb had brought them to its splayed and jagged foothills, and Micah's gaze rested on the narrow pass high above. He raised a hand and tugged at the brim of his hat. He clenched his jaw. Bit of luck, and they should get over it before the sun set. But as he let his hand drop back to his side, he couldn't resist stealing a sideways glance, hoping that the speck in the sky might have gone, and his mouth twitched with disappointment when it had not.

It had become larger, and Micah told himself that it was probably just a carrionwyrme scanning the weald for something to scavenge. Or a screechwyrme. Or one of them snatterjabs whose warbled call Eli had taught him to imitate. But then Thrace spotted it and let out a cry of unbridled joy—and Micah knew his worst fear had been realized.

The whitewyrme approached, his long neck arched and gleaming between two powerfully beating scalloped wings. Aseel in flight was a magnificent sight, his great silver-white body gleaming bright against the darkening clouds as he circled overhead and came in to land.

Micah turned to Thrace. She was standing stockstill, her head raised and hair hanging loose over her shoulders, which were braced and slightly hunched. The soulskin that clung to her lithe body glowed in the eerie yellow-grey light. Her face had never looked more beautiful. The full lips were parted, the dark eyes were wide and filled with such joyful anticipation that Micah felt himself shrink inside.

He wanted to say something to her. That he was glad for her. That he too was pleased to see Aseel

235

alive and well. That he hoped nothing would change . . .

But the words wouldn't settle, and those that did struck him as silly or insincere, and when he had finally decided what he would say, it was too late. Unable to wait a moment longer, Thrace had bounded forward across the rocky slope. Micah took a step after her, uncertain, and was relieved when Eli's heavy hand stayed him.

'Leave them, Micah,' he said gently.

Micah nodded and watched helpless as Thrace leaped gracefully up over the rocks, towards the head of the narrow pass, away from him. He watched the rhythmic judder of the black lance gripped in a single hand, and her long hair that fluttered behind her like a farewell. And his stomach cramped. And his mouth felt dry. And when he swallowed, the ache in his chest grew all the more intense.

The whitewyrme landed on a narrow spur that overhung the pass, his outstretched legs steadying him as his claws grasped the rock. He flapped his mighty wings till he was balanced, then folded them upon his broad sleek back. His tail was raised, the arrowhead tip flicking from side to side. White smoke snorted from his nostrils, and as the girl ran towards him, he lowered his neck and breathed harder, and the pair of them abruptly disappeared inside swirling white clouds.

'She will leave us,' Eli observed, and sucked in air through his teeth. 'Now her wyrme has returned.' He nodded, as if to himself, but then glanced at Micah. 'Wyrmekin are different, lad. They are as wild and untameable as the wyrmes they ride.' His blue eyes scrutinized Micah's face, and Micah felt himself reddening. 'Believe me when I tell you,' the cragclimber said, 'however much you wish it, you can never expect them to return your feelings, or be bound by them.'

Micah nodded. 'You heard us talking last night?'

'I did,' Eli admitted, 'and it brought back powerful memories . . .'

The clouds of smoke had cleared, and at the head of the pass Thrace and Aseel were moving with strange languid gestures of hand and claw, of tilted heads and sweeping limbs, and Micah saw that their bodies were the exact same shade of silver-grey, so that when Thrace was before him, her body seemed to melt into his.

'She's telling him of all that has befallen her,' said Eli. 'And he is doing the same. Kinship has no need of words.'

The whitewyrme showed evidence of recent injuries. The tips of his wings were scorched and tattered in places and there were scratches along his flanks. But Thrace ignored these. Instead, Micah watched as she reached up and traced the jagged black scar of an old wound that ran down its sinuous white neck. He saw her eyes close, her body judder . . .

He turned away. His mouth tasted stale. It was an intrusion, and Thrace deserved better from him.

When he looked back, moments later, the whitewyrme had taken to the air once more. His wings were open and full and beating hard, with no hint of any weakness that might have been caused by the tattered edges Micah had glimpsed. He soared up into the sky, and for a moment Micah dared to believe Thrace might have stayed behind, to continue with them on their journey . . .

But the spur was deserted.

It was a foolish thought, Micah chided himself, fumbling in the folds of his jacket for his spyglass and holding it up to his eye. When he focused on the whitewyrme, his gaze fell at once upon Thrace's slender figure, which was braced against the creature's clavicle and vertebral spur, her thighs gripping tight and the long black lance held at her side. She had raised her hood over her head, concealing her face, and apart from the lance, she and Aseel seemed to be one and the same. Neither of them looked back.

Micah felt a hand pat him on the back, then rest upon his shoulder and squeeze lightly, and he turned to see Eli looking at him. 'Let her go,' he said.

Micah raised his spyglass once again. Aseel and Thrace were flying over the pass, a single dark shape against the yellow-grey sky beyond, which, even now, was blurring with falling flakes of snow. Then they were gone.

Micah sighed, and turned to Eli. 'What now?' he said.

'We go on to the gutting tarn,' Eli said simply, 'for that is where Thrace is surely headed—and where I shall settle my own score with those kith.'

As they started on the long climb through the pass, Micah followed Eli in silence, the cragclimber's words repeating themselves over and over in his head. *Let her go. Let her go.* Micah picked his way arduously over the screestrewn trail, the heavy backpack pressing down on his shoulders, anchoring him to the earth. He pushed back his hat and looked up into the empty grey sky.

'I can't let you go,' he whispered.

FORTY-ONE

Where had Solomon got to? What could be taking him so long?

Leah climbed slowly to her feet. The cumbersome sidewinder, chipped and scratched from heavy use, was clutched in both hands, and she silently cursed the fact that she had not cranked and loaded it herself.

But that was Solomon's job—and Solomon was nowhere to be seen.

The stranger was standing on a low screemound. He was stick-thin and had a shock of hair that looked like teased sisal. At his scrawny neck were several strings of tiny wyrmeteeth, and the tattered shirt and raggedy breeks he wore were covered with scrawled signs and symbols.

'You stop right there,' Leah called.

The man didn't appear to be carrying a weapon, leastways, none she could see. Yet there might well be a small knife or a spike of some sort concealed in his flapping rags.

'Greetings,' he called out, his voice, hoarse and rasping. 'Ichabod's the name. Ichabod, the truth-seeker. Stone prophet and visionary.' He grinned. 'I declare you're the first living thing I've clapped eyes upon that ain't scaled and winged since I came to these hills.'

He made to step off the screemound, one bony hand outstretched, but Leah

240

stopped him by raising the sidewinder to her shoulder.

'That's far enough, preacherman,' she warned. 'I ain't fixing to make a new acquaintance.'

The man's eyes had strayed, and he was looking right past her at the camp, where their equipment was spread out on the wyrmeskin for all to see, along with the backpacks, cooking pot and water gourds.

And the sack.

It was tethered to a heavy boulder close by the blackened remains of the fire, and as Leah glanced round, it moved, angular shapes writhing beneath the rough material. She turned back to face the stone prophet, whose eyes had narrowed.

'What's that you got in the sack?' he asked, jumping off the screemound and taking a step towards her.

'What's that to do with you?'

'Thought I saw it moving, is all.' He paused. 'Wouldn't be trading in live goods, would you?'

He took another step towards her, his eyes glistening.

'That's no concern of yours.'

'So you wouldn't mind if I took a look then?'

'You take one step and I'll shoot you down like the no-good suntouched heaven-pedlar that you are . . .'

The man raised his hands. 'Surely it ain't worth threatening old Ichabod over?' His eyes bored into Leah's. ' 'Specially with a crossbow that ain't cranked nor loaded . . .'

Ichabod's hand slipped into the folds of his tattered shirt and Leah flinched and backed away, still clutching the all but useless sidewinder. When

241

he withdrew it, she saw that he was holding a small liquor flask.

'Care for a swig while we talk the matter over?' Ichabod said, smiling gap-toothed as he approached her. Leah could smell the sour odour of his unwashed skin and the rank grease of his hair. 'Finest green spirit in all the wyrmeweald,' he told her, grinning lopsidedly. 'Smooth as soulskin . . .'

There was a sudden humming sound, followed by a tinny clank, and the flask exploded in the scarecrow's hand. Leah spun round and flung herself down onto the wyrmeskin behind her, scattering the carefully laid out equipment in all directions. She turned back, green eyes hard, a wyrmebarb grasped in one hand and a serrated harpoon in the other—only to find that the stone prophet had fled.

'Did I get him?' said Solomon, approaching the camp moments later, grinning, his strong even teeth white against the blue-black stubble of his jaw. In one hand he held a slim spitbolt; in the other, a brace of plump manderwyrmes, their striped bodies limp and wings dangling.

'No,' said Leah darkly. She laid the weapons aside and climbed to her feet. 'But you did his liquor flask a mortal injury.' She kicked the remnants of the tin bottle at her feet.

'Who was he?'

'Just some crazy preacherman out scavenging, I reckon.' Her eyes narrowed as she pushed back her hair from her face. 'What took you so long?'

Solomon shrugged and held up the manderwyrmes. 'Had to do some hard climbing to snag these, Leah. Climbed nigh on halfway up those bluffs before I could get me a clear shot . . .'

The vermilion cliffs were home to manderwyrme, spike back and blue wing colonies, that nested in a squawking, flapping, flame-spitting cacophony in the shallow caves and ledges of its upper reaches. It was a good place to camp, though that was not why they were there.

Solomon searched the jumble of equipment scattered across the rock until he found a gutting knife, and then set about skinning and filleting the manderwyrmes. Leah went across and untied the sack, carefully opening it and tethering the whitewyrme by the neck when its head appeared.

It had grown, she noted, its yellow eyes already darting and alert with an intelligence that made her uneasy. Soon it would be too big for the sack, and too strong for the tether, and what was more, this whitewyrme would know it.

Solomon tossed over chunks of the freshly butchered manderwyrme meat and Leah fed them to the whitewyrme, taking care not to let the creature's snapping needle fangs nip her fingertips. It ate voraciously, pausing now and again to scrutinize her with a yellow eye.

'We can't wait any longer, Sol,' she said when the wyrme had eaten its fill and she had forced it back into the sack with tugs on the choke-chain and encouraging prods from a rock-spike.

Solomon was crouched over the fire, gently coaxing a flame with the last of their fuel. The clouds had thickened, and a bitter halfwinter wind was now cutting across the plateau.

'I surely know it,' he conceded, dropping meat into the cooking pot and beginning the makings of a stew. 'It's just like Jesse to get distracted by some

243

fool side-business over there at the tarn, when right here is the source of our returner's wealth. But you know Jesse, Leah. Never would listen to reason.'

Solomon peered over at the sack, which no longer writhed with agitation, but now rose and fell gently.

'It's bad enough we've lost Esau's muscle to the nursing of Beth's injury,' said Leah, and shook her head ruefully. She was packing up their rucksacks before the yellow-grey skies fulfilled their promise of snow. 'She'll die of it for sure, for it takes kin to heal kin wounds. We're only gonna meet up with the one of them at our winter den. You and I both know it.'

Solomon nodded, and stirred the pot.

'But now Jesse ain't showed up, and I'm fearing it'll just be the two of us on this here venture. And that scares me, Sol.' Her nose crinkled. 'Specially when I think of where we have to go,' she added.

'I surely know it,' Solomon repeated, rubbing a hand over his stubbled jaw.

He pulled at the cord round his neck and took a small leather pouch from under his tunic and loosed the tie. Tipping out its contents into a cupped palm, he raised it for Leah's inspection.

'Three opals, one sapphire and a half-cut blackstone,' he said, as Leah looked down at the small dull stones in his hand. 'That's it. That's all we've got to show for our long years of toil and tribulation up here in the high country, the five of us—and we must be 'bout the hardest flint-heart kith around, by my reckoning.'

He turned the gemstones over in his hand, then slipped them back into the pouch, which he concealed beneath his coat. He looked up, and the flames gleamed on his shaved head.

'But now we have the means to turn that whitewyrme into a fistful of wealth we can scarcely imagine.' He raised his hand and clenched it. 'Think of it, Leah, wealth that'll buy us a fine estate back on the plains, just like we always dreamed of, and a farm apiece for Esau and Jesse into the bargain—and all of it will fit into this fist of mine. Returner's wealth. And if we have to go into the caverns of the keld to get it, just the two of us, then I say it's a risk worth taking.'

Solomon's eyes sparkled, and Leah smiled as she leaned forward towards him. She placed her hand on his.

'Returner's wealth,' she said, and kissed him.

FORTY-TWO

Thrace braced herself, her eyes narrowed against the blizzard of small hard snowflakes that flew at her as Aseel soared across the sky. They pattered against her soulskin; they stung her face, her hands, her eyes.

The whitewyrme's powerful wings beat up and down, his shoulder muscles rippling rhythmically beneath her with every movement. The long arch of his neck stretched out before her, while behind, she could feel the constant sweep of his tail as Aseel adjusted to the evershift of the icy wind.

Gripping hold of his jutting shoulder ridge with numb fingers, she leaned across and stared down into the streak and smear of the landscape below. It was bleak here, treeless and scrubfree, with steep cliff-faces and jagged stacks, and boulderfields with deep perilous crevices crouched between the jumble of huge irregular slabs. It was a harsh trail to cross on foot, but up here on Aseel's back, it raced past with every wingbeat, like a fast-flowing river.

She sat up straight and tasted the flakes that clung to her lips with her tongue. They were cold and pure, and tasted of the sky.

Thrace leaned forward, wrapped her

246

arms around the whitewyrme's neck, her fingertips seeking out the jagged scar, her cheek pressed against his smooth glassy scales. She felt the warmth of his body on her cold skin. She breathed in his rich musky scent and felt a tiny, yet unmistakeable, shudder pass beneath her touch.

She raised an arm tentatively, pressed her nose against the palm of her hand and breathed in long and deep. It was still there, faint but detectable, the taint of kithodour.

Aseel had noticed it the moment she'd run up to him back at the high pass. He'd recoiled with a judder and bared his fangs, and she had stepped willingly into the billowing clouds of wyrmesmoke that poured from his mouth, bathing her, cleansing her, scouring her body of the fetid odour.

Yet she could still smell it on her hand.

The smell of kith; the smell of death—and they were one and the same. Dead wyrmes. Their rank odour had been everywhere. In the oil kith burned, the boots and clothes they wore, the skins they lay down and slept upon at night. The stench, rank and distasteful, was in their pores, their hair, upon their breath . . .

Her eyes darkened and her pulse quickened.

'It *will* leave me, Aseel,' she whispered, 'this smell of death.'

The whitewyrme tensed beneath her, and Thrace flinched at the sound of the ugly guttural words that had come too easily to her lips. She tensed, and then sat back, arching her back and tilting this way and that as she attuned her movements once more to the sway of the neck and the sweep of the tail.

Aseel understood, and he stretched his wings

247

wide and glided on the rushing currents of the wind. He had accepted her back, and she was one with him.

Thrace's gaze softened. The boy, Micah, was new to the weald and had yet to acquire the kith odour. The scent of his skin had been warm and sweet, she remembered, like aromatic leafcrush or fresh-trodden moss. He was not like the others. Not yet. She recalled his awkward looks and gestures that said so much more to her than his stilted faltering words.

'You interest me . . .'

But it was not just curiosity she'd detected in those wide eyes, but something deeper and more intense. Something that had made her burn inside.

Beneath her, Aseel shifted, but Thrace was too lost in thought to notice. Now, the icy wind dragged at her suddenly tense and stooped body, and Aseel became aware of a burden upon his back, heavy and snagging, and he flexed his shoulders and beat his powerful wings in vexation.

Yes, he'd been reunited with Thrace, but she seemed different—and both of them knew it.

In apology, Thrace relaxed her muscles and balanced herself once more, and the rhythm returned to Aseel's wingbeats. She would not allow this kith boy into her thoughts, she told herself—would not allow him to destroy this feeling of exhilaration.

For that was what kith did. Every last one. They sullied and desecrated. They spoiled everything they touched. They stole wyrmelings that had taken long decades to hatch; they slaughtered whitewyrmes and murdered their kin. They ran their foul hands over helpless bodies, groping,

248

probing. She could still taste the rancid rag that had been stuffed inside her mouth . . .

She gripped the lance tightly, her body flexed and her face a grim mask. Beneath her, Aseel thrust his neck forward, opened his jaws, and a great yellow and white plume of flame roared before them, turning the driving snow to wisps of steam.

The landscape sped past below them in smudged streaks of muted colour. Stained browns and smeared ochres. And far in the distance, like a droplet of blood on pure white skin, was redwater. Though as they approached, Thrace realized—with a jolt that she hoped Aseel would not notice, but knew he would—that it was the kithname for the place, uttered by the kithwoman, that had lodged inside her head.

The gutting tarn.

FORTY-THREE

'Never thought I'd say this,' said Eli, turning to Micah, 'but I'm surely beginning to miss that talkative tongue of yours.'

Micah shrugged and stared disconsolately into the distance. Eli turned back and resumed his steady tramp up the screeslip of the mountainside towards the high pass.

'It's that kin girl, ain't it, lad?' he said a while later. 'Kin's ways are different from ours, Micah. Like I told you before, they're wild, untameable. We can't tread the same trail as them, no matter how much we wish we could.'

Behind him, Eli heard a muffled grunt, followed by a long sigh. A while after that, closer to the top and with the snow already falling, Eli spoke again.

'You let me know when you want to rest up, son. We've got two days ahead of us. More, if this weather sets in.'

And this time Micah didn't manage a single sound, and Eli swung round with half a mind to chide him for his lack of response, only to see that the boy had heard, and was nodding, and he recognized the look of keen bleak despair in his eyes.

'The gutting tarn, the place where we're headed,' Eli began, as he fell into step with the silent boy, 'it's quite a sight to behold.'

Micah nodded.

250

He'd felt disinclined to talk ever since Thrace and Aseel had left them the day before, yet the cragclimber's voice had kept breaking into his thoughts, and though he knew Eli was endeavouring to buoy up his spirits, he was in no mood to listen. He'd fallen back a ways, to dissuade him from such endeavours, but Eli himself had slowed his pace and now was walking beside him—and despite himself, Micah found he was beginning to listen to the cragclimber's low rumble of a voice.

'But it's the *smell* of the tarn,' Eli was saying, and his face screwed up. 'That's what'll hit you first. Gutsmen use the tarn because its sides are steep and ridged—well-suited for leaving the organs they gut to drain, while the texture of the rock itself is just right for fleshing and scripping down carcasses. But such work comes at a cost.' He glanced round at Micah. 'The lake's dead,' he told him, his grip tightening on the handle of his walking staff. 'When the wind's in the right direction, it gives off a putrid stench that can be smelled from miles off.'

Micah pulled his tattered cape tighter around him, listening intently.

'Them gutsmen are a rough lot, even for kith,' Eli went on. 'They live in fortified rock barrows close by the tarn, despite its foul odour, and their only interest is the distillation of flameoil, wyrmemusk, gall-tincture and the like from the organs they harvest. And they are wasteful in their greed for these things. They think nothing of slaughtering a wyrme for a single gland or growth that they deem valuable, and simply abandoning the rest. For the only thing these tarn gutsmen are

251

interested in is accruing returner's wealth, so that they might leave the high country and return to the plains . . .'

Eli hesitated, reached up and gripped the brim of his hat, pulling it down against the snow, which had started to fall. He tugged at an earlobe.

'Returner's wealth,' said Micah. 'That's what I came to the weald for . . . Though I had but the haziest notion of how to come by it.'

'Anything of high value that is small enough to be carried back to the low plains counts as returner's wealth,' Eli told him. 'Powerful elixirs, some might choose; rarest wyrme ivory for others, or best of all, precious gemstones—though acquiring them means descending into those dark dangerous places beneath the mountains . . .'

'And why are they best?' asked Micah, fascinated.

'Because,' said Eli, 'they are the easiest to transport on the perilous, oft-times fatal, journey back from the wyrmeweald. Kith have had to learn that the hard way. Returner's wealth is no use if it's too heavy or bulky to be carried safely back, and few kith are up to more than a couple of journeys.' He smiled wryly. 'The wyrmeweald would be full to bursting if people from the plains could come and go with ease, but as it is, few survive the journey up here, and fewer still survive the return. They're not like kin . . .'

He hesitated, aggrieved by his mention of kin that would bring Micah right back to the very thoughts he'd been endeavouring to distract him from. But the boy didn't seem to have noticed.

'Where's *your* returner's wealth?' he asked.

'I don't have none,' said Eli evenly. 'I don't need

252

it,' he added, 'for I don't aim to return, Micah. Not ever. The wyrmeweald is my home.'

*　　　*　　　*

They rested up in a damp hollow shortly after crossing the crest of the pass, when the snow became too thick for them to continue with confidence. Eli used some of his precious flameoil to tease a fire from sodden firewood. Micah sat before the hissing blaze, legs outstretched and the bottoms of his breeches steaming. Carefully, he eased off his finely tooled boots and examined his tired and aching feet. The nails were unfamiliar grey and the skin was white, and when he inspected the soles, he saw the telltale signs of creeping skinpeel.

He fumbled in his backpack and found the small pot of salve that Jura the wyrmekin had given them. It seemed an age since Micah had lain in the cavern behind the waterfall and listened to her whispered conversation with Eli. Opening the pot, he methodically rubbed the aromatic whiterot salve into his feet, one after the other. The cragclimber had cared deeply for the wyrmekin, and she for him. Perhaps that was what had kept him in the wyrmeweald all these years. Thrace's face came into Micah's mind, and an ache tightened his chest.

He arose early the following morning, hardbitten with raw cold, and he stamped his feet and hugged his arms to his body until the sluggish blood in his veins started to flow. He'd have liked to warm himself by a fire, but Eli seemed anxious to move on, and he had to content himself with blowing warm air onto his fingers as they started down the rockside.

The previous day's snowfall was wet and soft beneath their feet, and dripped from jutting rocks. They headed down over the stepped rock almost as quickly as Thrace had suggested, and entered the broad gulch as the pale-grey sun was halfway up in the sky. The snow here was melting in earnest, and Micah's boots broke through its slushed surface and onto bare wet rock beneath. But then later, the sky brightened and the wind chilled. Underfoot, the snowmelt froze and crusted over once more and the dripping fell silent as icicles began to form at the tips of the jutting rocks.

'Seems like the weather can't quite make up its mind,' Micah observed.

'It's a fickle season, halfwinter,' Eli nodded. 'Folks can be deceived, and many have perished, believing winter to be finished before it has even begun. But it's on its way, fullwinter, Micah, and that's a fact, and when it does strike, we'd best be in the winter den, not on the trail, or we shall not survive.'

He raised a shielding hand and surveyed the trail ahead. When he looked back at Micah, his pale-blue eyes looked concerned.

'Halfwinter's the time for taking stock and preparing for the harshness to come, not undertaking a journey such as ours.' He shrugged. 'But it seems it cannot be helped, if them that's wronged us are to be held to account.'

The cragclimber hesitated and stared into the distance, and Micah knew that he was thinking of Jura, and the hideous carnage in the cavern behind the waterfall. Now, it seemed, it was Micah's turn to distract his companion.

He scanned the bleak landscape and frowned. 'It's mighty quiet,' he ventured. 'I ain't seen a single wyrme, Eli, not for a day or more—'

'That's because you don't know where to look, greenhorn,' the cragclimber broke in with a smile.

A hundred yards or so further on, Eli paused and poked his walking staff towards a disturbance in the snow.

'Squabwyrme's been here,' he mentioned casually.

There were shallow impressions that, now he looked more closely, Micah could see might well be tracks. They were splayed and set increasingly far apart, and adjacent to them were sweeping semi-circular marks, first on one side, then the other.

'Dumpy little critters at the best of times,' Eli was saying, 'but with winter approaching, they get so fatted up they can scarce raise theirselves airborne. They take a run up, wings outstretched and flapping, rolling from side to side, before . . . There. They finally take to the air.'

Micah saw the crumpled white ridge Eli's staff was pointing at. Beyond it the surface of the snow was untouched.

'Flying back to *their* winter dens in the weald caverns. Wyrmes know this halfwinter won't last long. You'll learn a lot about surviving just by observing their ways,' Eli told him.

Micah nodded, then realigned the heavy backpack on his shoulders and stamped his cold feet.

'Have you got your spyglass to hand?' Eli asked a little while later as the gulch levelled out onto a tree-scratched plain. Micah tugged it from the inside of his shirt. 'Train it yonder,' Eli told him, pointing far to his right.

Micah did so, and his gaze focused on a cluster of low pines, their dark needles shot with the blush of red berries.

'See them?'

Micah frowned. Then he did see them; a dozen or more tiny tatterwyrmes, each no bigger than his hand, their ribboned wings flapping as they hopped from branch to branch, plucking at the berries and stuffing them into their snubsnout mouths. Eli had his own spyglass raised.

'Probably their last good feed before fullwinter hits,' he was saying. 'They bury themselves beneath the tree roots and wait it out for the thaw, trusting to their body fat to see them through.'

They tramped on over crunching snow, with Micah growing hot as he struggled to keep up with the cragclimber's urgent stride. With this talk of winter and all, Eli seemed eager to get to where they were going in short measure. The sun had reached its high point in the sky—which wasn't that high at all—and was already sinking back down. Their shadows lengthened. The air grew colder still.

Micah scanned the far horizon. Thrace had told them the gulch would take them most of the way there—to redwater, as she had called it—but the end of the broadcut ravine had come and gone, and the land had opened up, yet Micah could see no sign of the tarn. At last, as the evening chill froze the snow solid and darkness closed in, Eli announced that they should rest up for the night.

They slept in the open beneath a moonless sky.

The stars sparkled bright, as if freshly burnished, and Micah awoke twice thinking dawn must have arrived, and rolled over chilled and disappointed when he found it had not. The third time he woke it was because Eli was shaking him.

'Micah,' he was whispering, his voice taut with urgency. 'Micah, get up.'

Micah's eyes snapped open and he sprang to his feet, too fast, and his head spun. 'What? What?'

'Over there,' said Eli, his voice hushed.

He was half-stooped, one arm around the boy's shoulders and the other pointing off across the cracked plateau some hundred yards off. Micah squinted and wiped the sleep from his eyes, and saw that the blur of angular boulders he'd seen were moving. Eli straightened up.

'Greywyrmes,' he whispered. 'A whole herd.'

Micah put the spyglass to his eye. He focused in, and the magnified circle abruptly filled with life.

There were two dozen of the creatures, or thereabouts, huge and lumbering, their grey bodies edged with black shadow in the dawn light. They looked to be grazing, scratching at the cushions of snow, then dipping their necks gracefully and nibbling at whatever they found beneath. They were slow-moving and calm, yet vigilant, with at least two of their number surveying the surrounding landscape at all times, necks erect and heads turning, while the others fed.

Micah recognized these wyrmes, he realized, for he had seen one of their kind before. It was back on the plains, the woeful creature sick and dying as it was goaded through the town square on that fateful night. How extraordinary and strange that sickly greywyrme had seemed to Micah back then.

257

It had probably been carried back as a wyrmeling, the returner's wealth of some desperate kith, and destined for a short life and slow death—a curiosity to be prodded and poked at.

As the herd ambled slowly across the plateau, Micah brought the spyglass round, and his gaze fell upon a gawky wyrmeling that was trailing some way behind the rest. It was thin and jittery, with raised wings and a head that looked too heavy for its scrawny neck, and when it noticed the others had moved on, it skittered to catch up on spindle legs. The greywyrme he had seen had probably started out just as young and free as this. It ran to a tall female, and the pair of them nuzzled together.

Suddenly there was a high-pitched screech, and the whole herd raised their heads as one. The next moment, they were stampeding. Some were running, attempting to fly, their legs a blur and wings flapping; some managed to take to the air, and skimmed low over the pink-tinged rock.

Micah pulled the spyglass from his eye. He saw the cause of the panic at once, a large sleek wyrme with green scales and deep crimson wings that were broad and scalloped and folded back as it dived down out of the sky at the scattering herd.

The wyrmeling was running as fast as it could, hopping and leaping as it went, struggling in vain to give lift to its infant wings. The female hung back from the rest of the herd, booming encouragement, then snapping and snarling at the predator overhead, causing it to pull out of the dive and soar up into the sky.

But then it was back, its limbs braced, yellow flame roaring from its parted jaws and its tail back behind it as rigid as a pikestaff. It knocked the female aside, sending her sprawling, and sunk its curved claws into the wyrmeling's back. It lurched, then righted itself, and with powerful beats of its wings, soared skywards. Dangling beneath it, the small creature struggled for a moment, then fell limp.

'Micah, quick!' Eli was shouting, and he grabbed his arm, and Micah turned to see the herd was heading straight for them, their wings flapping and their great grey bodies grazing the ground as they churned up snow and shale with their powerful legs. 'Here. Jump down . . .'

'My backpack . . .'

'Leave it!'

Eli dropped down into a narrow crack between two slabs of rock, and Micah joined him, ducking down just as the first of the greywyrmes thundered overhead. He skitched round, craned his neck, and looked up to see the terrified creatures skimming over the gap above him, one after the other, their cries sharp and keening and their terror pungent sour.

The pair of them emerged when the last one had passed, and Micah watched them hurtle away in a spray of frozen snow. The predator wyrme, along with the hapless wyrmeling, had gone. Micah went to check his backpack, which had been kicked and trampled across the rock. His gourd was punctured, but the pack itself had stood up well.

'Fearsome predators, redwings,' Eli commented.

Micah nodded as he hefted the backpack onto his shoulders. 'Better a life short and free,' he said, thinking of the greywyrme in the town square, 'than a longer one of pain and suffering.'

Eli looked at the boy and nodded thoughtfully.

REDWING WYRME

'Like I said, Micah, lad, you can learn a lot by observing wyrmes.'

*   *   *

It was late in the afternoon, the sun hidden behind slatecolour clouds, when they topped the second ridge of low hills. The land dropped sharply on the far side, then rose again in a slope of undulating terraces. Wind blew in their faces and Micah grimaced as the rank choking odour of blood and offal filled his nostrils.

He glanced at Eli, but the cragclimber seemed oblivious to the stench. He was staring into the distance, where black shapes circled slowly in the icy upcurrents of the halfwinter sky, hundreds of them.

'Something's wrong, lad,' he said, rubbing his jaw as he surveyed the carrionwyrmes. 'Sorely wrong.'

FORTY-FOUR

The gutting tarn lay still and eerie quiet. High above, the squalling shrieks of the circling carrionwyrmes were lost on the snow-flecked wind, the sulphurous wyrmebreath that hung heavy over the sheltering bowl of the tarn keeping them temporarily at bay. The heavy slabs of rock that blocked the entrances to the fortified rock barrows at the water's edge stood ajar, the dark interiors of the low stone buildings flame-blasted and soot-blackened.

The body of a man, gaunt and grey-grizzled, lay a little way off, a gutting knife in one hand and a half-sliced wyrme gizzard in the other. Death had caught him by surprise, the expression on his upturned face a strange mixture of fear and something approaching disappointment. His thick leather coat was stained with his own blood—at the chest and at the shoulder—where the kinlance had run him through.

Beside him, his companion, his head slumped forward into a crudely carved bowl of gleaming kidneys, was wearing a thick apron patterned with plashed blood. The angle of the neat black wound through his throat suggested that the kinlance had skewered both gutsmen in a single thrust.

Outside the rock barrows lay four more

gutsmen, each turned to silhouettes of cinder as they fled towards the safety of the low stone buildings. They lay awkwardly in death, their bodies bent into unnatural angles.

At the entrance to the first barrow, the body of a tall man with a tangle of red hair was sprawled halfway across the scorched threshold, a charred crossbow in his hands, the bolt cranked and ready to fly. At his side, a woman with thick grey plaits, wearing a stiff gutter's skirt and heavy boots, was draped over the slab of rock she'd been attempting to pull across the doorway when sharp talons had ripped her midriff apart.

On the slate roof of the neighbouring barrow lay the smashed body of a hefty-looking gutsman, seized by the same talons and then dropped from a great height.

Outside the scorched stone buildings, a pile of wyrmeskins had been turned to a pyre and reduced to a mound of ash; splintered crates of offal smouldered, giving off twists of oily smoke. Tools and nets and gutting paraphernalia had been smashed, shattered and burned.

Along a ways, on the other side of the blood-red lake, and reflected in its stagnant waters, was a tall gutting rack. Jesse was spreadeagled across the rack, his hands and feet nailed to the diagonal crossbeams of blood- seasoned pine by rock-spikes.

He was leaning forward, as though in the act of diving, his downturned face reflected back at him in the tarn's red waters. They mirrored the dried blood at the lips and chin, and the mouth, from which the tongue had been torn away at the roots, the way kith cut out the tongues of kin who will not speak, and a filthy rag had been balled and thrust into the bloody hole, a corner protruding from between rotten teeth.

Skewered to the front of Jesse's chest, with his own knife, was the large heart of a great whitewyrme.

The waters of the lake rippled as a sudden snow flurry penetrated the dip of the bowl, and the smoke thinned to reveal the figures of a cragclimber and a boy standing on the lip of the tarn. Overhead, the cries of the circling carrionwyrmes grew more insistent.

'Thrace,' Micah said numbly, and lowered his spyglass. 'Thrace did this.'

FORTY-FIVE

The wind rose and the air cleared, and the
carrionwyrmes spiralled down out of the
sky to gorge noisily upon the dead. The
two kith walked side by side, their heads
lowered, and this time neither of them
objected to the other's silence.

Despite the brightness of the sky, the air
was harsh with the cut of winterchill. Their
shadows were long and gangling. They
crested the jagged ridge to the west of the
tarn, and made their way down the long
shallow slope toward the vast lake in the
distance. As they came closer, Micah saw
that the surface of the lake was covered in
a latticework of pale-grey crackle-ice, all
apart from the far side, where wisps of
mist rose from a bubbling pool that looked
deep and was fringed by grey rocky
outcrops. He caught the whiff of sulphur.

'It's a hot spring,' Eli told him, and a
scowl spread across his leathery features.
'The gutsmen from the tarn bathe there . . .'

Micah nodded. He felt grimy and
footsore, and the idea of soaking in the hot
spring was certainly inviting, despite the
eerie miasma of steam that hung over it.

Eli seemed to have read his thoughts,
for he shrugged. 'You go ahead if you have
a notion to, boy,' he told him. 'I'm gonna
get a fire started before the light fails.
Catch us some fish.' He turned his head

265

along the shore and thrust his jaw forward. 'There's a favourable place in the lee of those rocks up yonder.'

'You don't mind . . . ?' Micah began.

'Why should I mind?' said Eli. 'Just don't ask me to join you.'

He had already started striding purposefully down the pitted slope towards his chosen camping place, his staff clacking at his side. Micah watched him for a moment, then turned and made his way round the frozen lake to the far side, where the pool bubbled and steamed.

He approached cautiously. The wind had dropped, the clouds had closed in and the hot spring was engulfed in shadow. He reached the water's edge, fine sandy gravel and broken shells crunching beneath his boots, and stepped up onto one of the grey outcrops of rock that jutted over the steaming water. A backdrop of dark craggy cliffs rose in a curving wall around the pool, with the moss and fern that clung to the cracks and crevices dripping sonorously into the water below. He walked to the end of the outcrop, and was enveloped by clammy warmth. He looked down.

Filaments of green weed fuzzed the steep sides of the pool. Down at the bottom of the clear water, he saw bubbles rising from the depths and shimmering up to the surface in shoals, before turning to belching twists of mist, white against the dark rock, like the wraiths of dead gutsmen.

Despite the warmth, Micah shivered. He took a deep breath and tore his gaze away from the writhing mist, then crouched down and dangled a hand loosely in the water. It was hotter than he'd imagined and silken soft. He sat back on the rock

266

and tugged off his boots. He pulled off his jacket, his shirt, his breeches and underclothes, and set them aside, then climbed back to his feet.

His skin smarted in the air that was, by turns, moistwarm and bladesharp cold. He splashed down from the rock onto the sloping sandy bed, and the hot water gripped his toes and ankles and rose up his legs to his waist as he took another step.

He squatted slowly down, and sighed deep with contentment as the hot sulphur-laced water hugged his chest and encircled his neck. It felt pure, cleansing, and he was about to dip his head beneath the bubbling surface when he saw the girl.

She was hunched by the water's edge, knees raised and clasped by her slender yet muscular arms. A hood hung down over her lowered head. There was blood on her interlocking fingers; there was blood on the pale wyrmeskin that clad her slim body.

Abruptly she looked up, and Micah saw that her face was streaked in blood also. It was smeared across her forehead, daubed down both cheeks and smudged thick around her mouth. She stared at him dully from beneath her hood, and Micah was unsure whether she recognized him or not. He opened his mouth to speak, but when he did so, the old familiar ache in his chest rose to his throat and turned his voice to a strangulated whisper.

'Thrace?'

*   *   *

Aseel wheeled round high above the clear lake and came in to land. Thrace was rigid and heavy as

267

stone. She clung to his neck, stiff and unyielding. And she remained stiff and unyielding as Aseel shrugged her from his back.

He stooped down and nuzzled the motionless body of his kin gently, but she did not respond. Something was wrong. Something was very wrong.

At the tarn, they'd been as one, effortlessly graceful and finely attuned to every deadly movement as they had killed the gutsmen. Then they had caught the kith with the straggly hair and the one eye; the one with the wyrmeheart in his pack. She had paid special attention to that one, while he had set about cleansing those stinking barrows with bursts of fire. When he'd returned and she'd climbed onto his back, everything had changed.

She was still and silent, and he could not rouse her. He'd thought the clear lake spring might help, but it had not.

As the yellow milky moon rose, the whitewyrme coiled his long sinuous body protectively around the hunched kin. He purred softly deep down inside his throat, and tendrils of warm wyrmebreath rose from his nostrils. But she seemed unaware that he was there.

Finally, when the dawn flushed the low sky with muted pinks and yellows, he gently uncoiled himself and climbed to his feet. He looked down at her, his yellow eyes unblinking.

She should eat. Perhaps that was what she needed. Damsel flies, fresh-caught and fire-scorched. They would be difficult to discover in the midst of halfwinter, larval and wingless and buried deep in the scree, but he would search until he found some.

He raised his head and flexed the muscles at his shoulders, stretching his wings and launching himself up into the dawn sky. He circled once, twice, above her, hoping against hope that the sight of him on the wing without her might rouse her yet, but it did not. He arched his neck and flicked his tail and, with powerful beats of his broad wings, soared off towards the distant range of suntipped mountains, barebacked, empty and alone.

*   *   *

For two days and nights, they'd watched and waited, she and Aseel, before they had launched their attack on the gutting tarn. It had been worth it.

At first, those blood-smeared kith had been cautious, emerging from their barrows in ones and twos like nervous skitterwyrmes, to carry out their rancid stench-filled work. But on the third day, *he* had arrived, and they'd come out to greet him and his stolen treasure, all of them excited and greedy for a glimpse of the heart of a great whitewyrme that he carried in his pack.

And at the sight of him, bile rose in her throat and the blood roared in her ears, and they had attacked.

Aseel had swooped, her lance had danced; talons slashed, flame spewed, and there was blood. Kith blood. And she had rejoiced in it.

Then they had cornered him, the one the kith called Jesse. Aseel brought him down with a blow from his tail and sent him sprawling into the gutting rack, insensible. Then she had done the rest.

269

A fevered rage gripped her as she took her vengeance. The kith, Jesse, would pay for what he and his companions had done; he would pay with his suffering and his blood. She would make sure of that.

But as she had gone about her task, the release she sought, the savage satisfaction at his terror, would not come. His pain did not ease her own, it only drove it deeper, like a shard of ice piercing her heart and spreading through her veins. Her fury grew cold and merciless in its disappointment. And when, finally, she drove the knife into the kith's chest, pinning the wyrmeheart to it, the full horror gripped her.

She stared at the corpse she had slaughtered, not a lancelength away, but so close that his blood now covered her, and no longer just saw the kith called Jesse. He was leaning forward, his face in shadow, and his long hair matted and tangled, obscuring his features. He was thin and gangly, awkward and vulnerable-looking in death.

He could be any kith hanging there. He could be Micah.

Thrace froze.

'Thrace?'

She could hear him now, inside her head, his soft voice earnest and concerned.

'Thrace?'

*   *   *

Micah stared at the bloodstreaked girl. Aseel was nowhere to be seen.

Thrace's eyes flickered, though whether with recognition, Micah was not sure. Her dark eyes

270

betrayed no emotion.

He stood up. The warm water trickled from his shoulders and arms and his skin steamed. He waded forward and stepped out of the pool. His teeth grazed his lower lip as he crouched down beside her.

He could smell the rank odour of death upon her. Splashed innards. Singed hair, scorched bone. The tang of the blood that covered her body, some of it brown and crusted; some smeared and red and still wet.

He cupped a hand below one elbow and placed an arm around her shoulders for support. She did not help him as he eased her gently to her feet, but neither did she resist. And when Micah took a step towards the hot spring, then another, she went with him.

Bathed in shadow, Thrace's eyes looked like two black stones. Her skin was pallid and her mouth twitched, but she remained silent.

As their feet stepped into the hot water, Micah paused. Thrace paused with him. He raised a tentative hand and pulled the bloodsplattered hood from her head, and her hair fell loose, and there was more blood, staining the ash-gold tresses red and matting them in clumps. At the sight of her, Micah felt an overwhelming wave of pity and tenderness engulf him, and he knew he had to wash this blood away, to cleanse this strange savage girl and rouse her from her frightening trance.

His hand was shaking, but she did not seem to notice as she allowed herself to be led deeper into the steaming green pool. The hot water rose slowly to their knees, then the sandy bed of the pool

271

beneath their feet shelved sharply, and they plunged in up to their shoulders.

Micah stood before her. He cupped water with his hands and let it trickle down over her face. With his fingertips, he gently wiped the blood from her cheeks and chin, and from the shell-like curl of her ears. The blood on her soulskin was dissolving and her whole body seemed wreathed in a cloud of red. Her dark eyes stared into his as he eased the bloodied wyrmeslough from her shoulders, from her arms, and peeled it down her body.

He cradled her in his arms and bent her backwards until her head touched the water. Her hair fanned out and Micah ran his splayed fingers through the thick hair and gently washed away the blood.

When he leaned back and helped her regain her footing, the last trace of blood was gone, and she seemed to see him for the first time. She stared at the scar on his chest, her dark eyes hardening, and her body tensed.

It was a kinwound, made by a kinlance. And kinhealed.

He flinched. He wanted to tell her that she had wounded him at the speckled stack, but that he didn't blame her—and that she mustn't blame herself. Or him. He wasn't a wyve collector; he'd been in the wrong place at the wrong time was all . . .

Before he could say a word, she reached slowly forward and touched two fingertips to the shiny nub of skin. Then she looked up into his eyes, her gaze penetrating and impenetrable.

'I did this?' she said.

Micah nodded solemnly. Thrace's nostrils

272

flared, and she breathed in, long and deep, her eyes still locked onto his.

Slowly, tentatively, Micah drew her closer to him, till their naked bodies met. Thrace tipped her head up; Micah lowered his. And their taut muscles relaxed in each other's hold as their mouths pressed together and their lips parted and their tongues touched.

FORTY-SIX

'I don't like it, Sol,' Leah was saying. 'I mean, the dark places beneath the mountains . . . There's good reason kith don't venture there.'

'We're going to be just fine,' Solomon reassured her. 'Trust me, Leah. I know the way. We'll be in and out of there in no time at all, and with more wealth than we know what to do with.'

Leah stared down at the sack. She kicked it.

'Don't you go scorching that leather none,' she warned. 'I won't tell you again, wyrme.'

The wyrmeling flinched, but did not make a sound. Its ridged head and wing-knuckles pressed out at sharp angles from inside the cramped sack, exposed and vulnerable.

'Hey, there,' Solomon protested gently. 'That's no way to treat our precious merchandise.'

'I hate it,' said Leah bitterly through clenched teeth. She kicked out again. 'I hate it. Hate it. Hate it. I wish we'd never found the damn thing . . .' She was shaking her head from side to side. 'That goddamn firebreath—and those eyes, Sol, staring right into me. I swear it's almost like it knows what I'm thinking. And I don't like it. It creeps me out, Sol . . .'

274

'You just keep your mind on the heap of riches it's gonna make us,' Solomon said, and he wrapped his heavy arms around Leah's body and drew her close. 'Returner's wealth, Leah,' he said, his head lowered and breath warm against her neck. 'That's why we've got to go where we're going. It's the only way, trust me in this.'

Leah nodded, and Solomon smiled and squeezed a little tighter. He looked into her eyes. Snow had started falling, fine and granular. It dusted their shoulders, their heads, their backpacks.

'Are we resolved in this matter, Leah?'

She nodded again.

'Come on, then,' said Solomon, easing himself away from her clutching grasp. 'Let's go down there.' He glanced up ruefully at the sky, where the clouds were curdled and dark and so low it looked like he could reach up and scratch them. Ice-chip snowflakes dropped into his eyes, which he wiped away as water. He lit the pitchdip torch. 'Leastways we'll be out of this weather.'

He reached out. Leah took his hand and they entered the tunnel together.

She glanced round at him. Despite the gloom, she saw that his eyes were wide and that there was a tautness to his jaw and lips. She didn't recognize the expression, for she had never seen it before, not on Solomon's face. And then she did.

It was fear.

'Happen we should remove our packs while we still can, 'fore we end up getting wedged tighter than a cork-stop in a liquor bottle,' he said. 'We can pick them up on our return.'

He kneeled down, shucked the rucksack from

his shoulders and propped it against the tunnel wall. Leah handed him hers, which he placed beside it. She felt lighter without the burdensome load, almost like she was about to fly, yet she also felt vulnerable without the reassuring weight upon her shoulders.

'What about this?' she said, holding out her spitbolt.

Solomon turned and observed the slender crossbow for a moment, his dark eyes narrowed, before taking hold of it. He gave Leah the flickering torch, pulled his own crossbow from his back and compared the two, eyeing their length and breadth, his gaze flicking from one to the other, then weighing the two of them on broad outstretched palms, the muscles in his neck and arms flexing as he did so.

'It's powerful and deadly compared to the spitbolt,' he said, raising the sidewinder higher, 'but it sure as hell is cumbersome. Then again, keld don't take kindly to kith bearing arms. I'm minded to leave both of them behind,' he said tersely, as if talking to himself.

Leah watched as he stowed the crossbows next to the rucksacks.

'Though it sorely grieves me to do so,' he muttered. '' Specially if it turns into a fight . . .'

'A fight, Sol?' Leah asked quietly, and was shocked by her voice, which was high-pitched and tremulous, like the voice of a frightened little girl. 'Are you anticipating a fight . . . ?'

She wanted him to reassure her. She wanted his deep voice to brush aside her fears, to tell her that there was nothing to fret about. But he did not.

'If the worst comes to the worst, I've got my

gutting knife,' Solomon said.

He picked up the sack with the wyrmeling, turned away and continued down the narrow tunnel. Gripping the torch, Leah followed as close behind as she could without tripping on Solomon's heels.

The tunnel widened out, and Solomon slowed to allow Leah to catch up alongside. He swapped the sack from one hand to the other and wrapped a heavy arm around her shoulders. He peered round at her and flashed an easy confident smile.

She smiled back, but as they continued walking, the cold and damp of the tunnel seemed to worm its way inside her, making her bones ache and her senses spark. There was an odour of decay in the air and, to her ears, the howlings of the wind were like the moans of undead things. Solomon's arm felt as burdensome as the rucksack she had left behind.

They kept on along the tunnel until it became too narrow to walk side by side. Solomon gave the sack to her, took the torch and led the way. Leah realized she was beginning to pant, plumes of her own breath billowing in the icy air as their pace increased. The smell of fear mingled with the odour of death, and it was her own. Inside the sack, the wyrmeling scratched and squirmed, and she chided it to be still.

They entered the narrowest tunnel yet. It got narrower still, then started to climb steeply. Leah's boots slipped on the loose stones beneath her feet, and she had to steady herself with one hand pressed against the wall, recoiling at its slimy texture.

All at once, the tunnel opened up, and Leah

277

stumbled after Solomon into a vast limestone cavern. Far above her head in the rocky folds of the vaulted roof, faint strands of light cast the cavern in skeins of green-black shadow.

'We're here,' Solomon said.

FORTY-SEVEN

Ichabod the stone prophet emerged from his hiding place.

He'd watched the two wyrmekith disappear inside the mountain. The yellow flame of the torch had flickered on the sides of rock for a moment, and then was gone.

His lop-sided gaze remained on the shadowed entrance as he jigged agitatedly from foot to foot in an agony of indecision.

Finally he turned away.

And then he was running. Running like he'd never run before. Madcap. Helter-skelter. Hurtling over boulders, slipping and sliding on scree, shatterrock, his tattered clothes snagging on thornbushes and spiky scrub. Falling to his knees, picking himself up, and running on and on, over rockmounds, through dry ravines and scrambling across bluffs and dry gulches. Running, running. Losing himself in the rhythm of his pounding legs and thumping heart. Losing all sense of time, of distance. Running. Running, running until he could run no more . . .

Eventually he collapsed, coughing and wheezing and fighting for breath.

At last, he seemed to gather his wits. Sitting up, he reached inside his jacket and pulled out a small leather pouch.

His fingers were shaking as he opened it

and tipped the contents out into the palm of his hand. Eight wooden marbles rolled into it, one of them larger than the others. Ichabod picked it up with forefinger and thumb. It was sweatdark and smoothed by hours of play, and the letter H had been carved neatly into the wood on one side.

He set it down upon the ground, and sorting through the others, selected a second marble, which he lay beside it. Then a third. And a fourth . . . Until all of them had been used up. His cracked lips tightened as he stared at the name he'd created.

HEPZIBAR.

He sat back on his haunches for a moment, then began rocking slowly backwards and forwards, tears streaming down his face.

'Heppy,' he moaned. He was weak-willed. He was cowardly. 'Heppy. Heppy . . .'

He wiped a sleeve across his wet face, then gathered the wooden marbles together with a single sweep of his hand. He slipped them back into the pouch, which he hung from his neck and tucked down inside his ragged shirt. Then he raised his head and looked around.

He was at the top of a tall ridged pinnacle. Down to his left was the rocky shoreline of a lake that was crystal clear and glazed with thin ice— apart from one corner, which was fed by a hot spring, its surface stippled by coiling twists of steam.

He would go down to the lake, he decided. He would soak his aching feet awhile in its warm waters.

The stone prophet climbed to his feet and began to walk down to the clear lake.

FORTY-EIGHT

Aseel spotted the bare screeslope from high up in the sky, the hot vents that pockmarked its surface wreathing the rocks in smoke and preventing the snow from settling. He swooped down and landed, and used his tail to sweep the rocky debris aside, then scrabbled urgently in the loose stones beneath. The damsel fly larvae he uncovered were purple and wriggling, and there were far more of them than he had need of.

He skewered them on his foreclaws, two or three to each one, till the talons were laden with succulent morsels. He cradled them to his chest, flexed his shoulder muscles and took to the air with swift powerful wingbeats.

The snow thinned as he soared over a crest of jagged peaks, and far in the distance, the fetid red gutting tarn came into view, with the clear lake just beyond, its waters like a huge turquoise gemstone set in the pure white of the snow.

It was only three days since he had returned to his kin from the mating. Flushspent and wounded, he had flown to the speckled stack to find her gone, and had set off at once in search of her. He had tracked her trailscent, and encountered only death. Death at the cavern behind the waterfall, death in the

281

camp on the high plateau, and when he had found her at last at the mountain pass, she was walking with kith, and their deathstench was heavy upon her.

There was something else that was different about her—but their reunion was so joyful that Aseel had put that from his mind. But he could ignore it no longer. Not after the gutting tarn.

She had willed it, that bloody vengeance on the kith. He had felt her passionate hatred, and accepted it. With their constant predations and wanton exploitation of the weald, the massacre was something the kith had brought upon themselves. He hadn't relished killing so many, but if it stemmed the advance of the two-hides, then such bloodshed was worth it, wasn't it? That was what kinship meant. Wyrme and kin fighting as one, more powerful together than alone—yet Thrace's lust for blood had surprised even him.

Afterwards, Aseel had thought, they would go to their winter refuge, their kinship as strong as ever. But something had changed in her; something deep and hidden from Aseel's unblinking yellow eyes...

He folded his wings back and swooped down lower in the sky, eyes fixed on the clear lake ahead. She was where he'd left her, on the sandy shoreside of the bubbling hot spring. She lay on her side, curled up in the warm mist, a blanket draped over her.

She was not alone.

A second figure lay behind her, his body folded into hers and head nestling in the curve of her neck. It was a kith, the boy Aseel had found her travelling with when he'd returned from his

282

mating. They were naked beneath the blanket, and heavy with kithscent. The boy's clothes lay in a disordered bundle by the side of the pool, while her soulskin lay beside them, carefully spread out on a flat grey rock. It had been cleansed of the gore from the gutting tarn, and the skin was now as white and glistening as the day Aseel had shed it from his own body.

The whitewyrme landed on the outcrop and stood, neck arching and wings outstretched, over the two sleepers. They didn't stir as he stared at them.

Had she also been called? he wondered, as he looked down at the girl. Had she been drawn to the boy the way he had been drawn to his wyrmemate? Had she endured the same ecstatic embrace, strange and powerful and savage . . .

Standing there by the hot spring, Aseel finally understood.

Yes, she had been called, and there had been nothing she could have done to prevent it. Aseel knew that now, yet still he shuddered with loss and sorrow and a sense of betrayal. He raised his forelimbs, the talons spread wide, as if about to strike . . .

Then, quietly, delicately, he removed the plump damsel fly larvae from his claw tips and laid them on the grey rock beside the soulskin.

Aseel turned away. Flexing his wings, he took to the air and flapped silently away, leaving the boy and girl locked together in their strange unknowable embrace.

FORTY-NINE

'Buyers or sellers?'

The words, soft and sibilant, filled the dark chamber. Leah looked at Solomon, who turned slowly round, his boots grinding on the gravelstrewn rock.

'Buyers or sellers?'

The voice was wheedling and insistent, and the acoustics of the cavern made it impossible to tell where it was coming from. Leah saw Solomon's hand grip the haft of his knife. If only they hadn't left the spitbolt and the sidewinder at the cavern entrance.

'We have something to sell,' Solomon said, his own voice echoing round the vaulted cavern.

'What have you got?'

The voice seemed to be behind them now.

Leah reached out and felt for Solomon's hand and seized it, and was comforted by its rough yet warm grip.

'Show me what you're selling,' the voice hissed greedily.

Solomon hefted the sack from his shoulder and raised it. 'This,' he said.

Leah tightened her grip on Solomon's hand.

'It's live goods,' Solomon said.

'You're after returner's wealth?' came the voice, querulous and mistrustful, now

284

from somewhere above.

'Word has it, you pay well for live goods, Redmyrtle,' said Solomon.

He let go of Leah's hand, and swung the sack down to the ground.

'Show me,' Redmyrtle whispered close by his ear.

Solomon flinched.

'And drop the knife.'

It clattered to the ground.

Out of the shadows came a pale milk-eyed wyrme, scabrous and stunted, scuttling on outsized rapier-like talons. It seized the knife, then hissed as a thin golden chain yanked it back into the blackness.

'Sh . . . show her, Leah.' Solomon sounded unnerved.

Leah crouched down and plucked at the knot.

'Need some help?' came a whisper.

Leah quivered with revulsion as a hand reached out from the darkness and touched her own. It was dry and gnarled and covered with a mess of blurred black tattoos, and it rested there for too long.

Pulling away, Leah opened the sack and the wyrmeling's head sprang up, blinking into the gloom. Beyond the pale shaft of light in which they stood, there was a stifled intake of breath.

'A beauty, ain't it?' said Solomon.

'*He*,' Redmyrtle corrected him, her voice now echoing from the blackness at the back of the chamber.

'It's a whitewyrme, as I'm sure you know,' Solomon said, turning his head as he tried to follow the direction of the voice. 'But if you're not interested,' he said, 'happen we can reach a bargain with someone else.'

'Not so much hasty,' the voice rasped, suddenly up close again. 'What do you want for him?'

'Make me an offer,' Solomon said.

For a moment there was silence.

'Hold out your hand.'

Solomon obeyed, thrusting an open palm into the shadows.

'Take.'

Solomon pulled his hand back. It contained a dozen or so small, pale-brown stones.

'Pretty,' he said, 'but I'm going to need more than a handful of honeygems for my trouble.'

Redmyrtle hissed. The tattooed hand reappeared and filled Solomon's palm with a spread of larger gems.

'That's more like it,' Solomon said. 'And such fine colours. White and purple,' he said, picking through them with his finger. 'Blue. Green . . .' He looked up, his dark eyes thin slits. 'I don't suppose you have any red stones.'

Redmyrtle hissed again.

'Now a red stone really would seal the bargain.'

Leah held her breath.

The gnarled hand held out a gemstone. It was smooth and red and large as a ripe plum.

Leah saw Solomon's eyes grow wide. This stone alone, she knew, was worth more than all the others put together. A smile spread across Solomon's face.

'We have a bargain,' he said. 'The wyrmeling is yours.'

The hand closed round the red stone, and another reached out and seized Leah by the wrist.

'The wyrmeling . . .' Redmyrtle's voice was

honeyed and eager. Her grip tightened. '*And* the girl.'

Leah started violently back. 'I ain't no piece of live goods,' she shouted, struggling to keep her voice from breaking up. 'Sol would never leave me here, ain't that right, Sol?' She heard her own heartbeat thumping at her temples. 'Sol, tell her. Sol . . . ?'

But Solomon Tallow said nothing.

FIFTY

Heppy awoke. It was that moment of drowsy confusion between dreaming and wakefulness.

In the cavern gloom, she saw her ragged sleeve as she held her hand before her face, and the rope that circled her wrist and snaked up to the rock-spike high in the shadows of the cave wall. But the dream in her head had not quite faded, and the cave and the rags and the chain made no sense to her.

Her father was beside her, his face gleaming in the firelight. They were playing that game they played together, and he was crooning that old lullaby she loved. They must have had a hard hike of it, for she was aware of the bone-ache of exhaustion that gripped her, and also a desperate desire not to be lulled to sleep, for if she did, she was afraid that he wouldn't be there when she woke up.

She tried to concentrate on the wooden marbles, the gleam of their polished surfaces, and the way they clicked one against the other. But it was no good. She was too tired and too comfortable, and the song wrapped itself around her.

'I will sing you off to sleep,
I will rock your cradle deep.
I will rock your cradle fine,

For I am yours and you are mine . . .'

And now she was awake, and the dream was fading. Yet the warmth remained, and the rise and fall of steady breathing. She reached out in the gloom and her hand touched something ridged and scaled.

Something that was alive.

She sat up and saw that she was encircled by a sleeping wyrme, white and sleek, wings folded, tail coiled protectively round her and wedged beneath a long tapered snout. As she watched, the wyrme opened its eyes, deep yellow and penetrating, and looked into hers. Smoke drizzled from its nostrils, and strange sounds like the whispering of the wind and the pitter-patter of falling rain emerged from its throat.

'Aysss . . . saaaah . . .'

Dream-addled and barely aware of herself, a name came into the girl's head, comforting and strong and needing to be spoken. She lay back and felt the wyrme's coils tighten around her. She could sense that he, like her, was lost, frightened, alone and seeking comfort in this closeness.

Heppy closed her eyes and melted into the steady rise and fall of his breathing.

'Asa,' she said.

FIFTY-ONE

Eli picked up a stick and stirred life into the embers of the campfire. He built it up with fresh logs, waited a moment for them to catch, then set a cooking pot on the blaze.

When the water came to the boil, Eli handcupped barleymeal into the cooking pot and the last of the fish from the night before, and stirred it.

The stone prophet opened his eyes, uncurled and sat up. He looked around, his face befuddled, his bleary gaze falling upon the cragclimber.

'You're awake, then,' Eli observed.

Ichabod nodded, then rubbed his eyes on the back of his fisted hands. He sniffed rodent-like at the air. 'Victuals,' he murmured.

Eli nodded. 'A spot of fish gruel,' he said. 'Looks like you could use some, preacherman.'

'That I could,' Ichabod confirmed, squirming beneath Eli's intense pale-blue gaze.

'So, what was it, green liquor or the voices of the ancestors?' the cragclimber asked coolly as he passed him a steaming bowl. ' 'Cause you weren't making a whole lot of sense last night. But at least you didn't try to bushwhack me with a liquid cosh this time,' Eli conceded.

290

'It was neither,' said Ichabod. He took a mouthful of the gruel. 'Ever since I was lightning-struck I've seen things a lot clearer . . . No, I had other matters on my mind last night.'

Eli stirred the cooking pot.

'I'm a useless cowardly failure,' Ichabod went on, as if talking to himself. 'Others enter—oh, yes—but Ichabod doesn't have the courage to follow them. Because I'm useless, useless, useless . . .'

Eli looked up.

Micah and the kingirl, Thrace, were walking towards the campfire, side by side, the low blanched sun casting long shadows behind them that blurred into one. Micah's face was flushed and his eyes shone bright as he stole furtive glances at the kingirl striding at his side. He was carrying her kinlance, Eli noticed, and Thrace was holding something in her hands, clasped protectively to her chest. The tight soulskin she wore was unfastened at the neck, the hood hanging loose off one shoulder, while her ash-gold hair fell in soft tousled tresses over the other.

'Micah, Thrace,' said Eli as they reached the fire, gesturing towards the ragged figure. 'This is Ichabod, the stone prophet.'

Micah nodded, though if Thrace had heard Eli, she gave no indication of it. Her mouth was small and tight, and her eyes were red-rimmed as she knelt down beside the fire and let the bundle she'd been clutching tumble into it.

'Damsel grubs,' Eli said quietly, and shook his head. 'Hard to find this time of year . . .'

Thrace said nothing, but sat back on her haunches and gazed at the roasting grubs in the fire. Micah was about to go to her, but Eli stayed him with a hand.

'Leave her,' he counselled.

The previous night, when the boy had not returned from the hot spring, Eli had gone in search of him, and had seen them bathing, Micah and Thrace. He'd turned away, his head full of thoughts of Jura, and his younger self . . .

When he'd returned to the campfire, he'd recognized the raggedy stone prophet slumped beside it, rocking to and fro and babbling quietly under his breath. And, despite their strange history, Eli had to admit he'd been glad of the company.

As the damsel grubs' hard carapaces split, the air filled with cracks and sputters and the sweet nutty scent of their toasting flesh. Thrace picked up a stick and pushed the grubs out of the fire, their sizzling skins grey with ash as they smoked on the rock at her feet. Then, fiercely, voraciously, the kingirl seized the grubs, one by one, oblivious to their heat, and devoured them, her sharp teeth tearing at their flesh as her slim body was racked by sobs.

Finally she was sated. She slumped forward, her mouth smeared in grease and ash, and the tears that coursed down her cheeks dripped from her chin, hissing and sputtering into the fire.

Eli looked down into the cooking pot. He stirred the gruel, then ladled some into a bowl. 'Micah,' he said, holding it out.

Micah tore his gaze away from Thrace, stared at the bowl for a moment, then shook his head. 'I ain't hungry,' he said.

Thrace seemed to have gained control of

herself, for she got to her feet and wiped her mouth on the sleeve of her soulskin. She fastened the collar, adjusted the hood and scraped back her hair. Her face was as white as the soulskin, and her dark eyes were bright and intense as she stared at Eli.

'Aseel has left me,' she said simply.

The wind that whipped off the frozen lake was raw and harsh and sharp as knives.

Eli nodded. 'I saw what you did to Jesse at the gutting tarn,' he said. 'Did you make him talk?'

Thrace flinched. 'The other two kith have the wyrmeling in a sack,' she said, turning away and looking out across the clear lake. 'But he refused to tell me where he was to meet them . . .'

'By all that is holy!' Ichabod exclaimed, laying down his bowl and getting to his feet. A smile came to his battered features. 'Two kith with a sack? It just so happens that old Ichabod might be of some use after all.'

FIFTY-TWO

Micah reached out and took Thrace's hand, and was surprised by the heat it gave off. She didn't pull away, but neither did she respond to his touch, nor look at him, and when he searched her face, he was uncertain whether she was even aware he was there. Her hood was up and her head was raised, and the kinlance gripped in her hand swung purposefully at her side as she walked forward.

A hot flush rose in Micah's face despite the bitter cold. The sky was sombre grey and full of snow that did not fall as the four of them crested the first crag, and they descended the steep incline on the far side.

When they'd emerged from the hot spring, the kingirl had looked so beautiful, standing before him washed clean of the blood and the acrid stench of the gutting tarn, her smooth unblemished skin glistening in the moonlight. Micah had scarcely been able to breathe at the sight of her, rooted to the spot, his heart hammering in his chest. It was she who had made the first move, wrapping her arms around him and drawing him close, holding on tightly as she pressed her open mouth to his.

The next morning, when they'd awakened, it had been awkward and shy between them. She had clothed herself in

294

the white soulskin once more, the second skin, the slough of her wyrme, and when she had crouched down next to the rock where the damsel grubs lay, she had trembled. And the trembling was nothing to do with him.

Now, as they tramped over the snowy ground, following the raggedy preacherman, Thrace was closed off to him once more, as strange and savage and unknowable as she'd been before they had lain together.

He felt Thrace's hand grip his arm. They had stopped, and Eli and Ichabod were crouching down behind a boulder.

'There,' Ichabod whispered excitedly and pointed.

Ahead of them, across a stretch of screestrewn ground, the pitted red rock of the manderwyrme cliffs stood dark against the evening sky. At their base, flanked by two pillar-shaped boulders, was a dark cave entrance. Some way to the left, on the edge of a steep escarpment amid the jumble of scree, a campfire flickered. As Micah watched, a figure clambered to his feet and stood illuminated by the firelight, his face turned towards them.

'Solomon Tallow,' Eli breathed.

FIFTY-THREE

Solomon Tallow.

There he was, alone and brazen, the shaven-headed leader of the gang of kith who had shamed her and tormented her, and who she had leaped from the speckled stack to escape. He had murdered Jura and slaughtered Jura's wyrme. He had taken the precious whitewyrmeling . . .

'Thrace,' Eli whispered. 'Thrace, wait.'

But it was too late. She was already up and running, lance in hand.

Solomon stared at her for a moment, then crouched down and seized the sidewinder that lay on the ground beside him. He drew back the spring, raised the crossbow to his eye.

The sidewinder cracked, and the bolt flew spinning towards Thrace. She threw herself to one side and heard it slam against a rock behind her and clatter down the cracks between the boulders. She glanced back.

Muttering furiously, Eli had ducked down and pulled his own crossbow from his rucksack. He loaded a bolt, quickly, expertly, while calling to Ichabod and Micah.

'You go that way, lad,' said Eli, pointing off to the right of the campfire. 'Ichabod, take the other side.'

From above them came the thrum of the

296

string being drawn and a soft click as Solomon Tallow slipped a second bolt into place.

Thrace rose and made a dash for the base of the cliffs, leaping one way, then the other, as she sprang lightly from rock to rock. Behind her, Eli must have let loose a bolt of his own for, up ahead, Solomon hurled himself to the ground.

The bolt whistled, then thudded as it ricocheted off a boulder. Thrace scrambled over the welter of scree towards the kith leader. She saw his big hands were shaking. She saw sweat glisten on his shaven skull. He was frightened, this one. This kith. She saw that. And that was her strength.

'Thrace, Thrace,' Eli hissed fearfully after her as she leaped forwards.

She was running now, agile and sure-footed on the uneven boulders as she dashed towards Solomon, vengeance the only thought on her mind. Her lance was levelled at him, cradled in the crook of her arm, just as if she was braced for an attack astride Aseel's shoulders, attacking in the only way she knew how. She was almost upon him. One leap, one thrust, and she would drive the lance through his vile kith heart. She lunged forward . . .

Only, she wasn't on Aseel's shoulders. She was alone.

Solomon jerked to one side and swung the heavy crossbow that was gripped in his powerful hands. It knocked the thrusting lance aside and slammed into her body with such force that she was thrown to the ground. Before she could rise, he was upon her. The cabled muscles of his arms crushed tight around her neck. His knife pressed into her throat—and Aseel was not there to fell this kith with a flick of his tail, or turn him to ashes with his

297

fiery breath.

Solomon looked up. There were three figures in the scree beyond the flickering light of the campfire.

'One step closer,' Solomon snarled, his blade pressing into Thrace's neck, 'and I'll kill the girl.'

Eli stopped. He motioned to Ichabod and Micah to do the same.

'Now how about one of you trail-tramps telling me what the hell this is all about? Here I am, minding my own business, resting up by my campfire, when this filthy wyrmehag comes at me from out of the shadows, screeching and hollering and ready to skewer me with that spike of hers for no reason I can rightly discern . . .'

'She had every reason, as you well know,' said Eli quietly. 'And so do I. You and your gang killed a dear friend of mine. They have paid with their lives. Now it's your turn, Tallow. Killing the girl won't make no difference to what you've got coming to you.'

'You're bluffing,' said Solomon. He jerked Thrace roughly round and backed away from the campfire, across the scree towards the edge of the escarpment, taking care to keep her between himself and Eli's crossbow. 'Back off,' he growled through gritted teeth, 'and I might just let her live.'

Holding the knife to Thrace's neck, he inched back onto the path that led down the steep cliffside. Micah leaped forward, his gangly body slight and callow in comparison with Solomon's heft. He gripped his hackdagger in his hand.

'I can't let you take her, Tallow,' he said quietly.

'You,' Solomon sneered. 'The greenhorn from the scrimshaw den.' He spat the words out with scorn.

Thrace felt the muscles in Tallow's arm flex as he raised the sidewinder and pulled the trigger. With a guttural cry, she twisted and clawed at Tallow's face, knocking the sidewinder with her elbow as it spat its bolt. Solomon recoiled with a snarl of rage, and Thrace's nails snagged on a cord at his neck.

She yanked it hard.

A pouch appeared from inside his jacket. The cord snapped, ripping the pouch and scattering its contents, a shower of glittering gemstones that shot out into the dark air.

Solomon flung Thrace aside and threw himself after the gemstones as they chinked and clattered on the scree at his feet and bounced over the cliff edge. But he was not fast enough. His hands grasped and snatched and closed round nothing as the precious stones fell into the blackness below.

And, off-balance and toppling in his desperation, Solomon Tallow fell after them. His anguished cry was abruptly cut short, replaced by the muffled clatter of tumbling scree that died away to silence. Eli crossed to the edge of the cliff and peered down into the darkness.

'If the fall hasn't killed him, the carrionwyrmes soon will,' he said. 'Either way, he won't be killing no more wyrmekin.'

Thrace paid him no heed. She was scrambling on all fours to where Micah lay in a crumpled heap on the edge of the escarpment. She fell to her knees beside him and tore at his jacket, her hands shaking as she searched for the bolt wound.

'He missed,' Micah said, his voice weak and dazed-sounding. 'You jolted his aim, Thrace.

299

You—'
    But his words were smothered by the kingirl's urgent kisses.

FIFTY-FOUR

'I'm going down there with you, Thrace,' said Micah.

They were seated upon a flat rock at the edge of the escarpment, the four of them clustered round a small fire that had blazed as it boiled their icemelt and charred their meat, but that had now dwindled to glowing embers. Night was all but upon them, and the cold was intense.

'I don't ask it of you, Micah,' the kingirl replied. She had set aside her lance and now held two of Eli's razor-sharp rockspikes in her hands. 'The wyrmeling is down there, and I must find it.'

'If you go, Micah, lad,' said Eli gruffly, 'then I go too.'

Ichabod the stone prophet climbed to his feet.

Eli looked up. 'You taking your leave, preacherman?' he said.

'No,' said Ichabod quietly. 'I have a score to settle with them keld myself,' he said, eyeing each of them levelly. 'And with three such as you, I figure I can settle it. At last.'

'A score?'

'Revenge,' said Ichabod, pulling a skinning knife from the ragged folds of his jacket. 'For what was robbed from me, and sold to them . . . Live goods.'

Ichabod kicked at the embers of the

301

fire.

'Well?' he said, wild-eyed. 'What are we waiting for?'

Thrace looked round, the expression on her face impossible to read. Then she nodded.

They stepped through the cavern entrance, Thrace up front. The sound of trickles and drips and eerie windhowls made the rock tunnels seem like the innards of some mighty creature. The reek of the dark air was meatfoul and sour.

They travelled through a labyrinth of tunnels, Thrace moving stealthily and silently, and the others endeavouring to do the same. Micah stumbled and tripped, and failed in his efforts to remember the twists and turns of their route. Ahead of him he could hear Eli start to pant. Behind him Ichabod fell heavily and cried out.

Thrace turned, her eyes blazing. 'Hush,' she hissed.

At the end of the tunnel, Micah saw a flash of light. Flames. Wyrmebreath.

They froze.

There was a hissing and the skitter of claws. Micah gripped his hackdagger tight. The jet of fire got closer, then was abruptly extinguished, and Micah heard a snuffling and wheezing, and the sound of the claws fade—that, and the sound of his own thudding heart.

Thrace took a side tunnel, and continued as silently as before. At every fork and turn they came to, she paused and sniffed the air, before continuing, following a scent that only she could detect. They passed the burned-out nub of a five-day torch. They passed piles of wyrme-droppings, acrid with the stench of the darkness itself. The

302

tunnel tightened its grip, till they had to dip their heads and hunch their shoulders. Eli, Micah and Ichabod moved increasingly slow and awkward, knocking elbows on the unforgiving rock, grazing their scalps. Thrace, agile and determined, drew ahead of them, a rockspike grasped in each hand as she charted a course deeper and deeper into the foul blackness.

And all the while, Micah grew more fearful. He couldn't help it. The rocks oozed foulness. The air whispered of death. At last, after what seemed to Micah like an eternity of stooping, shuffling and blindly reaching out, they came to the end of a tortuous scritch-scratch tunnel.

Thrace turned, a finger to her lips, then beckoned. They stepped out into icy coldness.

Micah heard the trickling of water . . .

He froze and stared up at the high vaulted ceiling, where a faint chink of light penetrated the gloom and fell upon a glistening white stalactite that hung down above the centre of a fetid black pool. A thin thread of water spiralled down from its tip.

'I've been here before,' he breathed.

Beside him, Thrace tensed as she sniffed the air, her rock-spikes raised. Ichabod gripped his skinning knife as Eli took the pitchdip torch from his belt and lit it.

'Over there,' he whispered, pointing to the far side of the pool.

In the shadows was another cavern opening, black and ominous. The four of them walked round the pool and approached the entrance. Holding the flaming torch above his head, Eli stepped inside. Micah and the others followed.

The cavern was smaller than the one with the stalactite, high-ceilinged and narrow, and the walls were pocked with shadows. The torch cast the chamber in an eerie flickering light.

A broad slab of rock stood on stone supports at the centre of the floor, its surface cluttered and stained.

There were cleavers, dark with smeared blood. Hatchets and bone-shears. A glinting jag-toothed saw. And wooden bowls of different sizes filled with chopped meat, and diced offal, and curved ribs, fringed with flesh and hacked to short lengths—the makings of a feast from something freshly butchered.

Micah had the intense feeling of being watched by many eyes, and turned slowly. His gaze fell upon the cavern walls. They were pockmarked with crude rock shelves, all of them crowded with staring human skulls.

Some were old and brown; some were pearly white beneath tattered skin, and with strands of long hair still clinging to the scalp. Some had good teeth, some had none; some had milk teeth set in tiny jaws . . .

'What *is* this,' said Micah breathlessly, his stomach churning.

'Live goods,' said Ichabod, his voice tight and constricted.

And when Micah looked round, he saw the stone prophet and Eli, their backs turned, staring down at the table. Micah crossed the dim-lit cavern to join them.

There, on the stone surface, was the severed head of a young woman. It had sun-flecked brown hair, sallow skin and high jutting cheekbones. The

STUNTED WYRME

full lips were drawn back over even teeth in a horrified scream. The eyes were almondshape and lake-green and stared back imploringly, their gaze shot with pain and fear and betrayal . . .

'Solomon Tallow's woman,' said Eli bitterly. 'Of all the wicked ways to eke out an existence in the weald, this keld has chosen the most wicked . . .'

All at once, out from under the table the stunted wyrme reared up, its jaws snapping and rapier-like talons slashing at Eli's throat. Micah lunged forward and plunged the blade of his hackdagger into one of the loathsome milk-white eyes, withdrew it, then thrust it deep into the creature's neck. With a curdled screech, the wyrme collapsed at his feet, where it writhed and twitched at the end of a golden chain as blood pumped from its severed throat . . .

'Sssssss . . .' The loud hiss came from somewhere above.

There was a whirring sound and a blur of light, followed by a fleshy thud. Ichabod staggered back from the table, a hatchet embedded in his chest.

The next moment, a cleaver whistled past Micah's head and a broadblade knife flashed down at Eli. The cragclimber threw himself to the floor, and the knife clattered on the rock at his feet.

'Up there!' he shouted, grasping the knife and throwing it.

Micah followed its flight. It flickered as it turned, then melted into shadow. There was a loud crack, and the knife abruptly flew back across the cavern. Micah didn't see where it landed. His startled gaze was fixed upon the ragged figure that clung upside down to the rock in the shadows of the vaulted ceiling.

306

It was back-stooped and shoulder-hunched, with thin stick-like legs, supplemented by two crutches clasped in the pit of each arm. Beadyeyed, beaknosed and with a mess of matted hair that was grey and red, like rusting ironwool. A heavy robe hung loose at the shoulders; layers of skirts and aprons billowed from the waist, threadbare and patchwork—squares of wyrmeskin, homespun, stiff striped canvas and grubby silk, edged with thin strips of lace, yellowed and limp.

A scrawny arm darted out and flexed, and another hatchet came spinning out of the shadows, sending Micah sprawling to the floor beside the stone table and the horrifying fare laid out upon it. Eli was hunkered down on the other side.

Redmyrtle scuttled over the ceiling, the hooks at her ankles and elbows and the spiked crutches a blur of movement as they propelled her silently across the pitted rock. She paused on the other side of the cavern, upside down and dangling backwards. Her grey-red hair quivered as she drew a murderous-looking butcher's knife from the folds of her rags.

'I slaughter each and all of you,' she rasped. 'I hack you to pieces. Then I feast.'

She scurried down the cavern wall towards the stone table. Micah looked up and saw Thrace uncoil herself from the rock shelf she'd been crouching upon, rock-spike in each hand.

He saw the savage rage in her face. Her mouth taut. Her dark eyes, cold and intense.

Scattering skulls and sending them clattering to the floor like ghastly hailstones, Thrace arched her body and hurled first one, then the other rock-spike at the cavern hag above her.

Redmyrtle used a crutch to deflect the first spike, but the second hit home and buried itself in the top of her leg. She let out a screech of pain and indignation.

Thrace shot out a leg and kicked away a crutch, and the hag fell, a flapping ball of rags tumbling from the wall and landing heavily face down on the floor. The kingirl was upon her in an instant. Her lithe muscular body pressed down on the hag's shoulders as she seized the creature's tangled hair and pulled her head sharply back.

'Where's the wyrmeling?' she hissed.

The hag snorted and struggled, and Thrace tugged back all the harder.

'Where is the wyrmeling?'

'Dead! Dead! Dead!' the cavern hag screamed.

'You killed it?'

'You kill my baby,' the hag snarled.

'You . . . you . . .' Thrace hesitated. She brought her head down, so that her mouth was pressed to the hag's ear, and she sniffed deep, and when she spoke again, her voice was ice-cold and incredulous. 'You were once kin.'

'Kin?' she rasped. 'Once, maybe . . .'

'And now you are keld.'

'I had no wyrme,' Redmyrtle spat. 'Never once. So I bought my beautiful baby . . .'

'That you stunted,' Thrace said, viciously twisting and yanking her hair.

'That I swaddled and bound,' the hag yelped, 'to keep him small. To make him fierce. To stop him from ever leaving me . . .'

'You dishonour the kin,' Thrace hissed, spitting out the words as her fingers slipped into the tangle of matted hair and her taloned grip tightened

308

round the hag's head. 'You are worse than the worst kith.'

A sharp crack echoed round the cavern as Thrace wrenched the hag's head to one side and snapped her neck. Redmyrtle fell still.

Thrace arched her back, her head raised and eyes shut. Tears streamed silently down her face.

'Let that be an end to the killing,' she said.

Out of the shocked stillness of the cavern came another sound.

'I will sing you off to sleep, I will rock your cradle deep . . .' A girl was singing.

Micah held out his hand to Thrace, who wiped her face on her sleeve and climbed to her feet. Spatters of blood trailed across the stone floor and through a low arched entrance on the far side of the cavern. They followed it. The song grew louder.

They ducked down and entered a small dome-shaped cave.

The wyrmeling, now half-grown and near to fledging, sat on its haunches, chained to the wall by its long sinuous neck. Beside it, a rope at her ankle, sat a girl of no more than eight years of age. She cradled Ichabod's head in her lap.

He was dead.

The girl stopped singing and looked up. 'He found me. Papa found me . . .' She stroked Ichabod's hair tenderly. 'I was stole. A man came to the rock barrow while Papa was sleeping. He was kind. He was friendly. He wore beautiful boots . . . He gave me a present, a pretty comb for my hair. He said that if I went with him, he'd show me more pretty things . . .'

Tears ran down her cheeks.

'I fell asleep, and when I woke up, I was here. And there was no man. And there were no pretty things. And there was no papa.

'But now . . . now, he has found me. *I will rock your cradle fine,*' she sang, as she held Ichabod the stone prophet in her arms, and wept. '*For I am yours and you are mine . . .*'

FIFTY-FIVE

High on the ledge, Hepzibar turned, her breath coming in clouds of mist. Beside her, Asa exhaled. Coiling wreaths of thick grey smoke encircled them both for a moment, before thinning and rising and drifting away.

The wyrme's new scales gleamed bright in the sunlight, while the skin he had sloughed—sheer and unblemished—now clung tightly to the girl's small frame, as white and gleaming as his own. As Hepzibar climbed onto Asa's back, it was difficult to tell where one stopped and the other began.

Deep down in the cavern, the whitewyrme had grown fast, and the previous night had shed his first skin. Thrace had helped the girl wrap it around herself and the wyrme had breathed his hot aromatic smoke upon her, until the wyrmeslough had tightened about her body and clad her like a second skin.

Soulskin.

Asa stepped back along the ledge, stopped at a rock that jutted proud of the cliff, and climbed upon it. The muscles at his shoulders bunched and flexed, and he raised his wings. As they flapped up and down, slowly at first, then growing faster, so the veins that coursed through them filled with blood; then they caught the air.

311

His talonspurs quivered. His scalloped skin tensed and was opalescent in the sunlight. Up and down, the wings beat, up and down, gathering strength and stirring the air as Hepzibar leaned forward and wrapped her arms round his sinuous neck.

Far below, the steep slope dropped away to the shimmering white plateau. Thick snow had rendered it featureless, covering the cracks and crevices, the boulders and scree, and the flat desolation continued white and unbroken to high distant crags, dark against the sun, where twists of smoke rose up from the highstacks and festercrags. The sky was blue there, but there were clouds sweeping in from behind, yellow grey and roiling and laden with fresh snow.

The first snowflakes began to fall. They fluttered down like white feathers, landing on the rock, where they settled; and on the wyrme's back and the girl's shoulders, where they did not.

Hepzibar gripped tight with her legs. Asa gave a shudder and craned his serpentine neck forward. His wingbeats grew faster, powerful and rhythmic, rising and falling on either side of the girl. They thrummed to an ever-quickening pace; they made the snow flurries swirl. Then, bracing his legs, he brought his wings powerfully down and leaped from the mountainside into the snow-flecked air.

They dipped for a moment, then rose up, their white bodies melting together as they soared higher and higher. They blurred in the snow, white against white, becoming smaller as they flew off across the sky.

On the snow-covered slope below, Thrace and Micah and Eli stood side by side and watched as the whitewyrme and his kin disappeared into the haze of the horizon. Eli shifted the rucksack on his shoulders and turned to Thrace.

'Micah and I have torched the keld's lair,' he said grimly, 'and buried Ichabod beneath a cairn of stones in the kith way.' He glanced back at the sky. 'And now you've taken care of his daughter, Thrace, we can move on . . .'

Thrace didn't move. Her gaze was still fixed on the horizon and Micah could see the look of longing in her eyes.

'Asa will take care of her now, in the kin way,' she said. 'He'll find a methusalah pine and fashion her a kinlance. He'll find their range, a day's flight in any direction from the eyrie he'll choose for them—a fume-cave, or a high festercrag—just like Aseel did with me . . .'

Micah heard the catch in her voice.

'Together, they will defend wyrmekind against the two-hides.'

Micah flinched at the unfamiliar term. *Two-hides*. She meant people. She meant wyrmekith.

She meant him . . .

'Just like you and Aseel did,' said Micah, feeling his chest tighten.

'That life is over for me now,' Thrace said, and turned away.

FIFTY-SIX

'The winter den is no more than a day away,' said Eli. 'And we'll make it before the blizzards,' he added with a trace of a smile, 'or my name's not Eli Halfwinter.'

The wind howled and whistled. The three of them hugged close to the small fire the cragclimber had made. Despite the blaze, the cold was intense.

'It's a time for holing up, fullwinter,' he went on. 'A time for reflection, for taking stock of the experiences of the past year . . .'

Micah glanced across at Thrace. The kingirl returned his gaze, and smiled. It seemed to him that, here in this flickering firelight, she looked more beautiful than he'd ever seen her.

True, her soulskin, once so white and sleek, now showed signs of wear. It was stained with blood from the caverns, and the sloughed skin itself had taken on a greyish hue and seemed looser fitting than before. Her hair no longer had the lustrous pearly shine it had possessed. Now it was windblown and prone to tangle, and tumbled loosely about her shoulders. But her face had softened, her eyes had lost their harshness, her lips seemed fuller, and the marble pallor to her cheeks had warmed to a pinkish bloom.

Eli pulled his blanket around himself and settled down to sleep. Thrace

314

shivered. Micah rummaged in his backpack and pulled out a thick leather jerkin, which he offered to her.

Thrace's nose twitched at the kith odour it gave off, but she took it anyway, and wrapped it around her shoulders. She smiled again, her eyes soft and tender. And Micah dared, for the first time, to believe that he and this strange kingirl might have a future with one another after all.

He shifted towards her and cradled her in his arms. He held her body tightly to his as they lay down beside the fire, close and warm, and drifted into sleep.

FIFTY-SEVEN

'Redmyrtle took a risk buying the wyrmeling,' the eel-mother hissed. Her voice pierced the silence like a rusting skewer. 'Yet it was a risk any one of us would have taken to possess a great whitewyrme.'

She regarded the other keld in the dimly lit cavern through mean yellow eyes. Around her corpulent shoulders, two sleek limbless crevicewyrmes hung listlessly, their thin tongues tasting the air. Blue Slake the poisoner raised a claw-like hand and turned his ruined face towards the guttering candle beside him. It sat in an elegant holder, a tripod of human thigh bones supporting an upturned skull.

'She was an excellent renderer,' he wheezed through the hole in his face where his nose used to be. 'And her flesh stew was second to none . . .'

'Maybe so,' said Cutter Daniel, the liquor bottles tied to his coat clinking softly as he spoke, 'but Redmyrtle was careless. She should have realized that wyrmekin would come after the wyrmeling. Kith can be manipulated, exploited, but these kin, they are dangerous.'

The distiller scratched his rat-tail scalp with long needlepoint fingernails. Behind him, his four slaves watched him warily, their eyes heavy-lidded with inebriation.

316

'Which is why the wyrmeling was such a prize.' The black-cowled figure beside the eel-mother spoke for the first time. Her voice was velvet soft and lilting, and the other keld inclined their heads deferentially. 'It would have been of great use to us. Our dear departed Redmyrtle understood this all too well . . .'

The eel-mother nodded in agreement, her grease-streaked chins wobbling as she did so.

'But now her death must be avenged,' the black-cowled figure continued. 'And for that we need the winter caller.'

'He is here,' said the eel-mother, and the crevicewyrmes around her ample neck hissed and shrank back as a huge figure shuffled forward out of the shadows.

It was clad in a coat of thick lakewyrmeskin, and a bone mask covered its face.

'You have their scent?' the black-cowled figure asked, her voice low and honeyed.

The winter caller nodded, dark eyes glinting from the sockets of the mask.

'Then find their winter den, and dig them out . . .'

FIFTY-EIGHT

Eli strode ahead, his walking staff crunching into the snow with every step as he probed for concealed rocks or hidden crevices. Micah and Thrace followed, walking hand in hand, keeping as close to his footprints as they could. Eli paused and looked ahead, then turned to the others.

The three of them were making good progress despite the heavy going. Snow had fallen throughout the night and lay thick upon the trail. It creaked and squeaked beneath their boots. More snow was fluttering down, the flakes grey against the icy whiteness.

'Once we've crested this next ridge, the winter den ain't no more than an hour's tramp,' he announced.

Micah smiled and squeezed Thrace's hand tightly, and they continued up the steep slope, both of them helping the other not to slip. The trail narrowed and curved, the grey ridged rocks crowding in from both sides.

Micah looked down, taking care where he placed his feet, and noticed that the heel of his boot was coming away. Letting go of Thrace's hand, he stopped to examine the damage.

The boot, once so fine and sturdy, had become sorely worn, he realized. The wyrmegut stitching that attached the sole

318

to the uppers had torn, and the heel was hanging loose.

Micah raised his foot and tugged at the heel, and as it came away, a cluster of bright gemstones tumbled onto the snow. Blue gems and green gems; purple, yellow and black gems, and some so natural clear it was like looking at something that wasn't properly there.

Micah looked at the boot, dumbfounded. Beside him, Thrace regarded the gemstones impassively.

His fingers agitated with excitement, Micah took his hackdagger from his belt and prised the heel off the other boot.

Two red stones, the size of stipplejay eggs, fell to the ground. They lay upon the snow like drops of blood.

Micah stooped and gathered up the returner's wealth, scarcely able to believe his eyes. He stared at the gems in his hand. This was the returner's wealth he had dreamed of, the reason he had come to the wyrmeweald. And to think, it had been in his possession all along.

It had belonged to that kith he'd encountered in the wastes, dead of thirst, but with a fortune hidden in his boots—the very boots Micah had taken from him and worn all this time. He could still see the man's sunken cheeks and hollowed chest, the staring eyes not yet plucked out by the carrionwyrmes that had circled greedily overhead.

The gemstones sparkled in his hand. What had the man done to get them? What hideous depravity did they represent?

And yet, they belonged to him now. He was rich. Back on the plains, he could live like a lord, with a magnificent estate, a stable full of fine horses and an army of servants to do his bidding. He could return and claim Seraphita . . .

He looked up. Eli was observing him evenly. The cragclimber shrugged and turned away. He had no interest in returner's wealth.

Micah turned to Thrace. She looked at him inquisitively, her eyes dark beneath soft corn-silver waves of hair. The soulskin that encased her body shimmered in the winter light; gold, magenta, iridescent blue and green, like oil on water. Her lips parted in a half smile.

'Don't worry,' she said. 'The den is close, and you'll have all winter to mend your boots.'

Micah smiled at the wild beautiful wyrmekin girl and let the gemstones fall from his hand. They punctured the flawless surface of the snow and disappeared. Snowflakes kept falling, filling in the holes, smoothing them away, until all trace was gone.

Thrace held out her hand and Micah took it. Together, they continued up the trail, towards the winter den.

EXODUS

The colony, a thousand strong, took to the wing and spread out across the sky in great rippling skeins. Here and there, hatchlings broke formation and dipped and wheeled with a natural exuberance, while around them, the older wyrmes flew with slow rhythmic wingbeats, pacing themselves for the long journey ahead. The sun disappeared behind gathering clouds as the great whitewyrmes pressed on resolutely towards the ridge of jagged mountain peaks on the distant horizon.

Behind them, the wyrme galleries lay empty. An ice wind whistled through the labyrinth of ancient tunnels, with their fluted columns of soft blue-grey stone, like a lilting lament. The ancient dwelling place of the great whitewyrmes had been abandoned.

The old whitewyrme was the last to leave. Slowly, reluctantly, he launched himself from the high rock, a vantage point from which he'd watched over the colony for most of his long life. With slow deliberate wingbeats, he rose high into the sky and followed the retreating colony.

The taint of the two-hides had become too strong to ignore. It was time to retreat further. Now, only the deep weald could afford them the protection they craved.

With a heavy heart, the old wyrme flew on.

As the colony melted into the distance, Aseel circled high above the abandoned wyrme galleries. Shunned and kinless, he had nowhere else to go. He landed on the high rock, folded his wings and bowed his head. Above him, out of a heavy grey sky, snow began to fall.